THE OTHER TWIN

KAREN ROBERTS TURNER

BROWN GIRLS BOOKS

For My Mother and My Daughter - the breath and heartbeat of my life

Acknowledgments

"In every thing give thanks . . . "
1 Thessalonians 5:18 (KJV)

I must first give thanks to the Almighty for the miracle that is my life. When darkness dawned almost a decade ago, God showed up and said, "Not yet." To Him be all honor, glory, and praise now and evermore.

I also thank God for blessing me with a gift of writing and assigning me to share that gift with the world.

Thank you to everyone who inspired, supported, encouraged, and challenged me to begin, continue, and finish this book. I appreciate that you saw what I sometimes did not. I could not and would not have completed this assignment had it not been for you all.

To my Aces - Mommie, Sondra, Alyia, and Kendall. I'm so grateful for your love, faith, and unconditional support of everything I undertake. You each keep me believing I am unstoppable. I love you forever and for always.

To my Squad - "Rev", Carla, Monica, Cassandra, Sheila, Sonya, and Iman. You were in my corner from start to finish, listening to my ideas, helping me name characters, offering feedback on storylines. You, along with my Aces, encouraged me until the last "t" was crossed and the final "i" was dotted. I'm humbled to count you among my sister-friends.

To the Brown Girls - Victoria, ReShonda, and Terri. Terri's book was the catalyst for my first conversation with Victoria about something I had started writing. "It's just a story," I said, "and it's not done." Victoria challenged me to finish the story. Then her encouragement, tough critiques, and patience allowed me to create a novel where "just a story" once lived. Terri, then a recent first-time author herself, shared my excitement as I reached writing and editing milestones. ReShonda and the rest of the team at Brown Girls Books brought us across the finish line in grand style. I am thankful beyond words for your belief in my creativity.

To my Church Twins - Michele and Reneé . Thank you for indulging my questions and sharing with me what living as a twin is like. While this book is *not* a story about your lives, I did want to make sure, on behalf of all the twins of the world, that I accurately represented the "twin thang." I'm grateful for your assistance in helping me achieve that.

To my favorite Millennials and GenZers - Alyia, Iman, Kendall, and Olivia. You guided me so I could speak in a voice that was relatable to your generations. Thank you for taking time to keep me on point.

To my Craft of Writing support group - Thank you for your comments, critiques, edits, laughs, and sandwiches. You totally rock.

To all of you who purchased my first novel, thank you for investing in my dreams. It has been an honor to share my story with you.

Peace & Blessings!
Karen

Prologue

F or our entire lives, Essence and I were textbook identicals. We looked exactly the same, from our chocolate brown complexion and almond-shaped brown eyes, to our coarse, shoulder-length, jet black hair. We walked alike, talked alike, and of course, we dressed alike.

Growing up, Essence and I had most of the same friends and loved playing twin tricks on them. We did everything together and hated being apart. When teachers separated us in elementary school "for our own good," I cried crocodile tears. Essence would wipe my face and say, "Just be brave, Bunnie. We'll be back together soon." Then we would hug and nuzzle noses.

My name − Ebony − was hard for her to say, so she called me Bunnie. I called her "Sisi," because she was my sister. Those names stuck.

I loved having Essence as my sister and even more as my twin. She was my first and best friend, and I was hers. We were each other's courage in scary times; comfort in hurting times; and happiness whenever we got sad.

We even had our own twin-sense, which meant we knew each other's thoughts and could finish each other's sentences. We could even talk to one another without actually speaking.

Even though we were mirror images, Essence was the

outfront twin. I was never far behind. Like when we ran track in high school, she might win, but I'd place a close second. Sometimes, we tied. No matter what, she always waited for me at the finish line, cheering me on. She outpaced me in other areas of our young lives, too – reading, doing chores, even getting dressed in the morning. However, she never considered her work done until I finished as well.

No one ever gave much thought to why I stayed a step behind. I was born a minute after her so maybe that's how God designed us. Whatever the reason, for my whole life, my twin sister has been the unattainable standard that I – and pretty much the world – measured myself against.

Who knew my life as my sister's twin would drastically change one day and send my world into a tailspin?

Chapter One

❧❧❧

I wake up early on this Friday morning feeling stressed and
anxious about the drive back to school. Seven hours in the
car with Essence will surely grate my already frayed nerves.
Sending one child off to college brings about a certain level of
tension for any family. Imagine navigating the return of two kids
at the same time. Add to that dynamic these once interchangeable, indistinguishable, inseparable twins have declared a silent
war on each other. Stressful? We're talking DEFCON-1. That's
the situation in our house right now as we prepare to drive from
D.C. back to Winslow, Connecticut to begin our sophomore year
at Bryce College.

Memories of my unforgiving freshman year weigh on me like
an elephant on my back. My high hopes and grand expectations
that college would provide easy academic success, an enviable
social life, and the romance of my dreams never materialized. My
grades? Far from stellar. My presence on the social scene? Sub-
par. Dating? Total fail. I felt like a complete disappointment and
desperately wished I could've hit Ctrl-Alt-Delete to restart that
whole experience.

My sister, unlike me, killed it in her first year. She made a ton
of friends, dated cool guys, and made the Dean's List. I was lowkey jealous watching her excel, but happy for her at the same

time . . . in the beginning. When she got tight with the popular mean girls on campus, she turned against me. Behind their backs, I call them the "DivaWannaBees" or DWBs. They wear expensive-looking clothes, carry knock-off Louis bags, and flood their IG feeds and SnapChat stories with staged pictures of them with other social imposters. Bad and bougie? Not. They may have the whole campus fooled, but not me. I know Essence and her friends are a bunch of fake snobs.

As much as I had hoped and prayed that my sister would rise above their bad influence, she formed an impenetrable bond with those girls and purposefully and painfully cast me out. To add insult to my misery, out of nowhere, she decided to untwin me just two months into our first semester.

Essence walked into my dorm room and closed the book I was reading; her way of demanding my attention.

"Ebony, we need to talk."

"Okay. What now?"

I always seemed to be doing, saying, or thinking something that she didn't like and this type of conversation had become routine for us. For me, it was exhausting. But she seemed to enjoy tormenting me.

"Well it's not a specific thing," she began. "It's everything."

"So, everything I do bothers you today?" I asked in amazement. "Well . . . I'm so sorry."

As insincere as it was, I wanted my apology to end the discussion. Of course, it didn't.

"Shut up and listen," Essence barked.

I hated for anybody to tell me to shut up. It was rude and disrespectful. Essence knew that but apparently didn't care. A foul clapback was my first thought. But remembering the advice my idol, Michelle Obama, gave - "When they go low, we go high" -- I took a deep breath and kept it high.

"Okay," I began, in a non-confrontational, you-have-my-full-attention tone. "What do you have to say?"

"I've been thinking." She hesitated. I couldn't believe she was scared to say what was on her mind after rolling up on me like the Big Bad Wolf.

"Okaaaay," I said, gesturing for her to continue, "come out with it, or leave me alone."

"That's exactly what I'm trying to do – leave you alone. No, actually," she yelled, "I need you to leave me alone. I'm tired of you always being in my shadow, following behind me, copying everything I do. You need to stop it. Now."

In my humble opinion, Essence had officially lost her mind. I never copied her. We're twins.

"Do you hear how ridiculous you sound, Sisi?"

"Don't call me that," she commanded. "I'm Es."

"You're crazy is what you are. You can't stop being something you were born as," I said with increasing bewilderment in my voice.

Showing no regard for scientific facts or any love she once had for me, Essence announced her position and it was final.

"I can do whatever I want and what I want is to not be hopelessly tied to you. Get your own life. Mine is no longer available for you to use."

ESSENCE DISCONNECTED HERSELF FROM ME THAT DAY, WHICH is still an inconceivable notion for me. We had always viewed ourselves as being two expressions of one existence and we treasured that connection. Our parents said God gave us that bond. Nobody but us understood it. My unanswered question was why would she want to throw all that away? But throw it away she did. Now, she's just mean to me every chance she gets.

"Hold up," Essence shouts, stopping me in the hallway outside my room. "That betta not be my *Crooklyn* t-shirt you got on."

Why she feels the need to yell at me this early in the morning, especially when she's standing three feet away, is another mystery I'll never understand.

"I have my own. I don't need to wear yours," I fire back.

"I don't believe you," she insists.

"So what."

"So, prove it."

Essence posts up in front of me with her arms folded waiting for me to respond. I ignore her. It never mattered until she got brand new if I wore her clothes or if she wore mine. Her untwinning me must've erased her memory of all the times when we bought the same clothes because we actually have the same taste, or the times she took my clothes without asking me and kept them. Oh wait, that just happened two days ago. I got so sick of her claiming my stuff was hers that I wrote my name in my clothes just like our mom did when we went to sleep-away camp in grade school.

"Bunnie, if that's your shirt I said prove it."

"You want proof? Here."

I snatch my shirt off and shove the tag with my name on it in her face.

"See, it's mine. Is this enough proof for you?"

She slaps my hand and the shirt away. With her nose turned up she says, "O-M-G, put your clothes back on. I can't believe you sometimes."

She can't believe me? Wow.

AFTER THAT ENCOUNTER, I DO EVERYTHING IN MY POWER TO avoid Essence as we make final preparations to leave. While our dad carries the l set bags outside, I take my travel essentials - ear pods, back-up phone battery, pillow, snacks – and sit in the car by myself. This alone time allows me to prepare mentally for this trip, knowing I'd rather walk over hot coals all the way to Winslow than ride in luxurious comfort anywhere near Essence. Actually, I'd prefer for her to walk on those hot coals - barefoot. Imagining that provides me with a moment of sheer delight.

Every trace of happiness vanishes as soon as our parents and Essence get in the car. She's already bragging about her big sophomore year plans.

"I definitely plan to declare my major and become more active in BSU and the Poli Sci Club, maybe even run for President. I'm also gonna apply for the Bryce Ambassador program, and my girls and I might pledge this year, too."

6

It takes everything in me not to scream "Stop talking." Doesn't she know the last thing I wanna hear is how she plans to conquer the world?

My salvation comes from the music streaming app I downloaded onto my phone. With a tap of the screen, a Drake playlist floods my ears and drowns out the grating chatter in the car. While most of the lyrics only distract me, the lines from *God's Plan* hit me deep in my spirit.

I been movin' calm, don't start no trouble with me.

Tryna keep it peaceful is a struggle for me.

I worry myself to sleep thinking about God's plan for me.

Chapter Two

✤

The drive to school takes what feels like an earthly eternity. The weather, for most of the ride, matches my mood. Dreary and gray. Essence fell asleep after our breakfast stop three hours ago so I've been spared her annoyance since then.

We reach Bryce Lane around two in the afternoon. An occasional burst of color pops through the otherwise dull landscape bordering this mile-long thoroughfare that leads us to the school. Once we reach campus, the scenery becomes alive as hearty green bushes now hug the road. Sun rays begin peeking through the clouds as if to announce our pending arrival. Rows of Bryce's signature yellow tulips accent Stone Gate, the century-old archway that serves as the official entrance to the college. Crossing its threshold spikes my anxiety level as the inescapable reality of another school year hits me like a ton of bricks.

My mind takes its own ride as we pass Founders Hall, the oldest building on campus. The official "Welcome Freshmen" banner hangs above the doorway of this grand edifice dedicated to Bishop Montague Bryce, the man who had the vision to build this school. That sign is so ironic for me. The only welcome Founders Hall ever extended to me as a freshman came in the form of frequent invitations from my academic adviser, whose office is on the third floor, to discuss my "underwhelming performance." Those visits left me feeling anything but welcomed.

The campus in other ways looks and feels deceptively inviting. Blossoms of every kind and color fill flower boxes in front of the buildings we pass on the way to our dorm, which enhances their external lure. But inside of more than one of them lay bits and pieces of my broken spirit and shattered hopes. In a week, these flowers will be dead, the signs will be back in storage, and Bryce will again show itself as the same dream-killing place it's always been to me; one I hoped never to see again.

After winding through move-in day traffic, we reach the dorm Essence and I will call home this year. Everyone here refers to it as "The Castle," but there's nothing palatial or regal about it. The Castle is actually a modern co-ed dormitory that resembles an urban apartment building. It's the only all-singles dorm at Bryce and the most sustainable living space on campus – green roof, solar panels, and lots of high efficiency gadgets. Our mom hates it. She says it destroys the charm of Bryce, which it does. But that charm can be pretty grungy and musty at times. I'll take this kind of life over charm any day.

The Castle's official name is Georgette Devers Castle Residence Hall. It consists of two identical towers, East and West, which are connected by a four-story atrium and indoor garden that supposedly will help improve air quality in the building.

At the end of freshman year, Princess Essence claimed she would die if she couldn't live in The Castle as a sophomore and because of her superstar status on campus, she got her wish. For reasons unknown to me at the time, I also got assigned to The Castle, right next door to Essence in East Tower.

Apparently, as I later learned, the culprit in Residence Life thought he was doing Essence a favor by "putting her twin nearby." Of course, she freaked all the way out. I wasn't happy about it either because it reinforced her stupid theory about me living my life in her shadow.

Needless to say, Essence made sure my room was reassigned. Now I'm down the hall but in West Tower. I have a nicer room now than I had before, so I'm not complaining. Essence still hates me being so close.

We pull up to the designated move-in area and take our assigned positions. Our father's masterful car packing and the helpful hands of the student volunteers make unloading quick and painless. Essence and I separately settle into our rooms, with our parents shuttling back and forth between us doing what parents do – nag and get in the way. Of course, Essence monopolizes most of their time, and for over an hour I'm alone in my room. Rather than do anything remotely resembling unpacking, I call my best friend, Taylor, who we call "Tay," to let her know I made it to campus with my sanity intact.

Tay and I became friends when we were in pre-K/K and, second to Essence, she was my best friend growing up. We could talk about anything I couldn't share with Essence, which was usually just stuff about Essence. Tay's a year younger than me and I like the idea of being the older, wiser one. Lately though, she's been the one dropping knowledge on me.

Tay chose not to go to college. When she first told me her parents were okay with it, I almost passed out. It still blows my mind.

"I can't believe your parents are letting you skip college to go to London for a fashion design internship," I told her when we talked a few days ago. *"I'm so hatin' on you right now."*

"Stop lying, Ebbie," Tay said. *"You know you've wanted to go to college your whole life. That's all you used to talk about. That was never my dream. College ain't for everybody. I might go one day. But for now, I'm pursuing my dream a different way, my own way."*

"You've always been a free spirit," I said.

"That's right. A free spirit walking in my own truth."

Tay had used that phrase as the caption for her high school yearbook page when she graduated a few months ago.

When our video-chat connects, her voice comes through first.

"Ebbieeeee. Hi, babeeeee."

This singsongy greeting has been Tay's way of saying "Hi" to me for years. It immediately boosts my mood. When I finally see her face, I greet her like I always do.

"Hey girl, hey." I pause and look closely at my screen. "Wait. Are you at the airport?" I ask.

"Yep," she says. "Headed to the UK today."

"But that's not till Monday I thought."

"It was, but I told you yesterday the fam decided to go early and spend the weekend being tourists or whatever. I don't know. I'm just glad to finally be going."

"Tay, you did tell me. I completely forgot. I'm sorry."

In her usual understanding way, Tay says, "No apology needed. You had a lot goin' on this week. Sooo . . . How did it go?"

She looks at me like she wants my answer but is afraid to hear what it might be.

"Awful," I cry out. "Sisi was unbearable." Turning up the whine, I complain about every bad thing that happened from the time I woke up to my parents dumping me off in my room while they go off tending to her royal meanness, who's already acting like she owns this place.

"I'm not sure how I can survive another year here," I whimper. "Something has to change." My words come out sounding like a declaration, but really, they're a desperate plea.

I didn't plan to spend this call doing this. And I'm sure Tay didn't expect it either. She listens, then gently tries to talk me off this ledge of despair.

"Girl, we had this same conversation so many times over the summer. I thought you were good. What happened?"

"I don't know. Now that I'm here, I'm just not feeling it."

"But why not?"

She waits for my response. I don't have one.

"Ebbie, I'll say again what I've said before. Maybe you need to hear it one more time so it can finally stick. You're so smart and so tough. I can't imagine you not being able to slay this year at Bryce. You always did impossible, zany stuff when we were kids. You were the brave one. Remember? Who always climbed to the top of the slide first? Who actually ate the mud pies we made in my backyard? And who was crazy enough to jump off the top of the monkey bars? That was all you. Before you went off to that school, you did anything you put your mind to. You had no problem making friends, meeting boys, and getting good grades. You graduated with the highest GPA of anybody I know. That's the Ebony I know. Maybe you forgot to take her to college with you."

"That's facts, Tay. That Ebony was nowhere to be found."

As soon as those words leave my mouth – *that Ebony was nowhere to be found* – everything besides my thoughts goes on pause for several seconds, while words, images, ideas, and emotions of all kinds, shuffle back and forth in my mind like a movie, alternating between super fast-forward and extremely slow rewind. It's so trippy in my head because all of this stuff is about me and Essence. Our good racing past so quickly I can barely recognize it. So much of the bad moving slower than the sloths in that *Zootopia* movie. I don't quite understand it, but I kinda know what it means.

I hear Tay's voice saying, "You alright?"

I'm not able to respond until the second or third time she asks. By then the chatter in my head and the "True Hollywood Story" of my life has stopped.

"Ebbie, you okay?"

"I'm not sure. That was weird."

"What was that? You kinda zonked out on me."

"Some kind of vision about me and Sisi. And all the stuff that has happened between us going back to when we were little. Oh my, God," I shout. "I just had an aha moment."

"Oooh. Like that Oprah thing? What was it?" Tay leans into the camera, anxious to hear about my revelation. Now she's tuned into me like I'm her favorite TV show.

"What I just saw somehow made me realize those things you said I was good at, all go back to Sisi. I did that crazy stuff because she did. I was brave because she told me to be. And I was cool, because she showed me how. Sisi made me who I was, which was basically a replica of her. That wasn't a bad thing then. But, it is now. Especially since she doesn't want a copy, a twin, or really even a sister."

Tay looks as shocked hearing what I'm saying as I feel speaking it.

"Ebbie, how can you even think she made you to be her copy? You're a good person; she's not."

"She used to be. You know that. We both worshipped her."

Tay cuts her eyes at me and says, "Worshipped," emphasizing the 'ed.' "Past tense," she adds.

"Whatever, girl. In my mind because we were identical twins we were supposed to be exactly alike. Right? But really, we weren't ever meant to be the same. Maybe it's not something I can explain to you, but that's what my vision showed me. Sisi was right."

Saying those words out loud makes me realize that Essence had *out*-twinned me long ago and she spent all those years making up for my shortcomings so we could continue to appear as one. That had to be so tiring. No wonder Essence eventually gave up on me. Maybe that's why she felt so much anger toward me, too.

Tay sits quietly for a few seconds absorbing what I'm saying. Then she says, "It totally sucks that you might be right about all that. But now what?" Tay never likes getting stuck on the problem. Her thing is moving to the solution.

"Good question and I have no answer," I reply. "Hopefully something will come to me just like that did."

"Aww man," Tay shrieks. "My flight's boarding. We gotta finish talking later, but as soon as I get an internet connection, we can start messaging again and figure something out. You got this, girl."

I love the faith my bestie has in me. If only I had that same faith in myself.

Chapter Three

My mom walks into my room and finds me sitting on the floor in the middle of mayhem.

"What in the world?" she exclaims. "Are you planning to do anything about this mess?"

"Eventually, but I can't deal with it right now."

She joins me on the floor. "What's going on, Bunnie?"

Her eyes pierce me with concern and in her voice, I hear her determination to fix whatever my problem is – no matter what it is. A momentary pause gives me the courage to share the latest twist on the struggle that is my life.

"I had this epiphany when I was talking to Taylor."

She interrupts me to say, "So that's why you didn't even open a box or a suitcase. You were on the phone running your mouth?"

"No, that's not why. But please listen. You already know how Sisi went through that whole untwinning thing with me," I begin.

She nods and says, "Yes, not one of her better moments."

"True. But maybe she had a point. Maybe I was taking up too much of her identity. Nothing about me ever existed apart from her because I've always tried to be like her. I'm not sure I even know who I am apart from being a poor duplication of Sisi."

Before my mom can interrupt me to tell me what I'm saying isn't true, I stop her.

"Think about it, Mom. How often did you hear people say, 'Sisi, you forgot your shadow?' Or, 'Sisi, where's your twin?' Everybody just rolled me into her."

"Ebony Gabrielle Morgan, where are you getting these stories from? That's absolutely ridiculous."

"Really, Mom? My whole name? Can you not pull that kinda rank on me right now? I'm just trying to explain my epiphany."

"And I'm trying to understand it, but I don't get where this is coming from."

"It's coming from my life," I say. My exasperated tone would ordinarily get me in big trouble, but it looks like she's giving me a pass today. More carefully, I continue with my explanation.

"Those are my memories. But you don't have to go back to my childhood for evidence. You remember the only reason I'm here is because Bryce wanted 'the other twin'?"

"Where in the world did you get that from?" she asks with a puzzled expression.

She's got to be kidding. First of all, she knows Bryce was never my choice. It was the school Essence picked. From the time I began high school, everybody knew I wanted to attend a college close to D.C. That was a big deal because it meant Essence and I would be breaking the pact we made on our first day of kindergarten never to go to separate schools . . . ever. We even sealed that deal with mud, glue, and our secret handshake. We used that same secret handshake to break our pact the summer before our senior year. Essence even helped me pick out the schools I applied to, making sure her first choice – Bryce College - was not on my list.

So to answer her question, I remind my mom, "After Sisi got accepted here Early Decision with a full scholarship, Bryce reached out to you and Daddy asking if 'the other twin,' not Ebony, they literally said 'would the other twin be interested in becoming a member of the BC family as well?' You guys didn't give me a choice. 'Apply or else,' was how Daddy phrased it."

She knows I'm right. But will she admit it?

"Don't count anything your father said against me. I never made any such statement and I'm still not sure you've got the story right. Even if they said that, it doesn't take anything away from you," she argues. "You applied and got in on your own merit. And you ultimately decided to attend Bryce. We didn't tie you down and force you to come here."

We need to be talking about my epiphany and figuring that out, not rehashing my college acceptance saga. But since she took this detour, we're gonna ride it out.

"You're right, Mom, I applied, and Bryce did accept me." She'll never hear from me how I did my best not to get accepted. I wrote a crappy essay, submitted my packet late, and told the admissions interviewer Bryce wasn't my first, or even my second choice. If I had tried, I couldn't have been more unenthusiastic about becoming a Bryce Panther. Bryce accepted me anyway.

"But remember," I continue, "they gave me a full scholarship, too. That made the decision for me as far as your husband was concerned."

She laughs. "He's your father, too."

"Your husband first," I say playfully. "But joking aside, from the beginning, coming here was the last thing I ever wanted."

"I'm really surprised by that," she remarks. "You seemed to be just as excited as the rest of us at the time."

"Yeah, I was pretending. Sorry. That seemed easier than telling you, well really telling Daddy, the truth. You probably would've understood. He would not have tolerated it at all."

Talking about the pressure my dad puts on me always makes me sad and my mom knows it. She says it's my dad's issue, not mine. After all these years, she still hasn't figured out a way to change his attitude toward me, so I feel like she tries to compensate for it by not judging me or pressuring me the way he does.

She says, "I'm not gonna lecture you about honesty right now because you already know, even when it's hard, the truth is always better." Shaking her head, she adds, "You really had me fooled."

"Yep. I had everybody fooled."

Except Essence. Call it our twin-sense.

"I know you're not happy about having to come to Bryce with me," she commented while we shopped for school supplies last year. "You know you can't hide anything from me. But good show for the parents."

"It's whatever," I replied. "I'm just an afterthought in this family. Nobody ever cares what I want."

No comment? No smart comeback? She didn't have one because she knew I was right.

A few minutes later, she said, "They're doing what they think is best. That doesn't mean they don't care."

By the time that day ended, Essence had me believing that Bryce would be good for us both, so I continued my charade. I couldn't fake my enthusiasm once the school year started and reality set in. What I should've done was tell my parents how I felt. But the burden of confessing my truth and disappointing them was too much for me to bear back then.

I try to move us back to the topic at hand.

"Mom, my feelings about coming to Bryce last year aren't the issue anymore, so can we go back to what I was originally trying to tell you?"

She does a thing with her head that looks like she's shuffling through her memory to get back to where this train derailed. She nods when she's there and I continue.

"I'm trying to explain how I was just the 'other twin' for my whole life, even up to when I got accepted to Bryce. When Sisi killed the twin part of the equation all that was left was 'the other.' The other what? The other nothing. That's what Sisi's untwinning did to me; it made me a nothing. I couldn't really put it into words before. But that's why I was so unhappy last year and that made it impossible for me to perform."

After several seconds of quiet reflection, my mom lovingly squeezes my hands and gives me a sympathetic smile. She's probably already figuring out a way to undo all of this. Because that's what moms do.

"I'm sorry you had those experiences, Lady Bug. I hate that you would ever feel like nothing. You are my world and I love you with everything in me. Never forget that. And know this. Sisi does not, I repeat, does not define you. Did she form you in my womb? Was she the one who nourished and protected you while every organ in your body developed? Did she breathe life into you? No, no, and no. God did all that. God doesn't make nothings. Not only are you something in God's eyes . . . and in my eyes, you, my darling baby girl, are something special."

Tears stream down my face as my mom's words sink into my spirit. She hugs me tightly as we sit together in silence. Her love for me radiates to my core and I melt into her arms. If I could stay here forever, life would be good. Knowing that's not possible, I memorize this moment and store it in a special place in my heart.

"Promise me, you'll never say you're nothing again."

"I won't. I promise."

After our talk, my mom finds the bin containing my linens and comforter and we make my bed.

"If you get nothing else accomplished today," she says, "at least you can sleep in comfort, not chaos."

About that time, my dad returns to my room.

"I came back to see if you needed help with anything, but I see you haven't done anything to need help with," he says critically. Then he announces, "Sisi is practically unpacked."

"Don't really care," I reply.

My dad scowls at me, causing me immediately to apologize for my disrespectful tone.

"Sorry, Daddy." But not sorry.

"It's fine," my mom interjects, heading off one of my dad's notorious Essence-Ebony comparisons, which invariably ends with him proving again why Essence is a better student, a better daughter, and maybe even a better person than me.

"She'll work it out, won't you, Bunnie?"

Chastised and feeling shamed, what else can I say but, "Yes ma'am." Like I have any other options.

Before my dad can say anything more, my mom stands up and declares the conversation over.

"Glad we worked that out. Now let's take the girls to grab a quick dinner before we get back on the road. It's already after six and we have an hour drive to Johnny and Yvonne's place. You know I need time to rest before the affair tonight."

That's right. When our parents leave us they'll be getting their party on old people style. Uncle Johnny, our dad's best friend since college, and Aunt Yvonne are celebrating their twentieth wedding anniversary. They rented a huge villa in Westbrooke and will be hanging out there all weekend with our parents and some of their other close friends. Meanwhile, I'll be stuck here.

My parents lead the way down the hall. Before we even reach my sister's room, we see her and a parade of undesirables – Essence's friends - streaming in and out of her doorway. We watch her transform as she reunites with her flock. This scene kills the minimal interest I had in spending any more time with my family. With my eyes, I plead with my parents not to force me to suffer through another moment with this person Essence has become.

Thank God they hear me.

"On second thought," my mom says, "the girls can figure out dinner on their own. They probably want to spend time with their friends anyway. We should get on the road."

Daddy calls Essence over and he and Mom say their farewells.

"Don't forget to give each other your room key codes," he commands.

"I already did," Essence brags.

"That's Daddy's girl."

19

"Actually we both already did," I say. "Not just her."

He doesn't acknowledge hearing me, but I'm not surprised.

Our parents walk me back to my room. As Daddy says good-bye, he sternly warns me to make him proud this year. My mom wraps her arms around me.

"You got this, Lady Bug," she whispers. "Just remember, you could never be nothing. You're so special and so worthy I can't even put it into words. God placed a beautiful light in you and you just need to keep shining your light. Nobody else has the light you have and you couldn't have copied it from your sister if you wanted to. It's time you let your own light shine, baby. And please stop looking back and bringing up all those sad stories. You can't change the past so focus on what's ahead. There's so much greatness waiting for you. Go grab it. And know we love you no matter what."

My eyes fill with tears. "Thanks, Mom."

She plants a dozen kisses all over my face, which usually annoys me. But today, those kisses make me smile and give me hope.

AFTER OUR PARENTS LEAVE, I START UNPACKING. IN THE process, I find a keepsake box filled with some of my old pictures and letters, my favorite childhood storybook, and some other treasures. My mom had me bring this box to school last year in case I needed some reminders of home. Curiously, it found its way back again.

When I remove the lid, I discover a note my mom gave me when I graduated from high school. It says, "Expect great things and great things will come." Under that, I find seven or eight photos from various dance recitals, vacations, birthday parties, and other momentous occasions. There's even a picture of me standing on top of the monkey bars with my arms raised high.

"Tay was just talking about this day," I say smiling. Not only did I amaze my friends by climbing to the top, I even jumped off and flew to the ground. My mother was yelling like a crazy lady because she thought I hurt myself. Lucky for me, the playground surface was made of rubber.

All the kids were clapping and cheering for me. They treated me like a superhero. Many days later my mother gave me this picture, which she snapped right before I jumped. Looking at it now and thinking about that day makes me feel good mainly because it was the first time I did something Essence couldn't do. After I jumped, she ran over, lifted me off the ground, and cheered with the other kids who had gathered around.

"Bunnie, how did you learn how to do that? That was incredible. Did you guys see that?" she screamed.

"I don't know but try it. It's easy," I said.

I tried to get her to jump, but she just shook her head.

"No way! I can't do anything like that. I'll leave that superhero stuff to you," she replied.

After reliving that day in my mind several times, and reminding myself how powerful and strong . . . and special everyone thought I was, I put that picture and my mom's note on the bulletin board above my desk.

The next thing I do, truly takes me back to when I was a kid. I pull the storybook out of the box and read it out loud to myself. Not only does it energize me in a way that only this book can, but it reinforces what Tay said - that once upon a time I really was the bravest kid in class and I really was the one who did the cool stuff other kids couldn't do. And not because I was Sisi's twin, but because I was me.

If I could do it then, I certainly can do it now. It's time to become that brave, can-do-anything Ebony again and start acting like "something special."

With that, my former self speaks a line to my present self from the book I just read - *"I think I can. I think I can. I think I can. I know I can."*

Chapter Four

I n my entire first year of college, I made exactly two friends,
Mercedes and Kendra, who everybody calls KK. They were
the only bright spots in my life and I'm thrilled when I get a
message from Mercedes in our group chat.

M: Hola Chicas. Just got here. This family is making me so loca.
Where y'all at? Can't wait to see u!

Me: Heyyyy! In my room. My people are gone. Staring at the
walls.

M: LOL Eb. Wish I could rescue u. Will let u know when they
leave. They wanna eat first. It's gonna be a circus. OMG

Me: LMBO. Ima order food. Not ready to hit the yard without
y'all. ☹

M: Aww ☹

K: Sup y'all?! Still @ JFK airport waiting on my delayed connection. Won't be in til late. Hit u up tomorrow.

Me: Yikes. Safe travels KK TTYT

M: JFK sucks. Sorry you got a delay. TTYS

Mercedes was my first real Bryce friend. We met shortly
before fall mid-terms in the library. That's where I spent most of
my time back then, mainly because I was failing Calculus and
falling behind in my other classes. Plus, the library was the only
place I didn't feel alone. At that time, my sister lived in a

different dorm, had a different class schedule, and had made her own group of friends, which included most of the black students I would have wanted to associate with. Once she claimed them, they were off-limits to me. She had also started phasing me out of her life as part of untwinning me.

Early on, I made friends with some of my white classmates, but they wore me out with their so-called wokeness. And if one more of those girls tried to touch my hair to satisfy her curiosity about my natural coils somebody was gonna catch hands. I had to leave them alone. That's when I met Mercedes.

She drew my attention because she had the body of J-Lo, the beauty of Queen Bey, and the fashion savvy of Rihanna. The bold colors she wore and her unexpected way of mixing patterns and prints made her stand out – in a good way. Not to mention, while I could barely manage to put on mascara and lip-gloss before my classes, that girl had her face beat to the gawds every day. Seeing her had me wondering how cool it would be to have her as a friend. One day, we finally met. It happened by chance, but she might've been an answer to a prayer I didn't even know I had made.

While I was studying in the library, Mercedes randomly came over and asked if she could share my table.

"Yes," I shouted, sounding way too excited about her joining me. She stepped back at first, but after looking me over, decided I wasn't crazy. She sat down across from me and introduced herself.

"Thanks," she said. "I'm Mercedes by the way."

What a perfect name for her, I thought. "I'm Ebony."

"Are you a freshman?" she asked.

"Yeah, sadly."

"Me too. But sadly is not good. One day you'll have to tell me that story."

I liked that she thought we would have future conversations. Right now, she had more questions. "Where you from? I'm from Miami."

"D.C." I said, not thinking my hometown could compete with hers.

"Oh, my God." she shouted. "I love D.C."

We heard a chorus of "shhh" from a nearby study group whose members apparently didn't appreciate her excitement. Mercedes and I both laughed and continued talking more quietly out of respect for the Einsteins around us.

"Like I was saying," she continued, "D.C. is so beautiful. My dad took us there a few times to see those Cherry Blossoms. I can definitely see why you might be bummed out about being at Bryce coming from there. That's how I felt at first coming from Miami."

"At first?" I asked with wide-eyed curiosity. "Why not still? Bryce is no Miami. You must be dying."

"No, baby, I bring my Miami heat wherever I go. I got over that freakin' Bryce boredom with the quickness. That's why my Mami calls me a party-in-a-box. I don't need the place to give me fun. I find a way to make it fun."

"Please show me the way."

"I gotchu," she said.

By the end of our conversation, I learned that my future best friend's full name was Mercedes Ana del Rosa Hernández and she was a pre-med major, originally from Colombia. Like me, she hadn't made many friends at Bryce to that point.

"It's hard meeting girls here," she confessed. "They're so catty. Not at all like my friends in Miami. My homegirls are so fly."

"Mine too. Making friends was never a problem for me until I got here," I told her.

"Well, whatever," she responded, rolling her neck and waving her hand. "We can be our own crew."

Mercedes and I did become a crew of sorts. At first, we just studied together a few times a week. We would spend more time eating and talking than in the books. That changed when Kendra joined our group.

Kendra and I met last year in hell, known to most as Calculus. She was one of the best students in the class. I had to be the worst, which was odd because my grades in AP Calculus in high school were always high. My brain just refused to function in that class. The teacher saw my struggle and asked Kendra to tutor me. My own pride or stupidity kept me from accepting her help until my mid-term exam failure. The fear of my father sent me running to her as soon as I saw my grade. Kendra put a lot of effort into helping me and we brought my failing grade up to a low C.

Second semester, we worked together a lot more, but didn't start hanging out socially until Spring Break when Kendra came to D.C. to visit her cousin. She and I met for a movie and ended up having dinner and going shopping afterward. We discovered we had a lot in common. We both ran track in high school, had the same zodiac sign - Virgo, and were obsessed with Michelle Obama. Before she left D.C., I made sure Kendra got to see the official portraits of President and First Lady Obama at the National Portrait Gallery. That probably ensured our inevitable friendship.

Kendra was the first person at Bryce to call me "Eb." She decided to give me a nickname, even though I already had two, just to make a point.

"If your sis wanna be Es, you need to be Eb. So that's what I'm calling you," she told me.

"KK's right, Ebony," Mercedes said. "You gotta do a new you."

Once Mercedes started calling me "Eb," my new name was here to stay.

When the three of us studied together, Kendra made me concentrate on Calculus, which forced Mercedes to do her own class work. Kendra was the drill sergeant who kept us on task, which we both needed and welcomed. By the end of the semester, our crew of two had grown to three.

WHILE I WAIT FOR MERCEDES TO FINISH WITH HER FAMILY, I try to place a food delivery order. Every option estimates a minimum two-hour delivery window. I'll be dead from starvation by then. My only choice is to go out alone, but the last thing I want to do as the first public act of my sophomore year is to venture onto campus by myself. That seems so pathetic to me.

Familiar voices in my head whisper, "You got this."

This isn't Tay or my mom speaking. It can only be my angels.

According to my Grandma Patsy, everyone has angels who watch over them. She told me about mine when I was about six or seven. After one really bad dream, I thought the creatures from this creepy cartoon show called *Fosters Home for Imaginary Friends* actually lived under my bed.

"You need to stop filling your mind with that nonsense," Grandma Patsy warned. *"None of that mess is real. Besides, Bible says God has assigned special angels to watch over you every day and night. So can't no monsters do nothing to you."*

About my angels -- I call them Stella and Lola. They're not the typical celestial beings you see in church with the long robes and wings. My angels aren't white either. They're richly melanated like me and I bet they're rocking hot outfits from some top designer's latest sustainable fashion line. They definitely don't have halos. They wear their natural locs as crowns.

With time, I eventually grew out of believing in creatures under my bed, but never outgrew my angels. They protected me from all the seen and unseen dangers that growing up brought – sleep away camp, my first date, my first kiss, learning to drive, and the worst, getting shots. They also worked overtime to keep me from completely losing it freshman year.

"Go for it," they whisper.

My spirit receives their encouragement, and I feel a renewed sense of confidence and bravery.

I know I can.

AFTER FRESHENING MYSELF UP, I STEP OUT OF MY ROOM AND notice Essence and her DWBs heading my way. Seeing them blows my entire mood. They walk past me without speaking. Before going into the room two doors down from mine, one of her friends must've made a snide remark about me because they all turn around, including Essence, and laugh in my direction.

Instinctively, I retreat back into the safety of my own room.

I thought I could.

But I can't.

Chapter Five

✦❖✦

If screaming could break the choking grip my sister has on my confidence, I would let one out so loud, it would be heard all across this campus. But such an outburst would surely result in referrals to all kinds of medical professionals and maybe even law enforcement. A better alternative is to deep-breathe my way through this setback.

Inhale.

Exhale.

Inhale.

Exhale.

I wait for another angelic push to walk out the door again.

A litany of words begins sounding in my head.

"You're something special."

"Let your light shine."

"You got this."

With my hand on the doorknob, I imagine myself moving beyond this moment on to the next, and then to the one after that. I'm determined not to let what has already happened ruin what is yet to come. My stomach reminds me that my original mission was to go out and get food. I make up my mind to move forward and jet out of my dorm before anything or anyone else gets in the way of my progress.

Once I'm outside, the campus feels familiar and not at all as lonely or daunting as I had feared. At the same time, there are so many new people walking about. Some even stop me to ask for directions. Imagine that. Each person I pass on my way to my destination - Food Truck Row - represents the possibility for something better. That gives me hope.

Food Truck Row, or The Row, is a popular eating spot from Friday to Sunday at Bryce. It's a quick seven-minute walk from my dorm. As expected, no less than twenty trucks and food carts are parked along both sides of a two-block stretch of Campus Drive. There's a choice of food for every desire – vegan and vegetarian, dairy-free and gluten-free, pizzas and patties, hot dogs and hoagies, Mexican and Mediterranean, sushi and salad, Thai and tacos, fried everything, and desserts galore.

I weave through the swarm of people who, like me, are searching for a culinary option that will make their taste buds dance. The fragrant aroma from each food vendor I pass pulls me in and my stomach is ready to commit, until I'm lured away by the smell of the seasonings and spices from the next vendor. My indecisiveness continues until I reach Tito's Tacos, which has a "move-in day" special and no line. Decision made.

After a short wait, I receive my baja fish tacos, sparkling limeade, and cinnamon dessert churros. This food looks and smells so good that I practically run to find a place to devour it. Not surprisingly, I end up at the Quad, which is a great place to park myself for a little while and enjoy my food.

With its central location on campus, the Quad is always busy with people, but even moreso today with all the families moving their kids into their new homes away from home. Like the rest of the campus, the Quad got dressed up for this weekend. The grass is beautifully manicured and new floral arrangements have been planted in each of its four corners. The statue of Bishop the Panther, our school's mascot, sits proudly in the center of the vast lawn wearing a fresh coat of black paint. Draped around Bishop's neck are three ribbons, one for each of the upper-classes.

At the end of Convocation on Monday, the Provost will add a fourth ribbon for the Class of 2022. Their ribbon will hang on Bishop until they graduate. After the ribbon-hanging, the entire campus body is supposed to rub Bishop's paw to ensure we all have a successful year. I might need to rub that paw twice to make extra sure this year works out in my favor.

The first available bench I find sits on the east end of the Quad near the the Campus Store and Multi-Cultural Center, or "MCC." This spot gives me a great view of the people. And they are straight entertaining me right now. The wide-eyed freshmen and their over-bearing parents dressed from head to toe in Bryce merch especially amuse me because that was us last year. Our parents were so ridiculous with shopping. They bought everything that said "Bryce College" and probably didn't use half of it.

The juniors and seniors are easy to spot. They're the ones posted up in front of the upperclassmen dorms, which surround the Quad on the north and south sides, or at their fraternity and sorority plots, which are located along the entire lawn. Some of those woke white kids from last year see me and wave. Thankfully, they keep walking. A few girls from my old dorm come over to say hello. We chat about our summer activities and room assignments this year. Of course, they're impressed I'm in The Castle. I listen to their conversation more than I talk. They eventually leave and I hope they know I wasn't being rude. But these tacos were giving me life and required my full attention.

Speaking of my full attention, across the Quad, I see someone who definitely needs that from me right now. That's either Zayn Malik or his lookalike. My brain keeps saying "look away," but my eyes refuse to obey. His messy, long, wavy hair gives him a bad boy edge. The motorcycle jacket and biker boots he has on make him look hot; sexy hot, not heat hot. But maybe that, too, considering it's like 80 something degrees.

Uh oh. He sees me looking at him. What now?

Unfortunately, I'm not able to turn away, but staring at a stranger staring at me feels weird. We make some kind of tele-kinetic connection with our eyes. He smiles and gives me a head nod. I smile back but quickly shift my focus to my food to hide the excitement dancing across my face. When I glance back up, he's walking toward me. Why can't I have a friend here to make what's about to happen less awkward? The thought of calling Mercedes crosses my mind, but it's too late. This Zayn lookalike is standing in front of me.

"Mind if I join you?" he asks.

"Not at all," I nervously reply, moving over to make room. He's even more beautiful close up but doesn't sound as enchanting as I expected. Points off for vocal quality. He also seems to only be about my height, which is 5'9" without shoes. My favorite heels have me coming in at just over 6 feet. This height challenge might result in more point deductions. I still welcome his company.

"I'm Donovan," he says as he sits on the opposite side of the bench. "Besides being the most attractive woman I've seen today, you are?"

He's quite the charmer. But that voice. It has an annoying scratchiness to it; again, not what I expected given the overall package. Focusing on his gorgeous face helps me listen to his conversation without hearing him talk. As difficult as that sounds, it works.

"My name is Ebony."

"Ebony. That's a perfect name for such a pretty lady."

"Thanks. I'll let my parents know you appreciate their work."

Essence used that line plenty of times when guys gave her the same kind of compliment.

He laughs. "And she's funny. You're obviously intelligent because you're at Bryce. Bet makers would call that a trifecta. Must be my lucky day."

Without thinking, I respond, "It must be mine, too."

That comment puts a big cheesy grin on his face. Meanwhile, I'm looking around for Essence because that sounded like her voice and her words coming from my mouth.

"So, what's your story, Ebony?"

"I'm not quite sure how to answer that," I tell him. "My story is still being written."

"Interesting." After a short pause, he says, "Do you think you have a chapter in your story where you can include me?"

Can I scream, "Yes?" Of course I can't. But I'm floored that a guy like this is even talking to me. I'm able to maintain my cool and give an appropriate response.

"Not sure about that since I don't even know you."

"What do you want to know? I'm an open book," he says spreading his arms out wide to make his point.

Instead of taking time to formulate a probing question, I blurt out the first thing that pops into my head.

"Is that jacket hot? It looks nice, but it is August."

He leans over and laughs. "You get right to the the point, don't you? That's kinda sexy."

Donovan's laughing smile goes back to that cheesy grin. Sexy is not a word any guy has ever used to describe me. I've been called cute, pretty, even stunning. But not sexy. I'm wondering what he sees that nobody else ever has.

"I'm glad you like what you see," he adds. "But to answer your question, no, it's not hot."

He shows me how the jacket is ventilated and has these perforated leather panels that keep him cool.

"What else you wanna know?" he asks, moving the conversation along.

"Do you ride?"

Wow, did I really say that? Great question, Captain Obvious.

"Yes. I do ride. My bike is the red Ducati over there," he says, pointing to a beautiful motorcycle parked on the grass near the senior dorm.

"Isn't there some rule about parking on the lawn?" I ask realizing he doesn't just look like a bad boy, he might actually be one.

"Rules are made to be broken," he responds. He moves a little closer to me and adds, "And to answer your next question, yes, it is a two-seater and yes, I do have an extra helmet and a spare hot jacket."

I chuckle and tell him, "That wasn't gonna be my next question."

"Okay then. Hit me with the next one."

This convo feels like a job interview, which I'm not feeling. And Donovan, at times, comes across as someone very stuck on himself; like the guys Essence dates these days. Not at all my type. But I'm surprised at how easy it is for me to continue a conversation with him, as superficial as it is. We move from talking about his motorcycle to that series of mundane questions college kids get asked so much that it becomes tiresome and annoying.

"Where are you from?"

"Where do you live on campus?"

"What's your classification and major?"

"What are your hopes and dreams?"

He gives no indication that my basic inquiries bother him. To the contrary, he's gracious and open.

"I'm a senior finance/international relations major. Not living on campus this semester because I'm doing a co-op in New York City."

He tells me about the co-op program and gets really excited talking about beginning his career in global finance and one day funding an international health equity non-profit. He also talks about other amazing ventures he has planned, world travel he hopes to take, and the huge impact he wants to have on the world. I'm more than a little bit impressed.

Donovan then makes a point of saying, "None of my success will mean anything without a woman to share it with and about fitty-'leven kids to carry on my legacy."

"Not fitty-'leven," I say, laughing. "That's a lot of kids. And you expect that from one woman?

"That's my plan. You interested?"

Giving him the side-eye, I let that question fall right to the ground with no verbal reply.

Donovan's problem is he goes from being this beautiful guy with mad swag to that sleazy guy in the club who starts professing his love after one dance. If Donovan wasn't so fine, I'd leave. But I'm feeling too hyped having a guy like him even talk to me, not to mention wanting me to have all his pretend babies.

"Let me stop messin' with you," he says. "Tell me, what's Ebony all about?"

"Still figuring that out," I say.

He runs through the same boring questions I asked him, but it doesn't seem like he's interviewing me. Actually, it feels like he's really trying to get to know me. To be so into himself, Donovan focuses intently on my every word, and even asks follow-up questions, which leads to me unexpectedly opening up about my painful first-year experience. I even talk about my complicated relationships with Essence and my dad.

"Bottom line," I say, after I've shared more with him - a complete stranger – than I have with anyone else in recent days, except maybe Taylor, "now I have to figure out what's gonna work for me, not just in terms of school, my major, and that stuff, but with my entire life. It's gonna take a whole new approach."

"Wow, Ebony. That's deep." His observation is frank and completely accurate.

Donovan leans closer to me. With a serious expression and convincing tone, he says, "Let me give you some advice. All that shit, excuse my French, with your pops, your sister, freshman year, let it all go. Freshman year is over. You can't go back. All you can do is move ahead."

"Yeah, that's what my mom told me."

"She's a wise woman," he notes. "A lot of us get off to a rough start, but who cares how you begin the race as long as you finish strong?"

"Hmmm." I nod in agreement. Donovan's words make sense.

He continues, "If your pops is like mine, he's hard on you because he wants your best. If you give him that, then it's not your problem if he ain't happy. It's his. You gotta decide whose race you're running, his or yours. Once you decide that, life will be a lot easier."

"Never thought about it like that," I say.

"I'm telling you. I learned the hard way and that's why I'm chasing my dreams and not going to med school, which was the plan my family had for me. It's liberating to declare 'No, I'm doing this my way.' My mom didn't talk to me for weeks when I did, but she got over it 'cause she knew I was right."

"Look at you, breaking this life thing down for me," I interject. "Should I be paying you for all this good advice?"

"You know I could never take your money," he says, "but I'm sure there are other ways you can settle your debt."

Sigh. We're back to sleazy club guy. I give Donovan the side-eye again. He returns my look with a smug expression and keeps talking.

"Now that sister of yours sounds like what my mama would call a piece of work."

"That she is," I say, chuckling.

"Best thing you can do for her, is give her what she wants. Leave her alone. Do your own thing. Show her you're as phenomenal as she is. And stop giving her so much control over your happiness."

Everything Donovan has concluded is right. I'll never please my dad, not as long as Essence is outdoing me. So, that shouldn't even be an aspiration. Essence doesn't want me in her life and I don't want to be in it. I'll need to figure out how to create my own existence in a place that's so full of her presence. Wow. To not know me, Donovan just fixed my life better than Iyanla could have.

"Hey Ebony, you still with me?

Donovan's question signals that I must've missed part of the conversation.

"My bad. Got lost in a thought," I reply.

"About me hopefully." The flirtatious grin he had earlier returns. I don't even wanna imagine what's going through his mind.

"It was. But probably not in the way you're thinking."

"That's okay. At least I got you thinking about me."

"You're a mess," I say, shaking my head.

Donovan and I continue talking about some good things Bryce can offer that he wants me to check out. He is happy about me living in The Castle and says it will change my life. His friend is a Resident Assistant, or RA, in East Tower, so he's already had a chance to hang out there.

As we continue our conversation, the lamp posts around the Quad flicker as day turns to dusk. Donovan and I notice them at the same time. We share stories of how, as kids we knew to get our behinds home when those street lights came on. Of course, being the perpetual rule breaker that he is, he admits he often stayed out until pitch dark.

"Nooo," I say faking disbelief.

He laughs. "Guess I've always had a little rebel in me. I got my share of behind whoopings because of it, too."

For a brief moment, I entertain the thought that this rebel might be fun to continue to get to know. But my inner voices think it's probably best to leave this one alone.

So I stand up and say, "Well, Donovan, I've really enjoyed talking to you. Thanks for the wisdom. You gave me a lot to think about. But I'm gonna take a cue from the streetlights and head back to my room. I've got so much unpacking to do."

"Aw, man. That's the worst," he says. "My girl always brings way too much stuff back to school and then gets mad when it doesn't all fit in that little piece of closet in her dorm room."

Wait?! Did he just say his "girl," as in his girlfriend, present tense? If this mofo has a girlfriend and is hitting on me like this, he loses all the points and all credibility with me.

"Your girl? You got a girlfriend?" I ask, sounding offended.

"What? Nah. Why you think that?" he asks, looking confused by my suggestion.

"You just said 'your girl always brings too much stuff back.' That sounds like you have a girlfriend."

"Oh, nah, I misspoke on that. I don't have a girlfriend. I had one. We broke up this summer. So I probably should have said my ex."

You probably shouldn't have brought her up." That tone had the essence of Essence all over it.

He laughs. "My bad. You afraid of a little competition?"

"I don't do competition," I tell him.

"Okay, Ebony. I hear you. I'm diggin' your confidence."

He got that all wrong. Confidence isn't the reason I don't compete for guys. It's actually because I have none, or very little I should say. These days, I'm probably my most insecure when I measure myself against other girls, and not just Essence. The last thing I'd ever do is go after a guy with a girlfriend or who messes around with a lot of girls. I'm just not made for that.

But whatever. I don't bother to correct Donovan's misthinking about my confidence level. He makes a few more suggestive remarks that are probably intended for someone more sure of herself than me. He seems to be developing the wrong idea about the kind of person I am. It's definitely time for me to leave before this conversation goes too far left.

"Well, on that note," I say, "I really do need to get going." Donovan reaches out and takes my hand.

"I can't let you go unless I can see you again. Let me get your number so we can hook up."

Essence would give him her number and he would call her. If I had a dollar for every time a guy asked for my number like this and didn't call, I'd be rich. Donovan seems like all those other guys in a way. But, there's something about him that draws me in even after telling myself to walk away. I end up giving him my number knowing I probably shouldn't.

"I'll call you later," he says.

Sure he will. I won't hold my breath.

Chapter Six

✥

As soon as I'm out of Donovan's sight, I send a group message to Mercedes and Kendra telling them about my new admirer, and to Taylor, even though she's on a plane and won't see it until tomorrow. Scrolling through my inbox, I find two unopened messages. The first is from my mom letting me know she put something under my pillow. Money, I hope. The second message is from Essence.

E: Hey. Came by your room to check on u.

Looks like this message came in when Donovan and I were talking. Maybe that's why I felt Essence all over my words. That would give our twin-sense a whole 'nother meaning.

As thoughtful as her message might appear, my own twin-sense tells me Essence just wanted me to know she checked on me. Maybe our parents told her to do it. I'm sure that's it. If she was really interested in how I was doing, she would've added 'U good?' or 'U OK?' to that message like she's done before.

Delete.

Back in my room, I rush to my bed, reach under my pillow, and find a journal.

"Today Is A Fresh Start" is imprinted in gold on the dark blue cover. Each page has a heading that reads:

Today I start fresh. I am better than I was. I am ____

37

How could my mom have known this would be perfect for my sophomore experience?

After thinking about it for a few minutes, in bold letters, I write the words **SOMETHING SPECIAL** on the blank line on the first page.

Friday, August 31, 2018

Hi. I'm writing this because my mom said it's true and putting the word NOTHING on this beautiful page would be lame. Between my vision, my mom's talk, and oddly enough Donovan's advice, I'm getting the message that I need to change how I see myself and maybe that will improve how life treats me. Sounds simple enough. It's worth trying. What I've been doing ain't working at all. Gotta start feeling special. ttyl

MY LADIES OF HIP-HOP PLAYLIST PROVIDES THE PERFECT soundtrack for unpacking and setting up my room. The Bad Gal Rih Rih starts me moving.

Work, work, work, work, work.

He said me haffi...

The music energizes me and, over the next three, almost four hours, I'm able to get most of my clothes and supplies unpacked and organized. As I'm about to collapse onto my bed from exhaustion, a text alert chimes on my phone. Mercedes must finally be free.

D: Hey Beautiful. Need 2 C U. Lets hook up

I'm in shock and just stare at the message. Then I read it multiple times to convince myself it's real. I didn't expect to hear from Donovan so soon, or at all. But a text message?

Me: Is this supposed 2 B U calling me?

D: LOL. Yeah. Come out and play

Me: Play? 2 late. 2morrow?

D: 2nite, PPLZ. Lvn in the AM for NYC. Need 2 c u again b4 I go

Something tells me to say no. My angels perhaps? It's almost midnight and Donovan is basically a stranger to me. But this could be my chance to shine my light. And he did say pretty please.

Me: Will make an exception this time

D: Cool. Meet me behind your dorm n 20 mins

Me: Y back there?

D: Legal parking

Me: LOL OK

Putting aside my fatigue, I change into something more suitable for a nighttime escapade – black leggings, vintage t-shirt, and a stylish zip-up hoodie in case it's cool tonight. I brush my hair and put on a little makeup. Once I feel sufficiently cute'd up, I go to the walkway at the back of my dorm and wait. And wait. Twenty minutes turns out to be a lot longer. My text and call to Donovan get no response. Just when I'm ready to give up, he sends me a message.

D: C U in 5

That's it? Where's the apology for making me wait? And why am I standing at the back door anyway, like I'm sneaking out the house?

None of this follows *The Code--Dating Rules To Live By*, a handwritten list of guidelines gifted to my sister and me from our older brother, Kingston, on our sixteenth birthday. *The Code* has been my guide for dating ever since then and this Donovan situation breaks every rule. Against my better judgment, I put *The Code* aside and stand around for the longest five minutes in history.

A rumbling in the distance announces Donovan's long-delayed arrival. He pulls up, takes his helmet off, and says casually, "Hope you haven't been waiting too long. Hop on."

Really? I'm not sure what Essence would do right now, but I'm kinda over this hook-up. And I don't care how gorgeous he looks sitting on that beautiful bike. The fact that I'm standing here with my arms folded across my chest and not hopping on should let him know this outing might be over before it starts.

Donovan must see I'm in my feelings because he looks at me apologetically. Points earned for reading my signals well. He gets

39

off the bike and walks toward me. His good looks disarm me and I drift into a daydream starring him and me, and maybe a beach or better yet, a mountain cabin. Then he starts talking, which kills the dream sequence. He still makes it hard for me to continue to have an attitude.

"You're not scared to ride, are you pretty lady?"

His annoying voice sounds very sultry right now and I'm wondering how he managed that. I take a second or two to refocus. He repeats his question with less inquiry.

"No," I say firmly. "But you know it's after midnight now. You shouldn't have me out here waiting all this time."

He grins and says, "You're right and I'm sorry, Cinderella. You not gonna turn to a pumpkin if you stay out past midnight are you?"

"What?" His question, as much as his lack of courtesy, bothers me. "That makes no sense," I tell him. "The stagecoach turned into the pumpkin, not Cinderella. If you're gonna tease me at least get the characters right."

In my head, I add, 'And don't mess with my Disney Princesses. I don't care how fine you are.'

Donovan steps back and raises his hands in front of him in retreat.

"Okay. Don't bite my head off. That was my bad. You're right. I shouldn't have you out waitin' on me this late. I'm sorry."

He takes my hand in his and kisses it softly. "Can this frog have another chance, Princess?"

My first thought is to say 'no' and go back to my room. But I don't. This rule-breaking, *Code*-violating, Zayn looking-like brotha has mad swag and that makes him quite irresistible right now.

"Fine, I guess." I respond with just enough pout for him to know he barely got a pass.

Donovan appears relieved. "Great. Let's get you set up." He walks me to his bike and asks if I've ever ridden a motorcycle before.

"No, and hadn't planned to ride one tonight," I say, looking at him skeptically.

"Come on. I promise to be gentle." There's that grin again.

Something in me is saying turn back, but still, I don't listen. I'm kind of intrigued by Donovan now. And no matter how much I tell myself he's not for me, I can't seem to leave him alone.

He gives me a quick lesson on how to properly ride a motorcycle beginning with where to put my hands and feet. Then he explains what to expect from the ride.

"I'm not gonna do any daredevil moves," he says, "but the bike will lean at times. I'll lean with the bike and you should lean with me. The most important thing for me is that you not move around too much. If you want me to stop, hit my shoulder. Hard. You cool?"

"Not really," I say.

I'm actually pretty scared about riding at all, and even more about riding with him. I don't tell Donovan that, which probably violates *The Code* as much as anything he has or hasn't done.

Donovan reassures me that he'll keep me safe. He gives me a helmet and a female biker jacket to wear.

"You got me wearing your girlfriend's stuff? It's like that?" I ask with a bit of outrage in my voice.

"My ex. And no, it's my stuff. But you don't have to wear it," he fires back. Sounds like he's getting a little attitude behind my comment.

He's crazy if he thinks I'd ride anybody's motorcycle without protective gear, so I put it on. I'm still thrown by him acting like we both don't know who this all belonged to. I don't say any more about it since it's obviously a sensitive subject. But that's more points lost.

"Where exactly are we riding?" I ask.

"I don't know. Wherever the spirit takes us," he says casually.

So, not only am I about to take a late-night ride on a motorcycle with a guy I just met, but he can't even give me our exact destination. I'm starting to think that this might actually be a bad idea.

"Are we leaving the state?" I inquire flippantly but kinda not.

"Of course not. We'll just ride around town, nothing too adventurous. Not for your first time."

That makes me feel a little better, but I still share my location with Kendra and Mercedes before I get on the bike. That way, if anything does happen to me, they'll know where to look for my body.

Chapter Seven

❦

When we zoom off, I hold Donovan's waist with both arms. The bike makes such a loud roar at first that my to heart drops into my stomach.

My body tenses up, I breathe faster, and squeeze Donovan tighter as I go from being afraid to being terrified. He must notice this change. When we stop at a red light about five minutes later, he turns to me and shouts,

"How's it going back there?"

"Scary," is all I can say.

"Just relax and enjoy the ride," he yells out as he speeds off when the light changes.

Eventually, the bike's engine settles into a steady, more peaceful and relaxing hum and I become less tense. Donovan's intoxicating scent flows freely through his fancy ventilated jacket, filling the air around me. I begin to lose myself in this experience, pressing myself closer to him and holding on to him more assertively, no longer because of fear, but just because he said I could.

Donovan starts taking curves and turns at faster speeds making the bike lean almost to the ground. No matter how agile his bike may be or how skilled of a driver he is, this maneuver frightens me every time and causes me to cling to him more tightly each time he takes me into one of those dips. The tighter I hold him, it seems, the faster and harder he rides.

We reach a stretch of straight open road and he puts the bike into what feels like turbo-drive for miles. When my capacity for this thrill maxes out, I punch his shoulder as hard as I can. He slows down and we ride at a more sensible speed until we reach a safe place to stop. Donovan parks the bike and we get off.

"You okay?" he asks.

"No," I shout, but he should be able to see that from the way I'm shaking.

"This was your first ride. I expect that reaction. The next time will be better."

"There won't be a next time. I can't do that again," I cry out in protest.

"Oh, really? So how you planning to get back to school? Ain't no bus or rideshare coming out here."

Dang. He's right.

We take our helmets and jackets off and Donovan leads me to a nearby park. There are no signs of human life out here now, but this area is probably a favorite of the locals, especially with the splash park and playground not too far from where we end up sitting.

Donovan and I talk and laugh about nothing in particular. He does bring up the twin thing again.

"So there were two of you on campus last year?" he asks, not expecting a response. "That's a lot of black beauty. How did I miss that?"

"Maybe you were busy with your girlfriend," I say in a light-hearted way.

"Okay. You got me with that one."

While we talk about the real reasons Donovan never saw me last year, we end up back on the subject of my freshman year woes. He again advises me to leave that experience in the past.

"You wanna shine now, you gotta grind now."

"Meek Mill fan?" I say, laughing.

"Oh you caught that?"

We start rapping the lyrics of "Dreams and Nightmares," poorly imitating Meek's facial expressions and hand gestures from the video.

Without me realizing it, Donovan closes the space between us and puts his arm around me.

"You're one beautiful chocolate woman," he says softly. "Bet you hear that all the time."

"Actually, I don't," I admit.

"That's hard to believe."

"Guess I'm just not quite the attention-grabber these days," I say with a tinge of sadness in my voice.

"Well, you certainly grabbed my attention. Now what do you plan to do with it?"

Good question. And one I hadn't given any thought to.

Donovan doesn't wait for my response. He caresses my face and neck, sending chills throughout my entire body. He moves even closer and asks me again, "You got my attention. Now what?"

Without thinking, I lean in and kiss him. At first, it's just a soft lip kiss. Then, I slide my tongue into his mouth. When it meets his, I lead him slowly into a rhythmical dance; a tango perhaps. Abruptly, I end our dance and unwittingly leave him wanting more. Meanwhile, I'm wondering where I learned to kiss that way because I've never experienced anything like that before.

"Wow. That was nice . . . and unexpected," he says of our first kiss. "Now you really have my attention."

Unexpected is right.

Donovan begins exploring my fingers, first with his lips then with his tongue. What have I started? This might be some kind of fetish for him. It feels creepy to me, so I take my hand away.

He responds by saying, "If you take that from me I'm gonna need to find something else to do with my mouth."

That sounds to me like he's waiting for a special request. I have none for him.

"You seem pretty smart, I'm sure you can figure something out," I reply.

And figure it out he does. Donovan puts his mouth to work.

After kissing up, down, and all around my neck, our lips meet again. He's in control this time and he kisses me more passionately than I kissed him. His is a hard, rugged kiss with dips and turns, much like our ride on his motorcycle.

I lose myself in the sensation his lips give me and allow him access to parts of my body no man has ever touched. He lifts my shirt and spreads kisses across my stomach and chest, lingering around my breasts. My body becomes aroused in ways and in places that are new to me and I give no thought to where this might lead until I feel the hardness of Donovan's body against my inner thigh.

Bells and whistles go off in my head and become louder the more aroused he and I become. Never did I imagine this experience being so noisy. Then it hits me. The clamor isn't the sound of pleasure pulses in my brain. These are all the safety warnings I've ever learned alerting me to impending danger. This has gone too far and at any moment . . . *it* could happen. But I don't want *it* yet. Not here. Not like this. Not with a guy I just met a few hours ago.

I squirm to try to escape from the compromising position I've gotten myself into, which Donovan must mistake for enjoyment. His movements become even more sensual in response to my attempts to free myself. Eventually, I break my lips away from his and manage to move my body parts away, too. Donovan looks at me but doesn't give me a chance to say anything. He pulls me back into a kiss. I push him away again.

"We should stop," I say.

Donovan doesn't acknowledge me with words. He caresses my arms, inviting me with his eyes to give myself back to this experience. He begins to rub me between my legs. My level of arousal skyrockets even as I'm saying to myself, 'not here, not like this, not with him.'

I'm on the brink of an explosion.

"Stop," I insist.

Donovan becomes still, but his body pulsates next to me.

He stares at me like he's waiting for me to unpause the action.

"We can't do this," I say.

He sits up and leans his back against the bench, freeing me to put my clothing back in place. I search his face for an expression or an emotion. He shows neither. It's obvious he's still aroused because his package is exposed, and what a package it is. I don't know what he planned to do with all that, but now that I see it, I'm glad I don't have to find out.

"What's wrong?" he asks.

"Nothing. This just isn't how I wanna do this," I explain. Donovan gets close to me again. Our bodies barely touch, but I can feel the heat of his desire.

"Tell me how you want it then. I'll make it happen."

The expression on my face must be unintentionally alluring because Donovan begins kissing me again. He takes my hand and rubs himself with it.

"Tell me how you want it," he whispers as he presses my hand against his body and his lips more firmly against mine.

The voices in my head holler, "Remember. Not like this."

I say "No," between each kiss. After the third "No," Donovan leans away from me and asks if I'm really saying no.

"I'm saying no, but . . ."

He shouts, "You can't say 'no, but,' Ebony. That's not how this is done." Now he sounds real irritated.

"How would I know that? I've never done this before," I yell back in my defense.

Donovan's eyes widen. In a calmer tone he says, "Wait. You saying you're a virgin?"

Before answering, I pause. "Yeah. Is that a crime?"

"Nah . . . nah it's not," he says as he stumbles over his words. "I mean, I just didn't know. You seemed real experienced to me."

"Sorry for giving you the wrong impression. I probably got caught up in the moment."

My apology is met with silence at first, followed by Donovan saying, "It's cool. Could've been me moving too fast, too."

"Yeah. Maybe," I acknowledge.

I'm still mortified, thinking that anything I said or did made Donovan think I would be cool having sex with him in a dirty park just hours after meeting him. That's not anything I would ever want to do. Yet, something about him had me one tongue tango away from doing just that.

After he gets his clothes situated, we walk to the bike and gear up for the ride back to Bryce. As he adjusts my helmet, Donovan stares at me for a few seconds and says, "You really had me going tonight. I'm getting turned on again just thinking about it."

I keep my eyes locked on him and feel my body warming up. "That makes both of us, but - " I begin to say.

"There you go with that but," Donovan says cutting me off.

"Let me finish," I say, interrupting him. "All I was gonna say is that this might work better if we actually got to know each other and dated first. It would feel more natural and less random to me if we developed a relationship before having sex."

Donovan shakes his head and lets out a long sigh.

"Ebony, you're a sweet, beautiful, probably delicious, chocolate woman. As much as I would love to be your man and give you days and nights of pleasure, I did the relationship thing. It didn't work out. I'm not ready to jump back into that. I just wanna have some fun with no obligations or responsibilities."

"That's not something I can do," I tell him.

"Guess that doesn't leave too many options for us, does it?"

"Nope."

I'm disappointed but relieved. Donovan is so far out of my league and I probably . . . no I definitely would mess up any romantic situation we had. This way is better for me and will spare me another Bryce heartbreak.

"Well then, let me take you home before your stagecoach turns into a pumpkin. Okay, Princess?"

"Sure," I say with a half-hearted smile.

"And here's some advice for you," he adds. "Next time a dude invites you out for a late night motorcycle ride, just say no. Or you might find yourself in a bad way. I'm not that dude, but you never know."

"Yeah. I get it."

That ends the conversation. Donovan and I ride back to campus. The bike roars less ferociously and takes the road less ruggedly now than it did when this journey began. My hearbeat falls into sync with the softer rumble of the bike. Even though we ride at a slow, steady pace I hold Donovan's waist tightly and take in as much of his scent as I can. I memorize the way he feels, how he smells, and the sensations his body gave mine. I enjoy my final moments with him. We'll probably never "hook up" again and I'm okay with that.

Chapter Eight

Before my eyes open fully the next morning, Mercedes and Kendra are blowing up my phone. When I answer their third call, they start talking over each other, making it impossible for me to understand either one of them.

"Wait a minute," I say cutting them both off. "One at a time."

Mercedes begins. "What the hell, Eb. Where were you and who were you with?"

Kendra adds, "And more important than that, why were you out alone at midnight?"

In my half-sleep state, I tell them everything that happened yesterday; beginning with my epiphany about Essence and me, then about meeting Donovan on the Quad. As I awaken more fully, I give them the whole story of our midnight motorcycle ride and almost losing my virginity somewhere in the middle of nowhere. I'm blushing just talking about it.

Kendra says, "That's right, Eb. Come out swinging on day one, YOLO."

Mercedes, on the other hand, does not approve. "No, Kendra. That's not right at all. Freakin' some stranger in the park? It's actually nasty. And stupid."

"There was no danger," I tell her. "He was cool. We hung out for those few hours and now it's done. He's not interested in anything serious so it ended before it really started."

"Aw man, that sucks," Kendra says. "But the semester hasn't even started so we've got lots of prowling time ahead of us."

"We?" I exclaim. "What happened to your boyfriend?"

She starts off, "If you must know. We still kickin' it. He just started at the University of Chicago. He's doin' his thing, so I'ma do what I do. He don't have a problem with it and neither should you. YOLO."

"So everybody is outta control doing this YOLO thing now," Mercedes screeches. "*Ay Dios Mio.*"

Kendra and I just laugh and assure her we're not out of control.

"But on the real," I tell them. "Last night was fun. Maybe a li'l reckless, but I couldn't help myself."

"Try harder next time, okay? Just slow down a bit." Mercedes pleads.

I say, "Sure, I'll go slower."

"Not too slow, Eb," Kendra shouts with laughter. "You gotta make up for lost time."

"Be quiet, KK and stop being a bad influence on her," Mercedes orders.

"I'm the exact opposite of a bad influence," Kendra replies. "Tell her, Eb."

"That argument is between y'all. My name is Bennett and I ain't in it."

Kendra laughs and says, "Ayyy. Good one. Gotta remember to use that."

"Just don't use it with me, Chica," Mercedes warns.

BY THE TIME WE END OUR CALL, KENDRA AND MERCEDES HAVE argued and made up. I've given them all the details about Donovan that I intend to share. And we've made plans to meet later and attend orientation together. I try to fall back asleep but can't, so I grab my journal and think about the word that describes today.

Today I start fresh. I am better than I was. I am ____

I write **YOLO!**

Saturday, September 1, 2018

Hi. Maybe it was crazy going out in the middle of the night with a stranger, but KK is right. YOLO--you only live once. I know D is out of the picture but the whole experience of meeting him and going out last night and the intimacy – I guess that's what I'll call it – did something to me. If I'm completely honest, I didn't want to stop. I know that's bad. Sorry. ttyl

AT TEN O'CLOCK, MERCEDES, KENDRA AND I MEET FOR orientation and spend the next six hours with the entire sophomore class being welcomed by school administrators and deans, getting reoriented on campus rules, attending awareness trainings, and suffering through forced meet-your-classmates activities. Even though attendance at this program is voluntary, the only way for us to get into the Bryce Back-to-School Bash tonight is to show we were here all day. The Bash, as we call it, is basically an indoor carnival. People are saying Travis Scott will be performing so everybody is hyped and we all obediently suffer through the most boring time of our young lives.

At exactly four o'clock, the last speaker in the last session concludes her remarks.

"That was painful," Kendra declares with a gasp.

"Yeah. The Bash better be worth it," Mercedes adds.

"It will be if Travis is there," I shout and start dancing.

Mercedes looks at me and shakes her head. "Save your energy for later." She then announces her plan to catch a quick nap. "Gotta be my best tonight."

Kendra and I decide to do the same and we all go our separate ways.

After some much needed rest, the three of us meet and walk to the Field House at around seven. Rumors are still circulating about Travis Scott performing.

"Hope it's true," Mercedes says. "That by itself would make those six hours in orientation hell not so bad."

I absolutely agree.

We wait almost thirty minutes just to get in because the Field House is packed. Kendra sees people she knows every few steps we take. Her popularity actually rivals my sister's, but her friends seem way more down to earth. Many of them I've seen before; a few even mistake me for Essence.

"Weren't we in Freshman English together," this one guys asks me.

"No, but I have a twin sister here, maybe it was her."

"Yeah, maybe. You seem a lot nicer than the chick who was in class with me anyway."

I shake my head and laugh. Yeah that was definitely Essence.

"I'm starving," Mercedes announces.

"Y'all know I'm always down to eat," I say.

"A'ight then. Hi Ho, Hi Ho, in search of food we go," Kendra says playfully.

We move through the crowd toward the food court set-up.

Along the way, we stop and play some of the carnival games. I try Skeeball, while Kendra and Mercedes enter a water gun contest. They lose to a freshman. Amateurs.

The three of us then join up with two guys at the ring toss booth. The one named Randell is definitely liking Kendra. They end up talking to each other and ignoring Mercedes, me, and the guy who was with Randell. The three of us amuse ourselves by playing more games until Mercedes gets refocused on eating. We signal to Kendra that we're leaving. She finishes her conversation with Randell and joins us.

"Did you just give that guy your number?" I ask.

Kendra proudly says, "Yep."

"Dang. You don't waste no time," Mercedes comments.

"Hey, when duty calls, I answer."

Kendra laughs at herself. "Is that part of your stupid YOLO thing?" Mercedes asks cynically.

Kendra scowls at her but doesn't say anything. Yet. The back and forth they're already having could easily turn into one of the nasty disagreements they sometimes get into. To avoid that, I get their attention back on food.

"Weren't we starving?" I ask. "Let's go eat." I grab Kendra's hand and walk toward the back of the Field House to the food court. Mercedes follows us, mumbling something I don't understand, but which I'm glad Kendra doesn't hear.

THE BRYCE BASH THEME - SUMMER IN THE PARK - IS emblazoned on a banner hanging across the entrance to the food court, which is really just a sectioned-off area of the Field House. It's probably one-third of the entire space and it's also decorated in the same carnival theme. The food is served buffet style and is the typical Bryce cookout menu – burgers and hot dogs (the beef, turkey, and vegan kinds), beer brats, baked beans, some nasty looking coleslaw, three or four varieties of hot and cold pasta, and some kind of tossed salad. Of course, there's not a hot link, rib, cob of corn or fried chicken wing to be found. My nose does detect kettle corn and funnel cake so that partially makes up for these other deficiencies.

With the exception of the coleslaw and those nasty brats, the food looks decent so each of us piles our plates with more than we can eat, for no good reason other than because it's free. It turns out to be a good strategy because we don't have to stand in line for a second helping.

The DJ has been playing all kinds of music since we got here. It's just background noise for us until he plays *Loves Gonna Last*. That song changes everything.

Kendra jumps up and says, "Aww, that's it right there. That's the Chi Stepping Anthem." She and some other Chicago people near us start dancing – Chicago stepping, of course. Maybe twenty more people come over and join in as the song plays. They turn the center of the food court into a dance floor.

"Westside Steppers, where y'all at?"

"Southside steppers stand up."

"Come through Riverdale."

Everyone is reppin' their hoods. Playful arguments start about whose crew steps the best and the trash-talking, non-Chicago people start shouting about how they can outstep anybody from 'the Chi.'

Mercedes and I watch the dancers and try to learn the steps from the sidelines. The dude who thought I was Essence earlier comes over and helps us out. By the time we halfway get the footwork down, this extended stepping set ends.

"Not bad for beginners," he says beaming with pride like he really did something. "Keep practicing," he suggests to me, "and you'll be ready the next time."

"Thanks," I say. "That's assuming I remember it the next time."

"Well, hit me up if you need a refresher. I'm happy to give you a one-on-one. Kendra has my number."

"Okay. Sure."

Turning to Mercedes, I say, "That's a whack way to say you want somebody to call you."

Mercedes agrees. "He wants you to go ask somebody else for his number when he could've asked you for yours? That's not working for me."

"Me either."

"So no YOLO with this one?" she asks jokingly.

"Definitely not," I reply with a giggle.

The DJ plays another step song, but the steppers don't like it, and actually boo him. Never knew people from the Chi were so gangsta with their music. He switches to a different song.

Pretty much everybody is up now and the entire food court becomes the dance floor.

. . . Left foot, let's stomp

. . . Cha cha real smooth

This might be the largest, and most ethnically diverse, group I've ever seen doing the Caspar Slide. Essence and the DWBs are across the room showing off. Randell's not far from them and it looks like he's trying to talk to another girl, which I point out to Kendra.

"Isn't that the guy you were just talking to over there all up in some other girl's face?"

She stops dancing momentarily to check out her competition.

"Please. Don't even insult me," she says. "That chick ain't got nothin' on me." She gets right back into her groove.

If she's not bothered, I won't be either. But on the real, this isn't a good sign.

As the slide song ends, the DJ begins a latin pop and hip hop set, kicking it off with Bad Bunnie and DJ Snake. That sends Mercedes into another dimension. She's completely lost in the music and I'm right with her. While we're gettin' it in, Randell finds his way back to Kendra and they go off together.

Because I need to know what they're up to, I grab Mercedes and make her come with me to follow them.

"W-T-F, I was doin' my thing?" Mercedes shrieks in protest.

"Kendra went somewhere with Randell and I wanna make sure she's okay."

"Eb, if anybody can take care of themself, it's that girl."

Maybe so, but I make her go with me anyway.

We eventually find Kendra making out with Randell near the vending machines. Mercedes turns to me and says, "Okay, you found her. Now what?" She gets my best eye roll.

"There's something about him that I'm just not feelin'," I declare.

"Well, it's not up to you. Can we stop spying on her? I gotta get back to my music."

Before I know it, Mercedes has already started walking back to the party, which goes on strong for another hour or so. At around eleven o'clock, Kendra finds us and breaks the news that Travis Scott isn't coming. She doesn't say anything about Randell

56

even though we know she's been with him all this time. Just when I'm about to ask her about it, Kendra gets excited and shouts, "Hey. It's time for funnel cake," and rushes off.

"Wait for me," Mercedes says. "C'mon, Eb. I need some cotton candy."

As if there is no cause for us all to be screaming "Stranger Danger," off we go to indulge in our doughy and sugary pleasures.

Chapter Nine

✿

What a difference a few days makes. When I got to Bryce on Friday, I was miserable with a capital misery. Never did I expect to have a vision that would totally change my view of myself, my sister, and our relationship. And I didn't envision ever meeting a guy like Donovan, who would open my eyes to see everything in a new way and take me on that ride on the wild side. YOLO. Perhaps best of all, who knew Mercedes and Kendra would so quickly fill the hole my sister left when she untwinned me. Between the Bryce Bash, the welcome back mixers and the Labor Day socials, we've been to more parties this past weekend, than I attended my entire freshman year.

It's hard to believe today is finally here. The first day of my sophomore year. Technically, yesterday was the first day, but all we had was Convocation. And I did rub Bishop's paw twice for extra luck.

Today, I'll have my first classes. Bryce always starts Fall semester classes in the middle of the week. That felt strange last year, but now, I'm actually excited. A short week means the weekend will be here that much sooner.

My goal for today has been 'get it done early.' Wake up early. Get dressed early. Leave early. Finish breakfast early. Make it to class early.

Two phone alarms guaranted I got out of bed on time. Unfortunately, a traffic jam in the bathroom delayed my shower. Then I ended up changing outfits twice. By the time I left my room and grabbed something to eat, I was running late. Through some force, my angels perhaps, I still managed to get to Lawrence Hall for my first class, Public Speaking, before the teacher.

The only reason I chose this class was because it's supposed to be an easy A and I need as many of those as I can get. Plus, I'm told it's a small class, which also works for me. I hated the freshman lectures we had in the massive auditoriums with a couple hundred students. That set-up really made me feel insignificant.

This classroom has the same stadium style seats as those bigger lecture halls, but with fewer rows and a fourth of the seats, it's way more manageable. To eliminate potential distractions, I still choose a seat closer to the front.

By the time the Professor arrives, the room fills almost to capacity, which according to the sign on the wall is sixty-five. That's not exactly a small class, but I'm stuck here now.

"Phones away, please. If I see them, I own them for the semester." Glad I never took mine out.

"Good Morning. I'm Professor Taurence Powell and this is Public Speaking 101. If this isn't the class you want to be in, please leave quietly. For those who dare to stay, I hope you downloaded the syllabus and made note of the assignment schedule, especially the first one, which is for today's class."

He continues, "You also should have acquainted yourself with the class rules. I don't tolerate rudeness, tardiness, or unpreparedness. I also don't accept excuses. You will learn that, and I quote 'Excuses are the tools of the weak and incompetent. They build bridges to nowhere and tunnels to nothingness. Those who excel in them seldom do anything else, therefore, there are no excuses.' Alright, let's move on."

I'm starting to question whether I "dare to stay" in this class after hearing that not-so-warm introduction. But Stella and Lola assure me this class is exactly where I need to be, so I brace myself for this scholastic journey.

After reviewing how we will be graded in the class, Professor Powell displays our first assignment on the smartboard.

You have 60 seconds to identify 3 facts about yourself that are unique only to you

"If you read the syllabus, you should have come ready to participate," he says.

The first six students he calls on are not ready at all. His commentary about their lack of effort is lengthy and brutal and ends with, "That's several minutes of my life I can't get back."

I didn't realize college professors were allowed to be so evil. In defense of those kids, who probably need therapy now, the syllabus said we would have to introduce ourselves in the first class. I'm sure they, like the rest of us, thought that meant the usual – name, class year, major, and hometown. That "unique to you" part has us all bent. The next group of students that gets called on take a pass on the assignment, probably hoping to avoid being ridiculed.

No such luck. Professor Powell calls each of them to the front of the class as "examples of not only of being unprepared but of cowardice as well." He adds, "You can achieve nothing in life if you are unready or afraid. You might as well give up if you're both. Maybe our next student will display more mental fortitude. Ebony Morgan, let's hear from you."

I don't move. . . waiting on that mental fortitude to kick in.

"Ms. Morgan, are you here?"

"Here I am," I say, raising my hand slowly.

"Are you waiting for a special invitation? Let's move it."

As I walk slowly to the podium, I take a few deep breaths. I've been thinking about what to say for the entire class, but suddenly I'm terrified and worried that Professor Powell will humiliate me like he did the others?

Deep breath.

I can do this.

"Hello, I'm Ebony Morgan. I'm from Washington D.C. If nobody else here is, that counts as one fact."

Of course, some kid raises his hand to say, "I'm from D.C., too."

"Okay. Never mind that."

I quickly move to the second fact I had prepared. "I'm probably the only one here named after a magazine."

"Nope, sorry my name is Elle," some girl shouts. "That's a magazine."

Uggh! "How about a black culture magazine?"

I wait to see if there might be an Essence, Jet, or Vibe, in the room. Thankfully there isn't, so I move on.

"My second unique fact, I hope, is that I have a twin sister."

"I got a twin, too," some kid in the back says.

Really people? Gimme a break.

"Well, mine is an identical twin sister. Do you have that?" I ask the interrupting voice.

"No. Twin brother."

"Well then, that's fact number two."

When I hear myself, I sound more annoyed than necessary, but really these kids are blowing me. Why won't they let me get through this? I mentally check myself and search my mind for anything else that might be unique to me. Where are my angels when I need them? Briefly, I consider sharing them as my third fact, but I would surely get laughed off this campus. Although, with my luck, somebody else in here would probably proudly admit to having their own angels, too.

As the seconds tick away, I stand in front of the class waiting for Professor Powell to bring this torture to an end because I know more than sixty seconds have passed. But no. He does like everyone else and waits for me to say something. Just when I'm ready to do like the classmates before me and take the coward's way out, a thought comes to me.

"Here's my third fact," I say proudly. Everyone perks up at the sound of my voice.

"My brother, Kingston, was named after the place where he was conceived."

Done. Instead of hearing cheers and applause, the girl sitting on the front row says,

"Well actually, that's the same for my brother Cleveland."

Really? That girl could've kept that tidbit to herself and no one would've known. I stare at her like she has two heads and mouth the word "why?" to her, or at least I imagine myself doing that. Professor Powell shoos me to my seat and he stands behind the podium.

"Thank you, Ms. Morgan for that valiant effort. You demonstrated what this entire exercise is about. Thinking on your feet with confidence and a little creativity."

Oh. Wow. Didn't know I did all that.

After my performance, the next set of students make a respectable showing. Everyone got stumped on the third fact.

Professor Powell then announces, "We have time for one more student. Cameron Gregory. Front and center, please."

Cheers and heckles break out from the back of the room when Cameron Gregory's name is called. When I look up to see why, I watch this amazing piece of eye candy approach the front of the class.

Ohh. Emm. Gee. I thought Donovan was beauty personified, but now I can say 'mine eyes have seen the glory.' Cameron Gregory is Donovan-fine but taller, at least 6'2 or 6'3, which is perfect for me. He's got a velvety caramel complexion that appears to have been kissed by the sun. His upper body is chiseled and I'm sure the rest of his body is, too. He probably looks as good as Odell Beckham, Jr. under that shirt. Let me sit up and give Mr. Eye Candy, hashtag my future husband, my full attention.

Professor Powell gives him a nod to proceed.

"I'm Cameron Gregory, from Brooklyn, Park Slope, and it looks like I'm the only one. So that's fact number one. The silence in the room confirms that he made it over the first hurdle. He shows his satisfaction by blessing us with his beautiful dimpled smile.

Without missing a beat, he continues. He must've given this assignment some thought like some of those other kids should've done.

"Number two . . . I play Basketball for Bryce."

A guy in the back yells out, "So do I."

Eye Candy quickly shoots back. "Man, be quiet. That ain't what I'm talking about," he says. "My boy, Chuck, over there is a good baller . . . on the JV squad, but I play Varsity Basketball for Bryce. I already know nobody else here does. So that makes two facts."

Chuck has the nerve to stand up and playfully say, "No applause, please," when Eye Candy gives him props on his ball playing. The guys sitting around him start laughing and talking back and forth, giving each other high fives. They cause a minor disruption. While Professor Powell reprimands them and restores order in the room, I enjoy my view of Eye Candy, who smiles and shakes his head as he watches the scene unfold. I'm trying not to stare, but once again, my eyes do what they want. Every so often, he glances in my direction. Could he be looking at me? Whether he is or not, I will literally die if he catches me gawking at him, so now my eyes will stay down.

When everyone becomes quiet, Professor Powell gives Eye Candy a signal to continue.

"Number three. My first name – Cameron - is my mom's maiden name."

"Mine, too," this kid named Stevenson shouts.

"Over here, too - Landon."

"Really? Damn, I mean dang. I just knew I had those three locked down. A'ight, gimme a second."

I'm not disappointed that he got tripped up on this last fact. That gives me more time with him. While he's off in thought, I sneak in a few stares.

"Got it," he says with a huge smile. "I'm six-feet-four inches tall. Nobody else in this room is my height."

The class is quiet. Eye Candy gave us three unique facts.

Professor Powell acknowledges his achievement with a "Well done." Without thinking, I show my delight by clapping and immediately feel stupid when no one else joins me. Eye Candy turns to me and smiles. Thankfully, his friends in the back of the room start cheering loudly forcing him to turn away.

Professor Powell makes a few flattering comments about Eye Candy's presentation and of course, reviews the rules of class conduct "so we have no more outbursts and unruly behavior." He then dismisses the class.

I watch as Eye Candy and his friends noisily leave the room from the rear exit. That moment when he smiled at me stays fresh in my mind.

While walking to my next class, I lose myself in a daydream sequence about our wedding and our honeymoon in Paris. We'll have three or four kids, who will hopefully all look like him. I've got somebody who already looks like me and I'm over it. Of course, Eye Candy will be an NBA star, which means I'll probably be on a reality show. By the time I get to class, Eye Candy and I are grandparents living our best life on a private island in the Caymans.

Chapter Ten

My Forensic Science class meets right after Public Speaking in Wright Hall, a brisk eight-minute walk across campus. I arrive just as Professor Elaine Kendall begins the course review.

"For most of the semester you'll work in teams, which I have already assigned," she explains. "When I announce your team, move around so you can sit with your teammates. These will be your permanent seats for the entire semester. Then take a few moments to review the first assignment in the syllabus with your team members."

My team includes two girls, Reilly and Jenna. Reilly is a sophomore Criminology major. Jenna is a freshman, undecided major, but probably leaning towards pre-law. They seem pretty decent. Reilly is the obvious leader in our group. She's already taken it upon herself to review the assignment, map out a project plan, create a timeline, and then give each of us several tasks. Jenna and I just watch and listen. Reilly is very smart, super organized, and determined to get an A on this and every assignment. I'm down for getting A's, so I don't mind doing exactly what she says.

"Are we all on board with the plan?" she finally asks when she stops talking and giving orders.

I wanna salute her and say, "Aye Aye Captain," but I prefer not to get kicked off the team. Jenna and I just look at her and nod obediently.

Reilly seems pleased, at least that's how I read her smile. She "lets" us fill out the forms Professor Kendall asked each team to submit at the end of class, which we do. After she inspects and approves the paperwork, she turns it in and gives us two thumbs up.

Then she asks, "Anybody got time for lunch? I'm dying for some pizza!"

"I can always eat pizza," I respond. "Count me in."

Jenna decides to join us as well.

EVEN THOUGH NONE OF US KNEW EACH OTHER BEFORE THIS class, we have no problem starting a conversation as we walk to lunch. Oddly enough, our first non-schoolwork related convo begins with questions from Jenna about Essence, of all people.

"Ebony, you have a twin here, right?" to which I almost answer "No," but the time it would take to explain wouldn't be worth it.

"Yeah, do you know her?"

"I don't, but she hangs out with my sister, Bianca."

I stand still and grab Jenna's arm stopping her, too. "Wait, Bianca is your sister?" I inquire in amazement. Bianca happens to be one of those DWBs that I can't stand.

Jenna sighs and says, "Yes, unfortunately." She then says, "Don't take this the wrong way, but why does your sister act like the world revolves around her? I mean she is such a . . . you know what?"

Jenna has this scared expression on her face, like I might punch her because she's talking bad about my sister. If Essence and I were cool, I might be jumping in Jenna's chest right now; but we're not, so she's safe. Besides, what she's saying is absolutely true.

"Look, I can't explain Essence," I tell her. "I don't know why she acts the way she does. That's her thing, not mine. But let's not get it twisted. My sister definitely has her issues, but Bianca is just as bad and sometimes worse."

"Bianca acts way different around Essence than she does around everybody else. She's such a faker," Jenna says.

"They all are. That's why I call them the DivaWannaBees, or DWBs for short."

Reilly, who has been quiet during this conversation, starts laughing. "I love that. DWBs. I know a few people who could be in that club."

Now Reilly wants to know more about Essence and how she'll be able to tell us apart if she ever sees her. Jenna jumps in and answers her.

"First of all, they wear their hair different. Essence has long hair now, but that changes a lot."

My sister does love her wigs and weaves.

Jenna continues, "Essence will also usually be with three or four other girls, like in Mean Girls. Did you ever see that movie?" she asks Reilly.

Reilly pretends to be insulted by the mere question. She leans back and says, "Duh, who hasn't? That film is a classic."

Jenna continues. "Okay good. So, they act kinda like that. But here's the big difference. If you say "Hi," Ebony would probably smile and say "Hi" back. Her sister wouldn't even acknowledge you. It's happened to me so many times. I thought Ebony was her when she walked into the class and I was like "This is gonna be miserable being in the same class with her." But then I saw that Ebony was too nice to be Essence. Bianca had already told me Essence had an identical twin here, so I figured I got lucky and got the good one. You two might look just alike, but you act nothing alike."

I high-five Jenna and say, "You're 200 percent right on that one."

Reilly now wants to know more, but I'm done talking about Essence.

They both look disappointed. They must know that we'll be

spending lots of time together over the semester and we'll have plenty of time to talk. Besides, I have a feeling that Reilly – the future FBI profiler or crime scene investigator - will not rest until she has all her questions answered.

After lunch, Reilly wants to get a head start on preparing for our Friday class. Unfortunately, I have to pass on spending any more time with her in order to get ready for my other classes, especially Sophomore Seminar and Introduction to Business. Both meet for the first time tomorrow and I still have lots of reading to do.

But I promise Reilly and Jenna that I'll come to the next class prepared and ready to work. Reilly promises to check on me to make sure. I do love her dedication . . . today. In a month, I might be telling a different story.

Chapter Eleven

❧

An all caps message from Mercedes is what my eyes see as soon as they open this morning.

M: EBONY ANSWER UR PHONE. BEEN CALLIN U ALL NIGHT!!!!!

How could she have been calling me all night when KK and I were with her at the BSU Ice Cream Social until after midnight? This is too much to process in my half-sleep state. I can't ignore the urgency of Mercedes' text, so I call her back. This better be important.

"First of all, why you ignore my calls? I been calling you all morning," Mercedes shouts as soon as she answers.

"It's still morning. Saturday morning actually, and I was tryna sleep."

"There's no time for sleeping. Have you talked to KK?" she asks.

"No," I reply. My eyes are fully open now. "But I see a few missed calls from her. She okay?"

"Well, lemme tell you what happened, then we gotta figure out what to do."

I already don't like the "we gotta figure out what to do" part of this story, but I listen.

"You remember that guy Randell that Kendra met at the Bash, literally one week ago?"

"The one who was messin' with that other girl while he was tryna get with KK and I tried to tell y'all he was no good?"

"Yeah. That one. So KK said they been hanging out since then and she kept that secret from us, which I went in on her for 'cause we both know she too hot for her own good."

"Mercedes," I shout, "stay focused."

"Sorry. Anyway, they musta got real tight because she felt it was cool to roll up to his room after she left us last night without even calling."

"No," I scream. I'm wide awake now and almost out of the bed.

"Girl. *Lissen.* It had to be two in the morning She told me and I'm sure she told herself that she was just going over there to 'talk'. . ."

I can picture Mercedes doing the air quotes.

She continues, "But really? Who does that? That girl had something nasty on her mind. Anyways, she said she got to his room, heard his music, figured he was awake and knocked. That kinda homely girl he was talking to at the Bash opened the door with only his t-shirt on."

I jump out of the bed and scream, "Shut up."

"Yeah. It's crazy, right?" Mercedes goes on. "So the chick said to her . . ."

"Let me guess. 'Trick, why you coming to my man's room this time of night'?"

"Basically, yes. Except she said "Bitch" not "Trick" and every other word out of her mouth was apparently a four-letter curse word. Then she and Kendra got into that tired 'he-must-not-really-be-your-man-if-he-tryna-get-with-me-but-he-up-here-with-me-now' thing."

My mouth is hanging open in disbelief.

"What did Randell have to say?" I ask.

"KK said he just stood there looking dumb. He got busted tryna run a game."

By now, Mercedes is laughing so hard she can hardly get a word out. I'm in shock.

Finally, she catches her breath. "But for real, you should call her. She said she tried calling you a few times before she reached me."

"Yeah she did. But I was knocked all the way out. Did she seem okay?"

"She says she's fine, but she might not tell me if she wasn't. You talk to her and see what you think. Then let's decide how to handle it."

"Sounds like it's handled if she said she's okay. You know she moves on from drama faster than anybody."

"Maybe. But make sure. Are we still meeting for brunch?"

"Absolutely."

As soon as my call with Mercedes disconnects, I call Kendra. She doesn't answer, but she does send a text.

K: Wassup?

Me: Just talked to M. Wanna talk?

K: Nah. Not trippin off that MF

Me: Lemme no if u change ur mind. Goin to brunch. U still comin?

K: Gimme a pass. Catch you later

Me: OK. TTYL

Kendra may act like this drama doesn't bother her, but how could it not? If anything like that happened to me I'd be humiliated and swimming in a pool of my own tears. But Kendra seems tougher than me in a lot of ways. And, she had to know that Randell "was sniffin' up other skirts," as my mom would say. It probably doesn't make this situation any less painful or embarrassing. I'll give her some time to process everything before I bother her again about it. It's probably worthwhile recording this foolishness in my journal before I go back to sleep.

Today I start fresh. I am better than I was. I am _____

I write **FEELIN BAD FOR KK**

Saturday, September 8, 2018

Hi. So KK got herself caught up with that dog Randell. I knew he

71

was bad but she didn't listen to me. She's on constant flirt even though she has a boyfriend. I don't get it. She says Randell was nothing but she's all in her feelings. All I can say now is, she needs to slow down before she gets really hurt. I'm still stuck on how she had time to run around with him. We've been together every night. This will remain a mystery unless she decides to tell us the whole truth. Unlikely. ttyl

"Hey, Chica, you look cute! That yellow is poppin' on you. You just need some animal print in there somewhere to really take it next level."

Getting a compliment from Mercedes about any outfit I'm wearing always makes me ecstatic. Of course she's right about the animal print. I hadn't even considered it.

"Noted. I'll remember that for the next time I wear this sundress."

"Did you reach out to KK?" she asks.

"Only by text. She said she didn't wanna talk."

"Is she coming to brunch?"

"Nope."

"Then we'll go to her after we eat."

Mercedes expresses all kinds of thoughts on how to handle Kendra's situation as we walk to Mocha Café. She's gone into her Olivia Pope fixer mode. If it was me, I'd be okay with her meddling. Kendra probably won't want the attention. I'll have to figure out a way to dial Mercedes back before she makes this situation worse.

As we cross the Quad, I notice a group of students approaching us from a distance – two guys surrounded by five or six girls. I'm positive that's Eye Candy. My heart starts racing and I get a fluttery feeling in my stomach, both of which intensify as he gets closer. Hopefully, I really do look as cute as Mercedes said I did.

When we're about six feet away, Eye Candy and I connect with an intense gaze, which we hold until we pass each other. I turn around to sneak a peek at him from behind and catch him doing the same to me. My heart starts dancing and I feel like doing the same.

While I'm lost in my Eye Candy moment, Mercedes drones on about . . . I don't even know.

"Ebony? Hello? I know you haven't been ignoring me and thinking about that fine boy we just walked past. He was checking you out hard."

"Girl, I'm so sorry but yeah. Haven't heard a word you said for like the last five minutes. That's the guy from my class," I announce with the excitement of the kid who found the golden ticket in the Wonka bar.

She laughs out loud. "That's Eye Candy? What a hottie. Why didn't you talk to him? You're so pathetic."

"You saw all those people he was with. You will not have me jumping out there embarrassing myself. One of those girls might have been his bae, boo, wifey, side chick, FWB, or whatever. Maybe they're all part of his freaky little harem."

"You sound crazy. I bet he's not like that."

She sounds confident, even though she has no way of knowing for sure.

"Well, I'm gonna need proof; direct evidence, not that circumstantial stuff." Alright. Come through Forensics vocab.

"Listen, Chica," Mercedes says. "If you let that fine boy get away after all the time you spent dreaming about your wedding and your kids and what not, you should be locked up because that's a crime. I saw him look at you. He likes you, Eb. It was all in his eyes."

"That doesn't mean anything. Guys look at me all the time and most of them just want to smash. I don't care to be a piece of meat to some guy. Especially some jock who's so fine he could have any girl he wants on this campus."

"Any girl except me. He's not my type," she points out.

"Well, good 'cause we might be fighting." I'm kidding. "But until I know for sure that he's not like Randell, I'll continue to admire him from a distance."

"Your choice," she says, "But you're still pathetic."

BY THE TIME WE REACH THE MOCHA CAFÉ THE ONLY CHOICES I'm thinking about are the ones spread out on the buffet. Mercedes and I sample food from each station to decide what's worth investing our appetites in. We both agree on the chicken and waffles and crab eggs Benedict. Mercedes isn't impressed by the paella, because her Mami's tastes so much better. Well, duh. I still enjoy it. She loves the lobster mac and cheese, which to me, looks like a stomachache waiting to happen. I pass on that.

We definitely eat our money's worth and finish our meals with an assortment of mini desserts – apple tart, brownies, red velvet cake, and key lime pie.

Once our bellies are fully satisfied, we pay our bill and plan our next move.

"Let's check on Kendra," I suggest.

"Good idea. Call and see if she wants any food."

My call goes to voicemail, but like before, Kendra sends a text.

    K: Hey
    Me: Hey how u b?
    K: Aite
    Me: Want company?
    K: K
    Me: Hungry
    K: A lil
    Me: K. We'll c u in 20 with your usual from MC
    K: Cool

KENDRA HAD ANOTHER GIRL, ALAYNE, IN HER ROOM WHEN WE arrived. Alayne lives down the hall and she's also from Chicago. After introducing us and talking with us for fifteen or twenty minutes, Kendra tells Alayne we're about to study, so she leaves.

74

"Why'd you tell her that?" I ask. "I liked her. Besides, we're not studying. We don't even have any books."

"She coulda just told her to get out, but that would be rude," Mercedes points out, as Kendra begins to eat the food we brought her. Chicken and waffles and a green smoothie.

"Exactly," Kendra says. "Thanks for the food."

Mercedes and I wait for her to bring up the topic of Randell, which she does after about fifteen minutes. The full story is pretty much a repeat of what Mercedes said earlier just with more curse words. There's a lot of anger in Kendra's voice, but I hear the sadness, too, even if she tries to hide it.

"Why am I even tripping?" she asks. "His ass was just something to pass my time."

"If that's true then let it go and be done," I suggest.

Mercedes, in her painfully direct way, asks the question that was on my mind; the one I decided not to ask out of respect for Kendra's privacy.

"Don't hate me for wanting to know this," she begins, "but did you have sex with him? 'Cause if you did, you might not be able to let it go so easy."

"Mercedes, that's none of your business," I yell.

She ignores me and looks at Kendra waiting for an answer. Kendra's silence should tell Mercedes this topic might be off limits for discussion, but she pushes anyway.

"KK, I'm really serious about this," she says, as if anyone thought she wasn't.

In a very controlled manner, Kendra responds saying, "That's none of your damn business. Discussion over."

Tried to warn her. Now Mercedes is sitting here with her feelings hurt. Kendra has an attitude. And nobody's talking.

This continues for about ten minutes. Kendra suddenly gets up and opens the door to leave.

"Hey, where you going?" I ask.

"Need some ice cream, y'all coming?"

"So that's how we doing this?" Mercedes says, looking at me.

"Guess so," I respond with a shrug.

And just like that, we're all good again. But, this Randell situation is totally jacked and I have a feeling there's more to this saga.

AFTER SPENDING HOURS WITH MY GIRLS, I'M EXHAUSTED AND can't get back to my room fast enough. A long hot shower is calling me but so is my journal, which I need to update before this day ends. I handle that first.

September 8, 2018, part 2

Hi again. The Kendra thing isn't as bad as I thought. Or maybe it is. She still isn't saying much. But that's not really the news of the day anymore because I saw Eye Candy on the way to brunch with Mercedes. OMG he looked so good. He was with a group of girls and another guy. We stared at each other but didn't say anything. Mercedes thinks he likes me and I should let him know I like him too. I'm not ready yet. I need to know what his status is before I put myself out there. What if he's like Randell? Or worse? I would die if I got played like Kendra did. I think I'll just wait and see what happens. Well that's it. ttyl

Chapter Twelve

A POPLEXY
    [ap-uh-plek-see] noun.

1. stroke
2. a sudden, usually marked loss of bodily function due to rupture or occlusion of a blood vessel.
3. a hemorrhage into an organ cavity or tissue.

THIS MADNESS IS NOT WHAT MY MORNING EYES WANT TO SEE -- a random word on the white board with no information or explanation. But at least we're done with that stupid "unique facts" assignment. That took three class periods and it was painful.

The whole class waits and wonders about this word. Some of us do it out loud; others probably do it silently like me. I'm also trying to figure out where Eye Candy is. He's not in the back with the guys he always sits with. After our encounter on Saturday, he's been on my mind constantly. The thought of seeing him today is what had me looking forward to class.

A student behind me mentions that Professor Powell is already ten minutes late and we should leave. Another student argues that the grace period is fifteen minutes. The back and forth debate between them becomes comical. When I turn around to watch, Eye Candy himself walks through that door in the back of the room. He immediately starts talking to his friends and doesn't look in my direction. That's okay because it gives me more time to admire him unnoticed. In the meantime, Cleveland's sister checks the Student Handbook online and confirms that faculty have a fifteen-minute grace period.

"So no one should leave yet," she admonishes.

Professor Powell rushes in at the fourteenth minute and gives us a lame "Happy Hump Day" greeting. I'm not the only one groaning in disappointment. He walks to the podium, apologizing for his lateness. He mumbles something about a taping running long. I want to yell, "No Excuses," like he does to us. I'm sure others in the class want to as well.

He then launches into an explanation about the word on the board.

"This will be another 'thinking on your feet' exercise," he says. "I will choose a volunteer then give you the word."

Is it just me? If you choose the person, can you still call them a volunteer? Maybe they should be called a volun*told*.

He continues. "You'll have one minute to use the word in as many different sentences as you can, without using the word to say you don't know what it means."

As scary as that sounds, I'm relieved to know that at least "apoplexy" is not the word for the day.

"The first volunteer for today, Delia Jacobs." The word namaste flashes on the board.

NAMASTE

[nuhm-uh-stey] noun

1.a conventional Hindu expression on meeting or parting, used by the speaker usually while holding the palms together vertically in front of the bosom.

DELIA LOOKS AT THE BOARD FOR SEVERAL SECONDS. AS WE wait for her to gather her thoughts, I quietly prepare myself to hear something from her that is sure to bring shame for generations. Delia is really smart, from what I'm told, but notoriously ghetto.

Delia opens her mouth and it begins: "Okay. First, there are probably many ways to use the word Namaste, but I will only talk about two of them. The first one is the one you would expect me to talk about. It's when people who do yoga and things like that start off in class by saying, 'Namaste,' and do this folded hand thing, like this." She pauses and presses her palms together. "I think they're saying, 'Hello, how u doin?' before the class jump-off since it's polite to say, 'Hello,' to people when you walk into class. Unlike some of the people here who have absolutely no manners and just walk in and sit down and don't say anything. Anyway. . . "

She has to roll her eyes to emphasize her point.

"They be sayin', namaste with they folded hands again at the end of the class. Kinda like they might be sayin', 'Thanks, we out.' Sometimes, you can bow when you say it, but you don't have to."

I'm stunned. What Delia is saying is completely whack. "Yoga and things like that?" and, "We out?" I just want to vote this chick off the island now. But she's still talking.

"The second way to use the word namaste is like when your friend wants you to go shopping or clubbing, and you don't feel like it. Or when Bae wanna go out, but you wanna stay at the crib. You could be like, 'Namaste home.' That means, "No thanks. I'ma chill till you get back. Thank You."

No. She. Didn't.

Delia does a curtsy and takes a bow as she walks proudly to her seat. My mouth is wide open, jaw probably hanging down to the floor. What just happened? The professor watches her, and amazingly is also speechless. Half the class is doubled over, laughing; howling actually. The rest are probably in shock; or maybe waiting for that guy to jump out of the closet telling us we just got punk'd. He never does. Exactly one kid in the back of the class slow claps Delia as she sits down.

After regaining control of the class, Professor Powell appoints two more "volunteers," who do better than Delia, but don't stand out as all that impressive. Then I hear his name. "Cameron Gregory." A tingle runs down my spine causing me to straighten up in my seat, focus my attention, and prepare to take him all in; and maybe even listen to what he has to say.

As he walks to the front of the class, I repeat his name to myself a few times. Cameron Gregory. That name suits him. It sounds strong. Solid. The name actually sounds like it says: "I'm fine as hail and y'all betta recognize."

Yes, you are, Mr. Gregory and believe me. We do recognize.

As he waits for his word, he has a serious, but confident expression on his face; maybe like one he would have before taking the winning shot in a big game, or before saying, "I do" at our wedding.

Professor Powell finally reveals his word.

STIMULATE
   [stim-yuh-leyt] verb
   1.to excite to activity or growth or to greater activity
   2.to function as a physiological stimulus to
   3.to arouse or affect by a stimulant (such as a drug)

I WATCH HIS FACE RELAX AS HE READS THE WORD TO HIMSELF. He gives the word a sultry smile and head nod. His face says, 'I got this.' Then he looks up at me.

Excuse me, Sir. Why are you looking at me now when I have no place to hide? We lock eyes for a fleeting moment, but it feels like forever. He gives me a bashful smile and says the word aloud, accentuating each and every letter and syllable. Or, perhaps the scene just plays out that way in my head.

Eye Candy continues to toss the word around a few more

times, pretending not to understand its meaning or how to use it in a sentence. Someone please tell him nobody would ever believe he doesn't know what to do with the word stimulate.

As if he can hear my thoughts, Eye Candy says the word one last time, more confidently, and proceeds with his commentary.

"Stimulate," he says, looking toward me.

My goal is not to react outwardly but on the inside . . . *issa party.* For the next minute or so he talks about something, perhaps related to basketball, but who really cares?

"I heard of this machine," he starts, "that some sports trainers use to stimulate the brain with little shocks. They say it makes players perform better. I'm not into using machines to stimulate me. I prefer natural stimulation. So, for me, if I want to be stimulated, I mean if I want my brain stimulated to improve my game or whatever, there's other things that can stimulate. Conversation can stimulate if it's with the right person. Things you see can stimulate. People can stimulate . . . even people you don't even know."

He uses the word stimulate in as many sentences as he can. The word sounds so sensual when he says it. He looks in my direction almost every time like he's inviting me to be his play-mate in this game. I'm helpless to resist. I accept the invitation and give him my entire attention for as long as he wants it. When his time ends, he has me in some kind of trance. After a few seconds, he releases the spell and we both look away. After that encounter, I've got to be all shades of red. Thank God for melanin so at least nobody can see it.

As Eye Candy leaves the podium, more than a few of the female students are watching him with dreamy, begging eyes. As he passes my row he steals another glance, then smiles as if to thank me for whatever we just shared. Now I'm sitting dreamy and begging, like the others. Those many shades of red rise again and I pray the power of the melanin continues to work in my favor.

After Professor Powell makes a few comments about Eye Candy's, "foray," which at first sounds to me like, "foreplay," he summons several more volunteers. All the presentations after Eye Candy's were entertaining, which made the rest of the class time pass quickly.

With about five minutes left in the class, Professor Powell proclaims "I won't try to accommodate another student presentation today, so I release you to the wild. Use this gift of free time to your scholastic advantage."

Release us to the wild? Scholastic advantage? This man has some serious issues, which at some point, when I'm not obsessing over Eye Candy and our future kids, I'll try to understand better, so my dislike of him doesn't keep me from earning an A in this class.

AFTER A PRETTY GOOD DAY OVERALL, I CAN'T WAIT TO UPDATE my journal.

Today I start fresh. I am better than I was. I am _____

I write **WONDERING**

Wednesday, September 12, 2018

Hi. So Eye Candy lowkey flirted with me today. I want to feel boosted but I'm steady wondering if he could really like me like Mercedes says. Why would he even be interested in me like that? I don't feel like I'm as fly as those girls I saw him with. Maybe Mercedes is wrong and my imagination is confusing me about what's real. I don't know. Too bad I can't talk to Essence about this. She would know exactly how to help me figure this out. ttyl.

Chapter Thirteen

Other than my stimulating Public Speaking class with Eye Candy, this week has been pretty unremarkable. My workload is building up, so I'm spending more time studying. Even today, when everybody on campus is kicking off the weekend at the pub or some other fun place, I'm in the library working on a paper. This sucks, but should please my dad. On second thought, nothing I do pleases him, so nevermind.

Kendra and Mercedes rescue me around eight o'clock and we take a ride downtown to Star Pho, a new Vietnamese restaurant Kendra has been pressed to try. Pho has never been my thing but, I'm loving the fish cakes we ordered and this noodle soup. Mine has beef brisket. Mercedes chose chicken. Hers looks and smells as good as what I have.

Kendra got fancy with her soup and ordered the one with tendon and tripe. She's adventurous for sure. It looks nasty, but she says it tastes amazing.

While we eat, Kendra gets a text message and tells us that BSU/ LATINX just announced they're having a kickback at the MCC tomorrow night.

"It starts at eight and is gonna be the perfect place to chill and get away from these colonizers," she says.

The particular colonizers she's referring to are the ones who have recently been causing problems by calling security anytime they see groups of Black and Brown students congregating. Or complaining about our noise.

"We're loud people. They need to get used to it and stop acting like our noise means we're mad or fighting, or comin' after them," she says.

"It's ridiculous," Mercedes adds, "We don't complain when they get in their groups or make their noise. They need to leave us alone."

"That's real," I say.

"So that means y'all wanna go?" Kendra asks.

Mercedes says, "If it's a party, you know I'm there."

When I tell Kendra I might need to work on my paper instead of hanging out, she's not having it.

"Work on it tonight and all day tomorrow if you have to. Just be ready by 8 o'clock," she orders.

Reluctantly, I agree to go and pray I don't regret this decision.

THE KICKBACK STARTED AT EIGHT. DESPITE MY BEST intentions, we don't arrive until shortly after nine. After spending all day Saturday researching and writing. I'm not as far along as I wanted to be, but I shut it down at around six, grab some food, and shift into party mode. It still took me forever to put a cute kick-back look together and that made us late.

The MCC is almost filled with people by the time we show up. All the cushioned seats that are scattered throughout the lounge area are occupied. Eight or so game tables are arranged around the room and people sit or stand around every one of them eating, playing cards, or busy on their phones and laptops. The pool table is in constant rotation. Dozens of other people are moving around talking, snapping pics, or making videos.

"This is the spot tonight," I say to Kendra. "Everybody's up in here."

"And they loud," Mercedes shouts.

"Loud and happy and ain't nobody mad about it," Kendra says proudly.

They're right. The groups playing cards are loud. The kids on their phones are loud. Even the guys playing chess are loud. The sound doesn't bother me because it reminds me of my family gatherings. The louder we are, the more fun it means we're having. That's probably how it is for most of us here. People being loud with life and enjoying each other without worrying about offending anybody or someone feeling threatened by our existence.

The students here seem nicer tonight, too. People we don't know come over to us and introduce themselves. People we do know actually take time to have conversations. Jackson Butler, President of the BSU, who goes by Jax, walks up and speaks. He and Essence might've dated last year. Maybe that's why he's talking to me. Or more likely, he probably has to greet everybody as part of his official duties. We talk for a while and he presses us about helping with the BSU Spring fundraiser. Kendra says "no" flat out, but I agree under one condition.

"So Jax, you know my sister and I don't play well together. If she's working on this project, too, you should probably ask someone else."

"She's not, so don't worry. And I understand what you mean. Es is . . . Es. That's all I'll say."

He's got a goofy "I still have crush on her" expression on his face so I don't bother to address his comment. I just let him move on to the next group of people he has to force himself to socialize with.

We chill with some girls Mercedes knows from her dorm, Danielle, Sofia and Jennifer. This guy named Javier joins our group with his friends and for a while, we listen to him tell jokes and make fun of people. His jokes are funny. His insults, not so much.

"Yo, that girl, Nina, over there, her butt so big, if somebody told her to haul ass, she'd have to make two trips."

Only the guys laugh. We all give him our "whatever" stares. My crew and I walk away.

"Y'all Randell is here," Kendra says, pointing him out to us.

He's got that girl we saw him with at the Bash holding on to his arm like he's some prize. Her ratchet outfit looks like something a stripper would wear; and not one of the classier ones.

"Is that the girl who you argued with?" I ask.

Kendra is giving them the most hateful look I've ever seen her give.

"Yeah," she finally says.

Within minutes of showing up, Randell's girl is already making a scene, complaining about the room being too hot, not enough places to sit, and no alcohol.

"What the hell kinda party is this?" she barks.

Somebody might wanna let her know this ain't *that* kind of party. Randell lets her make her noise. He's probably scanning the room for his next side piece anyway. He spots Kendra and walks in our direction. His girl follows him.

"Uhh, I think they're coming over here. Let's go somewhere else." That's my easy solution to this imminent problem.

Kendra says, "I ain't going nowhere."

"Me neither. Why should we leave?" Mercedes asks, not expecting a response. Nobody told me my friends had such thug tendencies.

Randell walks up to Kendra. "I need to talk to you," he demands. "Alone."

"No," Kendra says without even looking in his direction.

His girl walks up and goes in on him. Then, pointing at Kendra she says, "Didn't I already deal with this problem. Why you over here talking to her?" She gives Kendra all kinds of disapproving looks. Randell ignores his girl's question, and tries to convince Kendra to go with him so they can talk. Kendra doesn't give either one of them as much as a glance.

"You hear me talking to you?" His girl sounds pissed.

"Tisha, be quiet. Damn. Can't you see I'm having a conversation?"

Now they're arguing with each other. Much of the other activity on our side of the room stops and all eyes turn toward Randell and his noisemaker.

Kendra gets up and walks away. "Let's go, y'all."

We follow behind her. Tisha moves quickly and stands in front of Kendra and starts talking smack. Kendra lets her babble on. I'm sure she doesn't want to get into a verbal, or physical, altercation with this girl, but it could come to that if Tisha doesn't back off.

One of the guys playing chess comes over and says something to try to defuse the situation.

Randell has the nerve to get mad at him for "disrespecting his lady," who has acted nothing like a lady since she got here. Other people gather around, including a couple of Kendra's homegirls, waiting for some kind of action to start.

Randell moves in between Tisha and Kendra and says to Kendra, "Ignore her. I'll handle it." He might as well be talking to himself.

"Nah, I got this," Kendra fires back defiantly.

She shoves Randell out of her way and moves in close to Tisha. They stand almost eye to eye. Kendra dares Tisha to say one more word to her about "the pathetic excuse for a man she so pressed about."

Words start flying back and forth between her and Tisha. Randell tries to gain control of the situation, but nobody pays him any attention. Mercedes and I try to get Kendra to walk away, but she refuses. Many more people are now standing around watching this madness unfold.

Out of nowhere, Essence and Bianca show up. I didn't even know they were here. We've walked around this room multiple times tonight and never saw them. Essence comes and stands in front of me and next to Kendra on one side. Bianca stands on her other side next to Mercedes. Strangely, all the arguing stops.

Essence then pulls Kendra away, steps up to Tisha and says "I'mma need you to back off from my sister and her friends or you're gonna have a problem with me."

Tisha looks Essence up and down, probably trying to figure out if she can back up her words. Trust me. She can.

When Tisha doesn't move, Essence repeats her warning.

"Maybe you didn't hear me. You need to leave my sister and her friends alone or you *will* have a problem with me. You got me?

Some girl pulls Tisha away and walks her out.

Randell walks up to Kendra like he has something to say. Essence glares at him and says,

"That's not a smart move, playa." With a motion of her head, she makes him aware that no less than five guys are ready and waiting to come to our defense.

He tells her he just wants to apologize to Kendra.

"Then do it from there," she advises.

Randell stands across from Kendra and says, "Sorry that situation went sideways. My girl crazy as hell. I hope we can still be cool."

"Boy, we were never cool," Kendra tells him. "And you and Thotianna can both kiss my entire ass and go straight to hell."

Kendra walks away and pushes a chair that accidentally hits Randell on purpose. Mercedes follows her out. Essence looks at me, laughs, and says, "Let me find out your friend is a hundred percent that chick. "

As she turns to leave she says to me, "You good, Bun?"

"Yeah," I reply. "Thanks for having my back."

"Always. I'd never let anything happen to you," she whispers. She and Bianca then disappear into the crowd.

When I find Mercedes, she's laughing and playing JENGA with a group of students from LATINX. Kendra's joking around with her friend, Brynn, and some other students, giving out card playing tips. They're over that drama already. Not me. I'm still shaken thinking about what might've happened if Essence hadn't shown up.

And I'm more than a little confused about her saying she would never let anything happen to me. She's the main thing that happens to me so what do her words even mean? I'll never figure her out, so I won't even bother to try.

At some point, this gathering becomes a full-blown party, with music, food, and unapproved liquid refreshment. Kendra is now talking to some guy who saw what went down with Randell and "thinks she deserves a man who will treat her right." I wanna tell him she has one at the University of Chicago, but that's none of my business. I'm just gonna sip my tea.

We leave the MCC around two in the morning. When I get to my room, I still have so many emotions flowing and decide to write in my journal. I open to a clean page.

TODAY I START FRESH. I am better than I was. I am ____
I write **CONFUSED.**

Saturday, September 15, 2018

Hi. I knew the Randell situation would be a hot mess and it is. KK almost got into a fight with his girlfriend tonight over his worthless butt. He's so lame. But KK has time enough for both of them. She's fearless. Unlike me. Essence came to our rescue tonight. That was strange. She usually doesn't care about hurting my feelings so why would she care if some crazy chick wanted to fight me and my friends? I'll probably never know why, but it felt good to hear her refer to me as her sister and to watch her defend me from what she thought was a threat. Just like she did when we were kids. She even said she always has my back. She has a weird way of showing it. For a few minutes, I had my Sisi back. I really do miss her. I can't believe how much I love her right now. ttyl

Chapter Fourteen

Sunrise Yoga at the lake sounded like a good idea when I signed up for it a week ago. At the time, I didn't know the night before and really the entire preceding week would be so physically and mentally taxing. I wanted to sleep in this morning, but I forced myself to come out anyway. I'm hoping this class will help me clear my head and recover from last night's mayhem with Randell.

About twenty of us gather on the lawn near Bryce Lake, mats in place as we await the instructor, Miss Abeya, who asks us to call her Bey Bey. Such a serene morning full of stillness. We watch the sun peek above the horizon, painting the hazy morning sky with brilliant hues of gold, pink, orange and red. This is my favorite sky. If I didn't love sleep so much, I'd wake up this early every morning to experience this spectacular showcase.

Bey Bey greets us to start the class. "Namaste, Yogis."

Collectively, we respond, "Namaste."

I laugh softly thinking about Delia's class presentation and her nonsensical assault on this word.

"Let's meet together on our mats and center ourselves for this Vin to Yin experience. Our journey today will bring both Vinyasa and Yin Yoga asanas into one practice to open ourselves for greater flexibility and energy flow while also fortifying and revitalizing our bodies and minds. Please take a moment to set an intention for your yoga practice "

When I've done yoga in the past, I never put much thought into setting an intention. I usually offered any word that popped into my head. Today, I want to make it meaningful.

Bey Bey directs us to speak our intention to the universe. "I am expecting good things," is my proclamation.

Deep breath.

"I am expecting good things."

Deep breath.

"I am expecting good things."

Deep breath.

"Now stand at the top of your mat with your feet hip distance apart. Bring your arms up and we'll begin with our Sun Salutations . . . that's right. From here, Downward Dog into your Swan Pose. Very nice. Now bring your knee between your arms and settle into our Pidgeon Pose. Breathe here for ten seconds "

For the next hour or so, Bey Bey shepherds us into and out of more animal poses than I've ever done before – Caterpillar, Butterfly, Dragon, Sphinx With each movement, I feel the release of tension and stress and the unlocking of joy within me. On her prompting at various points throughout the class, I affirm my intention.

"I am expecting good things."

Deep breath.

"I am expecting good things."

Deep breath.

"I am expecting good things."

Deep breath.

Bey Bey brings us out of the Seated Lotus Pose and directs us to lie down on our backs.

"Now assume our Shavasana and let your bodies fully relax into the pose. You can bring your arms over your head for a full stretch."

Laying here, stretched out in this pose, I'm just empty and could really go to sleep, but Bey Bey has other plans for me.

"Roll over on your side and slowly return to your Seated Lotus Position. Breathe In . . . Breathe Out. Cover your heart with your hands, Yogis and just breathe. Reaffirm your intention if you like."

"I am expecting good things."

Deep breath.

"I am expecting good things."

Deep breath.

"I am expecting good things."

Deep breath.

"Open your eyes and allow your bodies to consolidate into your practice."

"Great job, Yogis, I'll see you next week right here on the mat. Namaste."

Together, we reply, "Namaste."

While my fellow yogis move around rolling their mats and packing away their props, I sit for a while longer, mainly because I'm drained and don't have the energy to get up.

I'm also enjoying the peacefulness and beauty of this morning. My mind is quiet for a change. For that, I'm grateful.

About fifteen minutes later, the morning sun is shining higher and brighter, a cue that it's time to head back to my room. On the way, I stop at the Bryce Fitness Center to get a drink from the Juice Bar to replenish myself for the walk.

The juicerista, that's actually what they call themselves, greets me with way too much excitement for eight o'clock in the morning.

"Morning, Morning, Morning. Good Sunday morning. What can I get you?"

Trying to match his enthusiasm, I laugh and give him a hearty "Good Morning to you, too. Can I have a large sunrise energizer with a wheatgrass shot please?"

Someone walks up behind me and says, "Make that two."

That voice. O-M-G.

When I turn around, Eye Candy is towering behind me.

"Hey, Miss Ebony Morgan," he says.

92

Thanks to my yoga zen, I stay calm and find the breath and words to respond.

"Hello, Mr. Cameron Gregory."

My previously quiet mind is busy once again, anxiously wondering what to say next, and what do I look like? Oh crap. What do I smell like?

The juicerista's voice pauses my rant. "Here you go two large sunrise energizers and two wheatgrass shots. Am I putting this on your tab, Cam?"

"Yeah. Thanks, man."

When Eye Candy gives me my drink, I thank him and say, "I'm impressed you have a tab at the Juice Bar."

He laughs. "Don't be. Just one of the perks of playing ball here."

"Nice perk."

"I guess." He downplays what to me seems like gold at the end of the rainbow.

"So what brings you here this morning," he says, "if you don't mind me asking?"

"Came for the juice after the sunrise yoga class."

"Oh wow. That's interesting. I'm not into yoga, but I do love a good sunrise. How was it?"

"The sunrise or the class?"

"The sunrise," he says.

That's was surprising. I thought for sure he'd say the class.

My first thought was to say, "As beautiful as on our wedding day," but he might not appreciate that I've already imagined many sunrises in our future life together. It's probably best that I don't share that information just yet.

"One of the most beautiful I've seen here," I tell him.

"Really? I'll have to check it out sometime."

"Didn't expect a Varsity Basketball superstar to be into sunrises."

"Oh yeah. Sunrises and sunsets," he says with a slight smile.

"And I didn't expect a yoga master such as yourself to be into basketball."

93

This delicious piece of eye candy has a sense of humor. With a chuckle, I reply, "I'm not."

In response, he says, "Maybe I can change that," as if he's asking permission.

"Maybe you can." Permission granted.

We both let that verbal exchange occupy our space for a few seconds.

I sip my juice drink and keep my eyes down for as long as possible while shaking off the daydream I'm having about me and him somewhere on our private island.

Eye Candy asks, "What's on your mind, Miss Ebony? You got quiet."

You are, obviously. I make up something to say. "Oh, I'm thinking about getting back to my room."

Eye Candy pretends to be offended. "Aw man. I'm boring you that much?"

"Not at all," I assure him. "In case you haven't noticed, I'm a little funky and really need to shower."

"I didn't notice, but it's cool. I should get to practice anyway."

Eye Candy and I leave the fitness center together. Before heading in our separate directions, I thank him again for my energizer.

"My pleasure," he remarks.

As I turn to walk away, I say "Guess I'll see around."

He responds, "Yes, you will."

Eye Candy is watching me. I can feel it.

Hope he's enjoying the rear view.

ONCE I'M FAR ENOUGH AWAY, I SEND A MESSAGE TO MERCEDES and Kendra in our group chat.

Me: I just talked to Eye Candy! OMG!

Kendra videochats me immediately. "Yo Eb, you scored. Congrats."

"I know, right? I'm about to explode."

"I can tell. I hope you stayed calm around him."

"Of course," I say.

"So what's next?" she wants to know.

"What do you mean next? Nothing's next."

"He didn't ask you out? Or at least exchange contact info?"

"No, and why is that a problem?"

Kendra doesn't appreciate my desire not to move so quickly with Eye Candy. Sure, we talked today, but I tell her I prefer to take this at my own pace and not speed into something I'll regret. I'd be wrong if I pointed out why moving fast is a problem using her life as an example.

"Just don't move so slow that you end up not moving," she insists.

Before I can address that comment, we get a message from Mercedes.

M: Gimme deets!!!

Kendra adds her to our call, and I repeat the story for Mercedes. She's not as disappointed as Kendra was that we don't have a date planned, but she also wants me to be more aggressive.

"Don't do the most," she cautions, "but flirt a little more."

Kendra disagrees. "A little? Do that and watch somebody else snatch him up."

When I've had enough advice I tell my friends, "I appreciate you both taking so much interest in me, but I got this."

They look at me like they doubt that I got "this" or anything remotely close to "this."

BACK IN MY ROOM, I REPLAY THE WHOLE EYE CANDY encounter in my head over and over. My insides are dancing and my heart is singing.

Maybe, just maybe, I finally did something right. This accomplishment deserves a journal entry.

Today I start fresh. I am better than I was. I am ____

I write EXCITED

Sunday, September 16, 2018

Hi. Eye Candy talked to me today. I can't believe it. I'm about to lose my mind, but this time in a good day. I really like him and I'm starting to think he likes me, too. He could be my Prince Charming. I can't wait to see. I need Mercedes and Kendra to chill though and stop trying to rush me. ttyl

Chapter Fifteen

Monday took forever to get here, especially after the rollercoaster weekend I had. I'm super excited because I'll get to see my future husband in less than an hour.

My friends were full of advice this morning.

"Be yourself."

"Don't act too pressed."

"Make sure you look extra cute."

"Stay calm."

They lost me at calm. How can I be calm when today could be the day Eye Candy and I move to the next level? To settle myself right now, I do some yoga breathing exercises, set an intention for the day, and document it in my journal.

Today I start fresh. I am better than I was. I am _____

I write **HOPEFUL**

Monday, September 17, 2018

Hi. Today I AM HOPEFUL. This might be the day that Eye Candy asks me out. We're definitely moving in that direction. Please let today be the day. And please help me to relax so I don't screw it up. ttyl

Before walking out my door, I check myself out in the mirror a few times to make sure I'm giving lots of cute, a serving of flirty, and a splash of sass. Check. Check. Check.

When I arrive for class, I quickly scan the room but don't see Eye Candy. Moments later, he comes in through the door at the front of the class and approaches me.

"Good morning, Miss Ebony."

"Hey, Mister Cameron."

I'm all set to offer him the empty seat next to me. But before the words come out my mouth, Cleveland's annoying sister takes it. I mean mug her, hopefully without him seeing it. He gives her a funny look, too, which I guess is the male version of what I did. But his expression says, "You wrong for that. Don't you see me over here shooting my shot?"

She's oblivious. And who has time to educate her? Not us because Professor Powell has made his grand entrance. Eye Candy goes to the back of the classroom and sits with his boys. Every few minutes I get the urge to turn around, but that would be the very definition of "doing the most."

My eyes focus on the instruction of the day. My mind, however, takes a journey of its own, which does not end until Professor Powell announces the end of class. While gathering my belongings, Eye Candy comes over to me.

"Dude was extra boring today," he says. "That class had me out."

"Yeah, me, too. He lost me about three minutes in."

Eye Candy and I leave the lecture hall together.

"So, Miss Ebony you got plans right now?"

"If you consider a class plans, then yes. I have a Forensics class."

"Forensics? Interesting. Didn't know they had a class like that here," he comments.

"Actually, it's an entire major," I tell him, "if you're into that *CSI- Criminal Minds* kinda stuff."

"That's dope." Eye Candy pauses, then with a bit of reluctance, says, "Okay if I walk with you to your class?"

"Sure," I say, sounding very composed, but inside it's rockets blaring and bombs bursting. Stella and Lola, please don't fail me now.

On the walk to Wright Hall, Eye Candy tells me he saw me or my twin the day he moved in.

"Whichever one of y'all had on that *Crooklyn* shirt, that's who I saw."

"That was me. My sister and I almost got into a fight about that shirt that day."

"Oh word? That shirt was nice. I see why you was ready to go toe-to-toe for it," he says laughing.

To keep the conversation upbeat, I'd prefer not to talk about Essence anymore, and especially not about us fighting. But Eye Candy, like most people, asks more questions.

To satisfy his curiosity, and to make our long, tortured story as short as possible, I just say, "For us, it's complicated. And not in a good way."

"Oh wow. You'll have to explain that to me some time."

I'm glad he's cool with my non-answer, but I'm not making any promises about sharing the details of how badly my sister has mistreated me this past year. Yeah, I don't want to think about it, let alone talk about it.

To escape this minefield of a topic, I turn the spotlight to him, "Why don't you tell me, what's your story?"

That was a line Donovan used on me. Why am I using it on Eye Candy? A voice in my head says, "because it works."

"My story? That's an interesting question, Miss Ebony. Never been asked that. You got me using my brain. I dig that."

Guess that line does work.

He continues. "If I had to sum it up, I'm an average guy with some above-average abilities, which I try to use to bring joy to the spaces I occupy. Just living life to make the people I love proud."

"Wow. That's a great story," I tell him.

"I'm sure yours is, too. Care to share?"

Honestly, I would say no if I were to say something. But,

thankfully, we reach my class and that gives me a way out of having to say anything.

"Maybe another time. Gotta get in there and catch some bad guys."

He laughs and says, "Guess I'll let you go then." But he doesn't. He holds me with his bashful grin. This is torture.

Please ask me for my number or something.

A few students from my class race past us.

"I'm late. I'll catch you later," I say.

He replies, "No doubt."

Chapter Sixteen

F orensics class is long and boring today. And very technical, which makes it hard. This class is another course I was told would be easy and would satisfy the general studies science requirement. Another lie. It does meet the requirement, but it ain't easy. And it's gotten worse with each class.

Today, we spend an hour reviewing the chemistry stuff we've learned, or should've learned, over the past two weeks in preparation for our first module examination next week. If my two pop quiz grades are any indication, I'm not even close to being ready for that test.

Professor Kendall, or Dr. Elaine, whichever we prefer, is a great teacher, but in this class, even the new brave, positive-thinking Ebony is riding the struggle bus. Listening to what the teacher expects us to know by next week has me feeling like I've failed before I've even started and that's a rabbit hole of emotions I don't even wanna go down.

Reilly announces to Jenna and me that "our group is gonna work with Wesley and his team to get ready for the test." They plan to split up the topics from the review guide and assign each of us a section to outline for the group. Jenna and I agree to work together on ours. Neither of us feels particularly confident in our knowledge, but we know what Reilly expects. Somehow, I'll have to find time to review this material again before I meet with Jenna and that has to happen before our first group session tomorrow afternoon.

As I leave the classroom, I'm feeling very burdened and over-whelmed by the challenge facing me. In my head, I calculate how many hours between now and our session tomorrow and try to figure out how much time I have available to get any of this work done. My conclusion? Not enough.

"Hey, Miss Ebony, why you look so down?"

I look up and see Eye Candy standing outside the door.

"Cameron. Where did you come from?"

"Nowhere. I've been waiting for you to get out of class."

"Really?" I say with questioning eyebrows.

Probably realizing that sounded a little crazy, he explains. "What I mean is, I wanted to ask if you were free after class, but you left me, so I waited for your class to end."

I'm trying to maintain my cool right now, but I'm super geeked Eye Candy is finally asking me out. Not to mention, he waited out here for almost an hour. Who does that? The voices in my head remind me to be easy with it.

"That's funny," I say smiling, "You know I didn't leave you. All I did was go to class."

"You still left me." He makes the cutest sad face and my cool starts fading away.

"Well, I'm sorry," I say. "How can I make it up to you?"

For the slightest second, I worry that my statement sounds like I'm suggesting an afternooner or opening the door for an equally crazy proposition from him. Luckily, he doesn't take the conversation that direction.

"Have lunch with me," he says.

Lunch I can handle. I say, "Okay, when do you wanna go?"

"Now. Unless you have another class," he says, trying to be funny.

My issue isn't another class; it's all that work I have to do before my group meets. But this is Eye Candy.

I rationalize away my need to study and be responsible

because this is the big play, so to speak, I've been waiting for since the first time I saw him. With the one condition that is mandated by *The Code* for every first date, I agree to go with him, but I let him know, "I've got something to do this afternoon, so I'll need to keep an eye on the clock."

The only reason I can tell this lie with a straight face and without stumbling over my words is because I've been saying it for years. Now, even when it's not true, and when I would prefer not to say it, muscle memory takes over.

My time limit, artificial as it is, doesn't faze him. Eye Candy flashes a victory smile. But I'm probably beaming more than him because his victory is my triumph.

Kendra and Mercedes would be overjoyed to know that Eye Candy and I are making progress, but I'm considering keeping this accomplishment to myself for now. There's still a lot I don't know about him; like whether he's really interested in me or if I'm just another girl to add to his collection. Only time will reveal the truth of that.

We agree on Antonelli's for lunch. He says "It's close and quick considering your tight schedule."

This is one time I wish he wasn't so thoughtful and considerate. But I do love Antonelli's, so I'm not complaining about his choice. I plan to order my usual, pepperoni and sausage pizza, and probably mention that a few times during our walk. Eye Candy suggests otherwise.

"You already know you love the pizza, so why not try something new like the chicken parm sub? I'm telling you that thing is the truth. It's a lot of food, though."

I had my heart set on pizza, but I'm liking that Eye Candy is interested enough in me to suggest a different option. He definitely earns points for that. And there's probably something in *The Code* about letting the guy show me what he's working with during this introductory period.

"I'll try the sub then, but if it's that much food, a small one is enough. It betta be good," I say with an 'or else' implied.

Eye Candy snickers, feeling absolutely unthreatened, I'm sure.

He goes to the counter and places our order. After getting our drinks, we find a table.

"The food's gonna take a minute so they'll bring it to us," he advises me.

While we wait, we continue the conversation we started on our walk over; how the basketball program at the school he went to last year fell apart when the coach left and how he ended up here.

"But why Bryce?" I ask. "The basketball team sucks and the school . . . isn't too far behind."

He laughs and says, "Tell me how you really feel?"

I have to laugh, too, because that was the old Ebony talking, but Eye Candy starts speaking and my chance to correct my statement is lost.

"First of all, Miss Ebony, the team used to suck. Not no more," he says with conviction. "Not to brag, but I'm here now and I'm changing the game."

"That's totally bragging, but I hear you, Cam-G," I say, playing into his bravado. "But if you're all that, couldn't you find any better school than Bryce?"

"We're gonna need to talk about why you're so down on your school," he says. "Bryce ain't bad. Kinda small, but I'm liking it here. But you're right, it wasn't my top pick."

There's something we have in common.

"I could've played ball other places," he continues. "But either the money wasn't right, the athletic program wasn't good, or the academics didn't cut it. The ball program here doesn't suck like you think and I'll definitely get some good playing time. But the real reason I'm here is this was the only school that offered me a full ride?

Something else we have in common.

"I'm not looking to head to the NBA, so my folks kinda told me I had to come."

Wow, three for three; a trifecta. Hmm?

Just as I get ready to ask several more questions, our food arrives. My new topic of interest is resting on the plate before me – lightly breaded chicken breast on half of an Italian roll, covered with oooey, gooey mozzarella and smothered with Antonelli's famous marinara. Actually, Eye Candy's grande sandwich is three times the size of mine and looks that much more delicious. We both got salads and garlic knots, too.

"It's the lunch special," the waiter says.

I'm stuck wondering how either of us is gonna be able to eat all this food. Eye Candy doesn't seem worried. He looks like he can eat his and whatever I don't eat of mine.

"Can I bless our food?" he asks before starting.

Stella and Lola start dancing in my head when they hear that. A guy who wants to pray? They are here for it and so am I.

"Sure."

He takes my hand. Shock waves move through my body. But, I stay in prayer mode by focusing on the words he says and not on how excited I feel having any part of his body touch mine.

"Bless this food, oh Lord, and the hands that prepared it. May it nourish and strengthen us for greater service in your name. Amen."

"Amen."

"You got a lot of food there, girl; you better eat up."

I hear words coming from Eye Candy's mouth, but I'm rewinding to the moment where he held my hand to pray. None of the guys I've ever dated prayed out loud. I don't know if any of them prayed at all. Now that Eye Candy has, I might have to add this as a new requirement in the *The Code*.

"Ebony." Hearing my name draws me back to the present moment and to Eye Candy wanting to make sure my food is okay.

"It's fine. I'm letting it cool off."

He accepts that response and gestures for me to start eating. This sandwich looks and smells so incredibly good that I don't need any more encouragement. Eye Candy has already started eating his. We eat and talk a little bit more about Eye

Candy's life before Bryce. Then he turns the spotlight on to me.

"What deep, dark secrets are you hiding, Miss Ebony?"

I almost choke on my food when he says that.

"What makes you think I got secrets like that or that I'm hiding them?" I ask.

"Everybody has something messy they don't want anyone to know about," he says matter-of-factly. "But then again, you seem pretty perfect to me, so maybe you're that one exception."

Perfect? Did the man of my dreams and imaginations just call me perfect? Maybe he's using flattery to get something from me the way Donovan did. Or maybe he's playing me like Randell did Kendra.

An angelic voice whispers, "Or, maybe he's not."

Valid point.

"Messy, I got. Perfect, I'm not," I say. "Remember I got that complicated twin-sister issue."

"You mentioned that briefly. Tell me about it."

I'm not sure what *The Code* would say about sharing the most personal and painful parts of me with someone who I'd like to keep around for a while.

I'd probably run from anyone with my same story, which is why my first reaction would be not to give him any more information. But something in him speaks to something in me and I actually want to share the real me, the entire me. The 'me' Essence discarded. The 'me' I've rediscovered. Even the 'me' that still carries the hurts, disappointments, and failures that I've buried, or at least tried to bury away.

"The deal with my sister is probably just a piece of my whole puzzle. Don't laugh at this," I warn. "Growing up, I used to think the hospital switched me at birth and put me with the wrong family because I'm nothing like them. People in my family fit the same molds; they follow the straight path. My brother went to Morehouse College just like my dad and granddad. They all went to business school and got jobs in banking or finance or for some Fortune 500 Company, blah,

blah, blah. My mom and her siblings all decided on their careers early in their lives and made plans for how they would get there. They all got it done. I'm not like them. I didn't grow up wanting to be anything. I still don't know what I'm doing here."

Eye Candy listens attentively as I share my mess. Like the people in my immediate family do, I expect him to trivialize or dismiss my feelings. My parents, especially my dad, are notorious for doing that. But he doesn't.

"That's gotta be tough," he says with compassion. "Parents can be our biggest fans and our worst foes. I know mine are. My whole life they really pushed me to play basketball, but then didn't try to understand how them splitting up killed my love for the game. Like yours, my folks didn't want to hear what I had to say."

"We've got a lot in common, I see."

"Yeah. We do," he agrees. "But I decided not to let them or anybody dictate how I was gonna live my life. I'm only investing my time in my dreams and spending less time trying to please people. It's a decision you have to make, too."

This sounds a lot like what Donovan was saying. At that moment, a strange feeling comes over me. It's like one of the boxes that I stored stuff away in and hidden somewhere in my memory pops open and I begin sharing.

"It's different for me," I admit to him. "You're great at basketball. I'm great at nothing. Apparently, I'm not even great at being a sister because mine basically renounced me as her twin."

Eye Candy interrupts me. "Wait, for real? How is that even possible?"

"Medically, it's not. Emotionally, yeah. She did it. It's been a struggle figuring things out ever since. To say I felt lost, doesn't even capture the depth of it. But I'm finding my way. Slowly."

"That's some messed up shit, I mean stuff. Not judging you but just saying. That's wrong of her to do that to you."

"Yep."

"Well, forget her then." He does a swatting motion with his hand. "Tell me what you dream about."

I can feel a huge smile forming across my face knowing I dream about him, our wedding, our kids, and our private island. There's no chance I'm sharing that with him today.

"All I do is dream," I tell him. "I'm always slipping in and out of a daydream, in case you haven't noticed."

"I've noticed," he says, laughing. "It's kinda cute, too." Then he says, "Maybe your dreaming is the key to figuring out what you want to make of your time here."

"Hmmm. Maybe," I say, pondering that possibility.

I can feel him eyeing me, perhaps waiting for me to say something else or perhaps wanting to say something himself.

"How'd you like the sandwich?" he eventually asks.

"Oh my gosh, it was delicious." My empty plate should have been the clue to that.

"Yeah, it's hard not to like. Kinda like you." That gorgeous face of his is beaming again.

"Keep saying stuff like that," I warn. "I'm gonna start believing it."

"Well get ready to start believing."

The look he gives me when he says that *almost* makes me leap for joy. Instead, I give him my very best, 'Let's do this,' smile.

After lunch, Eye Candy walks me to my dorm, and we exchange numbers. It's almost impossible for me to keep my mind on studying after that, but the echoes of my father's voice saying, "Make me proud," keep me from straying too far into my dream world. My study time is well spent, but I can't stop savoring the hours I spent with Eye Candy.

Those details get documented in my journal.

Monday, September 16, 2018, part 2

Hi again. I expected something great to happen today and it did. And best of all, I stayed calm. Eye Candy and I had a lunch date. He actually waited for me after class. I guess he really does like me.

Maybe not as much as I like him, but he's definitely crushing on me. We talked about so much. And he wasn't turned off by my issues. He still doesn't know everything. If he sticks around long enough he'll find out. For now, I like that it's just us who know what we're doing and there's no pressure from anybody else to make me nervous. More good things to come. ttyl

BEFORE I CLOSE MY EYES TO GO TO SLEEP, I GET A TEXT ALERT on my phone.

EC: Hey Miss Ebony. Thanks for hanging with me today. Sweet dreams.

Immediately, I jump out of bed and start dancing around my room.

"No need to be calm now," I say out loud. Then I actually do settle back into bed and reply to his message.

Me: Hi Mr. Cameron. It was my pleasure. I hope your dreams are sweet too.

Am I really supposed to go to sleep knowing Eye Candy is thinking about me right now? That's impossible and I lay in bed for hours imagining us sharing all kinds of future experiences, until sleep eventually does find me.

Chapter Seventeen

I hate rain. And I absolutely hate rainy days that come after rainy days. I've tried my best to embrace rain considering it's a meteorological certainty. Sure, plants and trees and marine life depend on it. But I still hate it with a passion. Not even my cute rain boots and matching rain jackets, which I only get to wear when it rains, have changed my attitude about it.

A rain cloud has stalled over Winslow, Connecticut and we've had two straight days of downpours. The forecast predicts today will be day three.

Interestingly, Essence and I share the same view about rain. The only difference is that Essence never took the time to invest in the proper rain gear. I'm sure she'll be barging into my room again to borrow a pair of my boots like she always does on days like this, even after she cut me out of her life. As that thought leaves my mind, I hear my door unlock.

"You up?" Essence shouts while walking into my room.

"No," I yell back.

She ignores me. "It's freaking raining again. I need something different to wear."

She searches through the bin where I keep my rain stuff. She pulls out my red boots.

"I'm wearing those," I say.

"Whateva," she declares. "They probably look ridiculous with my outfit anyway. I'll take the yellow ones. And this jacket."

"Yeah, okay," I reply even though it's really not.

"Later." She slams the door on her way out.

"You better return all my stuff," I scream, knowing she can't hear me and if she could, she wouldn't care.

I don't have the mental energy to be mad at Essence for being so entitled and disrespectful. I just hope she gets drenched today.

After she leaves, I lay in bed trying to fall back asleep. The blaring of my alarm about a half hour later jolts me out of bed. This weather is sapping all my drive and killing the good mood I've enjoyed courtesy of Eye Candy, who Kendra says is "coming at me with a full court press."

Getting a text from him instantly brightens my day. It's just the sun emoji with #liquidsunshine typed below it. He thinks calling rain liquid sunshine will help me not despise it so much. Actually, his early morning texts, which he's been sending me every day since our first lunch date at Antonelli's, are what turn my gray skies blue. After responding to his message, with a smile emoji, I push myself to shower and get dressed. My outfit today has to withstand the elements, so that takes some extra time to put together. Once I'm ready, I head out to battle Mother Nature.

A GUST OF WIND DESTROYS MY UMBRELLA HALFWAY TO MY English Composition class so I detour to the campus gift shop to buy a new one, which leaves me only enough time to get a muffin and juice from the coffee bar in the back of the store for break-fast. Leaving from there, I get splashed by a car that speeds past me. By the time, I walk into my classroom, my muffin isn't edible, I'm drenched and late. I regret wishing this fate upon my sister. Karma is a . . . .

My only comfort is that pretty much everybody in class is in the same condition. Wet coats and soggy boots line the walls and fill empty seats. While I complain about how wet my clothes are, a couple of kids are dealing with wet laptops that now don't work. If I had to deal with that problem on top of everything else, I'd quit school today.

The sky opens again while I walk to my business class. I'm miserable and barely pay attention once I get there, which is not much different from how I usually spend my time here. I'm only registered in this course because my dad forced me to take it. Needless to say, I hate it.

By the time class ends, the sky looks a little brighter. Mercedes sends a text asking me to meet her at Central Dining for lunch. I'm starving since I didn't eat breakfast, so I agree. As I walk to meet her, I pray for a break from any more liquid sunshine.

That prayer must not have gotten higher than the clouds above my head because the sky opens when I leave the building drenching me again. By the time I get to where I'm supposed to meet Mercedes, I'm even more miserable than before and I probably look even worse. When I find a table, I peel off my wet coat, then text Mercedes to let her know where to find me. She responds quickly.

M: Hey Chica, it started raining real bad. Didn't wanna melt LOL so I came back 2 my room. Dinner later before class?

That's so messed up. Just like her, I could be in my room dry. Instead, I'm sitting here alone and soaking wet. The best response to her text is no response because what I'd like to say could risk ending our friendship.

A day like today requires comfort food, which today will be a cheeseburger, fries, and warm chocolate chip cookies.

I'll also get some chicken Alfredo for later, just in case I decide not to come back out for dinner before my seminar tonight.

After picking up my food, I settle at my table and select a calming playlist to provide a soundtrack for this dining experience. While eating, I marvel at the number of people who come in dripping wet with no coats or umbrellas. It's been monsoon raining for days. Did they really think they had some special ability to stay dry without any gear at all? I'm soaked and I left my room prepared.

My rain-shaming continues until Eye Candy and his crew walk in. He looks like no water even touched him. Or maybe wet on him just magnifies his fineness. Seeing him puts a smile on my face.

He notices me and comes to my table while his friends get in line to eat. I'm sure I look like a train wreck, but there's nothing I can do about it. Besides, the voices in my head remind me that on my worst day I'm at least a six, maybe even a seven. Today is hardly my worst day. It is my soggiest.

"This is a treat, seeing you on a Tuesday." His broad smile is like a ray of sunshine.

"Yeah, but too bad you have to see me like this."

"What I see looks pretty good," he says.

"Aww thanks."

Now that I know him better, I can accept and appreciate his compliments. Especially on a day like today.

"You staying for lunch?" I ask.

"Nah. Gotta grab and go. Still have another class and then a workout before practice."

"A workout and practice? That's a lot."

"That pre-season tournament is this weekend so we've got some new plays to fine-tune."

"That's right. You did mention that."

Eye Candy's friends are yelling across the cafeteria for him to come get his food.

"Those dudes have no home training," he says. "Let me bounce before they get us kicked out. I'll call you after practice, if it's not too late."

"You can call me anytime," I tell him. Anytime at all.

WHEN I GET BACK TO MY ROOM, I CAN'T GET OUT OF MY WET clothes fast enough. I take a hot shower and cover every inch of my body with a relaxing lavender body lotion and put on dry clothes. After giving myself an hour or so to decompress, I start reading for class. Midway through the first article, I notice my neglected journal under some textbooks so I take a moment to vent.

Today I start fresh. I am better than I was. I am ____

I write **OVER THE RAIN**

Tuesday, September 25, 2018

Hi. Today started out awful. The evil I wished on my sister came down on me, literally. I'm sorry God. Please take the curse away from me and keep me dry when I go back out to class this evening. Eye Candy was a bright spot. Thanks for sending him my way. #liquidsunshine ttyl

Chapter Eighteen

A s soon as I walk into Central Dining for breakfast this
morning, I head for the waffle station. I'm not surprised
that Mercedes is already in line. She raves about these waffles
and would eat them every morning if she could.

"Hey, Chica, hurry up and come get in line with me so you
can beat the rush. Just bring your bag."

As instructed, I join her in line and she begins my lesson,
Waffle Station 101.

"People get overwhelmed with the choices up there and
freeze. It makes the line take forever when that happens," she
continues. "So think about it now. And trust me, you don't ever
want to be in this line when it's more than five people. You'll
wait all day to get your food."

On the low, I'm impressed with how Mercedes has this waffle
line reduced to a science, but at the same time I'm a little
worried about my girl. How much has she thought about this?
However much I wanna judge her, everything she said is absolutely correct. This line crawls along. By the time we get to the
front, I'll take almost anything on a plate. She orders some fancy
fruit combination while I keep mine simple . . . chocolate chip
with whip cream.

Once we get our food, Mercedes leads us to find Kendra. On

the way, we stop at The Grille and she piles a dozen or so bacon strips on her plate.

I look at her and say, "No offense, but that's a lot of bacon. You eating like you just got out of jail."

"Be quiet," she snaps back. "I'm craving bacon. And what Aunt Flow wants Aunt Flow gets."

"Ohhh, I see. My bad. Let me be quiet. Go 'head and handle your biz."

I throw a few extra slices on her plate for laughs. I know all too well how demanding the red monster can be.

We see Kendra at a table by the window with two guys we don't know. I'm not in the mood for company this morning.

Kendra has an assortment of "keto-friendly" food items laid out in front of her. This is her latest diet fad, which she's been doing for about a week. She dining on sliced avocado, eggs, spinach, and nuts, which she must have snuck in because this is a "nut free" community.

"Nuts are contraband on campus, you know that right, KK? I think you can get sent to the electric chair or something if they catch you with them?" I give her that warning in a joking, but kinda serious way.

She cuts her eyes at me and pops a handful of cashews and peanuts into her mouth.

"That's real talk, KK. You should listen to your girl," one of the guys says.

She ignores him, too, and continues to eat her nuts, stopping only long enough to rail on Mercedes' plate of bacon.

"Yo. What should be against the law is all that bacon."

"I'm craving bacon," Mercedes makes known. "Go back to eating your illegal nuts and let me have my peace."

One of Kendra's friend says to the other one, "Watch out, man. She craving bacon. You know what comes next? She gon' be throwing that bacon in a minute."

"I know right . . ." he says, ducking to avoid imaginary bacon being thrown at him.

The guys have their own private comedy moment, laughing,

and giving each other hand slaps. Mercedes and I both throw bacon at them to shut them up. Kendra checks them and us.

"Can everybody just chill the ef out." She then makes the introductions. "Rahj and Damien, this is Mercedes and Ebony. Y'all, these are my homeboys."

Mercedes says to them, "You guys are freshman right? I can tell. I would say it's nice meeting you, but I'm not sure yet." That's payback for the bacon comment.

Damien starts to say something, but Kendra squashes it and changes the conversation at the table.

"Y'all heard anything about the joint the Party Mafia is throwing tonight?" she asks. "They sent out a text blast late last night."

Damien and Rahj say, "Nope," almost in unison.

"What's that?" Damien asks.

Sounding like she's giving them the Wikipedia explanation, Kendra proceeds. "The Party Mafia is a group of white guys, all juniors and seniors now, who throw dope parties a few times each year. They call themselves the Party Mafia because they think they're killin' the campus party scene. Don't give me that look, D, that's what they say. I didn't come up with that mess."

Mercedes adds, "Their promos always say stuff like: "It would be a crime how much fun you can have," or "People will be dying to be seen with us."

Kendra says, "Yeah, it's weak, but the parties are lit."

Rahj leans back in his chair and folds his arms across his chest. He looks like he's replaying in his head what Mercedes said, trying to make sense of it. I feel him on that.

"Let me get this straight," he finally says. "They actually think referring to themselves as a mafia makes them socially acceptable?"

"That was my reaction, too, when I first heard about them," I yell out. Maybe Rahj has a little more sense than we gave him credit for.

Kendra dismisses our concerns anyway.

"It doesn't matter what y'all think. Their parties are the ish and they're getting paid. It's all about making money moves."

Mercedes shares a few more details about the party. "The gimmick they're using tonight involves a made-up VIP guest list. If they see your name on the list, you go right in. If not, they make you wait in another line and pay ten dollars. They arbitrarily decide whose name they see on the list, which has to be the lamest promotion stunt ever."

The guys listen in disbelief. Damien says, "Lame is right."

Kendra then says, "Lame or not, it's the first real party of the year and nothing else is happening on campus tonight. It'll be packed."

"You know," Mercedes interjects, "ladies get in free before eleven-thirty, so we," Mercedes emphasizes "we" and points in a circular motion to me, her and Kendra, "need to be there before that time. Fellas, y'all are on your own."

"Wow, that's messed up. Y'all just gon' leave us out there?" Rahj asks.

Kendra says, "Don't hate the playa . . . "

"Okay, I see how you do. Me and D will just have to catch up with you there. Gotta make it to this class now. Y'all be good."

After Rahj and Damien leave, Mercedes complains about the guys taking up the time I was supposed to be using to update them on Eye Candy. Then she adds, "The Rahj one is kinda cute and he might be worth keeping an eye on for the future."

"No, Mercedes." Kendra reminds her she vowed "No dating younger guys. Not until we're in our thirties when it might be more to our advantage."

"Whateva. I'm still gonna keep my eye on him. He might blossom and be different by his junior year."

"That sounds like stalking for real." Kendra says laughing.

"I'm not listening to y'all anymore. Can we talk about Mr. Eye Candy please?" Mercedes turns her attention to me.

"Yeah. Spill it, Eb," Kendra says.

Dang. Almost got away without an inquisition.

"Alright. All I'll say is, things are moving along nicely. We had lunch again this past Monday and we sat together in class on Wednesday. He's walked me to class a few times. We've been texting a lot. We talk sometimes. He's definitely earning Prince Charming status."

"Okay, Eb. That's what I'm talking 'bout," Kendra says clapping and cheering me on like I just ended global warming.

Mercedes is not happy I kept this info from them.

"I didn't want to say anything too soon," I confess. "And you guys put a lot of pressure on me to speed things up. I can't do that."

"That's Kendra, not me. Get that straight, Chica."

"Hey, I just give advice," Kendra says. "Take it or not. It's no pressure."

"Whatever. That's all I got. Can y'all be excited?"

"We are, right Kendra?" Mercedes asks.

"Absolutely."

Neither of them sounds convincing, but I don't care.

Since I have nothing more to report, we change the subject of conversation back to the party.

"We going tonight, right?" Mercedes asks.

Kendra says, "Yeah, I'm down."

I say, "Me, too."

"Good. Then Eb, can we meet in your fancy room at nine-ish?"

"That's fine. *Mi casa es su casa,*" I reply.

"*Muy Bien Amiga,*" Mercedes says giving me a little proud mami clap. Then she says, "So nine o'clock and don't wait till the last minute to think about what you wanna wear. We're going for more sexy. Maybe Mr. Eye Candy will be there."

Wouldn't that be nice?

Chapter Nineteen

G etting ready for this party is taking on a life of its own. First, as always, I run through multiple outfit changes. I waste too much time and make a huge mess. I'm trying to look cute in case Eye Candy shows up, which is now a real possibility given his last text message.

Me: Coming to the Mafia party?

EC: Not sure depends how I feel after practice. RU going?

Me: Yep

EC: Maybe I'll come thru then

Me: Hope so

When I finally commit to an outfit, I already know that Mercedes will hate it because, one, it's solid black. She thinks color is always better. Two, I've got my 'girls' all covered up. Her definition of sexy is more cleavage.

I'm not doing cleavage tonight. Instead, I'm wearing a fitted, backless mini dress to highlight my other *assets*. She might not like it, but Eye Candy won't complain if he sees me in it. But nobody will ever see me or the dress if I can't get my hair to cooperate. For some reason, I'm not having any success getting this hair snatched. The only people who know how to handle my hair better than me are my mother, who isn't here, and Essence, who I refuse to ask for anything. I'd rather put on a wig on;

except, I don't have one. I'm screwed and realize that I have to ask Essence for help.

We've seen each other a few times this week, but haven't spoken. I hate to have our first actual conversation being me asking her for help. I can hear her now bringing up all that "You're living in my shadow," crap again.

Then I remember how she jacked my rain gear for a week.

She owes me. Time to cash in.

Me: Having hair issues. Can u plz help?

Short and to the point. No begging. No making deals. Will you help or not? Counting the seconds until she replies, I pray for a similar short and to the point response. No lectures. No commentary. Just a yes or no, but preferably a yes.

About two minutes pass and she hasn't responded. A "no" would be better than being ignored. As soon as I start working on a back-up hair plan, my door opens. Essence walks in and isn't yelling for a change.

"Are you trying to wear it up or something?" she asks. Her tone is surprisingly humane.

"Yeah, and I'm trying to add this ponytail," I say, holding up a bundle of hair similar in texture to my own but longer and with kinky curly coils.

"Well you're a long way from getting there and a low ponytail would look better and probably be easier. Sit down. Let me do it."

Sometimes I can't stand my sister, because I didn't ask her what would be easier. I told her what I wanted. But she's wearing her hair up in a bun, and would never allow my hair to look anything close to hers. I'm still grateful for her because without her help my hair would be an unruly afro on top of my head and I wouldn't be able to leave my room.

Essence spends about fifteen minutes brushing, pulling, parting, and smoothing until she makes every strand of my hair and my edges obedient and perfectly snatched.

"Okay, stand up. Nice. I do good work. You should put that flower you took from me and never gave back in your hair. It'll look cute with that dress. I guess you'll be at the Mafia Party tonight, right?"

"That's the plan."

"I'll be there too, but we have VIP access so you probably won't see me. Toodles."

"Thanks, Sisi, I mean Es."

"Whatever." She leaves my room on the same broom she flew in on.

Once I'm all put together, I twirl around in front of the mirror and check myself from all angles. I absolutely love how she did my hair, but I'll never say that to her. After snapping a few pics and sending them to my friends, I start my makeup and get ready for our pre-party shenanigans.

I spot my journal on my desk and realize I didn't make an entry today. Might as well do it now.

Today I start fresh. I am better than I was. I am ____

I write **READY**

Friday, September 28, 2018

Hi. Tonight is the first real party of the year. I am psyched. My squad is coming over to pre-party and do make-up. The day was almost a disaster because of my hair. I had to ask Sisi for help which I hated having to do. She did it the way she wanted not the way I asked. Still controlling me. Hopefully, we can stay far away from each other tonight. Also hopefully, Eye Candy will actually come. He said he might. That would be more awesome than words could describe. Gotta bounce. ttyl

KENDRA ARRIVES CLOSE TO NINE-FIFTEEN WITH SMOKED wings and nachos smothered with guac and some low carb cheese mess. She's in shorts and a t-shirt. She responds right away to the 'I know you don't think you're going anywhere with me looking like that' look I give her.

"Clothes are right here. Nachos and a white dress don't mix."

"Facts," I say with an approving chuckle.

Mercedes follows shortly afterward with sliders, sodas and a lot of commentary.

"Why you wearing all black, Eb?"

Knowing her comment is more of a statement than a question, I don't even answer.

Kendra laughs and says "Ignore her, Eb. She just mad 'cause you serving looks.

Mercedes fires back. "Don't get me started on you KK. Get your entire self together then you get to be in this conversation."

"I'll do it after I eat. Until then, I'm just gonna get on your nerves."

"You do such a good job at that, too."

"I try," Kendra says as she devours another mouthful of nachos, dripping sauce on her t-shirt.

Talk about serving looks, Mercedes outshines us all in that gorgeous floral wrap mini dress. With those four-inch heels, she's giving legs for days. I'm scared of that plunging neck line though. She could end up giving a peep show if she's not careful. But as she moves around, I can tell she's taped down. Of course the fashionista would take that very necessary precaution.

Everything she's giving is fire, but the choice of zebra print belt and shoes confuses me, considering the floral pattern in her dress.

"You always get a pass to talk about everybody because you're usually flawless, but what's on your feet with that dress? Do those shoes even match?" I ask.

Mercedes looks at me like I just challenged her to a fight.

"Let me explain something to you. Animal print is a neutral. It goes with every freakin' thing."

"In what universe?" I ask.

"In the universe of every civilized fashion forward human being. Keep up, Chica."

"Oh my goodness . . . You are crazed," I yell.

Kendra starts laughing uncontrollably.

Mercedes says something to us in Spanish and basically ignores us until our amusement fades.

"Yo Eb, your hair is looking good," Kendra says. "Is that a new ponytail?"

"Brand new actually."

"Who makes it?"

"You know it's Yaki, but Essence did it for me, if you can believe that. I was struggling, looking like Buckwheat," I tell her.

"Wow, what did it cost you? A kidney?" she says sarcastically.

"LOL. No charge, other than her funky attitude. But I'm sure I'll pay for it later."

We hear a knock on my door.

"That better not be somebody complaining about my music."

"That happens to you too?" Kendra asks in disgust.

"These girls are so ridiculous. Everything is too much noise for their delicate ears. I'm not answering the door. They can call security." I say.

The knocking continues. Then Mercedes remembers, "Oh yeah, I invited two of the girls you met at the MCC, Danielle and Sofia. That might be them." She starts toward the door.

I'm trying to figure out why Mercedes would invite basic strangers to my room to hang out with us and not even tell me.

She welcomes *her* guests in. The Sofia girl is from Dallas, Texas and greets us with a cheery, "Hey y'all." She has a pizza and some sodas in her hand. Danielle, who's from the D.C. area, doesn't say much at first. She smiles and hands me a bag of still hot '24Hour' cookies. Because I love these cookies and pizza is my source of life, I smile and welcome *our* new friends into my home.

Mercedes becomes singularly focused on how Sofia and Danielle look.

"Loving the outfits ladies, but you need some more pizzazz on those faces. Danielle, your black girl magic is looking too vanilla, and Sofia your Latina fire isn't even sparking. You too, Kendra. Stop feeding your face so we can paint it. Ebony, help me out here."

Mercedes goes into her makeup bag and adds some dazzle to Sofia's face. I take on Danielle. While Kendra waits her turn, she blasts the perfect playlist and our final party prep goes into full effect. We have a lot going on -- eating, loudtalking, loud music, makeup and lashes flying everywhere. Mercedes and I battle each other for the best spot in the mirror to apply finishing touches to our own faces and hair.

Mercedes is on final outfit approval. I'm in charge of making sure we all have on enough, but not too much, makeup. The makeup also has to be wear-off-able, so as the night goes on we still look good in case we can't escape to touch it up. Of course, all of this pandemonium gets documented on IG and Snap Chat with about a billion pictures and story updates.

After Mercedes approves of our outfits and I feel like our faces are all properly beat, we see the time and collectively let out a gasp. "We gotta go."

Chapter Twenty

We leave for the party around 11:15pm and make the ten-minute walk to the gym at Stuart Hall. We have to wait in a pretty long line, which moves slowly for several minutes. I'm pretty sure a snail moves faster.

Essence and her DWBs come near where we're standing.

"Check my sister out. Ready to party," she says loudly as they look us over. "I had to do her hair. And that's probably my dress she has on."

Bianca chimes in with, "It doesn't matter what she has on. They'll never get in. Connor said they're only admitting VIPs now."

They walk off, leaving a trail of mocking laughter.

Kendra says, "You said she was gonna make you pay for helping you with your hair. I'd say she just did."

"She's so stupid. This dress isn't even hers and she knows it."

"That's just rude," Danielle says.

Mercedes wisely observes, "We have a bigger problem. If Bianca is right, we have zero chance of getting into this party."

Just when I'm ready to suggest we do something else, like hit the lame campus pub, I notice a guy from my Business class. He's part of the Mafia crew. We've chatted before, but nothing too involved. When I point him out to my friends, they suggest calling him over. One of us can fake-flirt with him and maybe he'll put us on the VIP guest list.

At their insistence, I do it.

"Hey, Brad. What's up?" I call out to him.

He walks over and gives me a big hug, probably trying to show off for his Mafia buddies.

"Hey, Ebs. You lookin' like a snack tonight."

Ebs? I'm cringing. My friends know I hate "Ebs" and I made that clear when Kendra decided she needed to call me "Eb." They also know they're the only two people in the universe who get to call me that. And Brad, I'm not your snack. Eww. Please unsay that.

My friends send me messages with their eyes letting me know that they're offering me as tribute, so I flash an appreciative smile and don't blast Brad for calling me "Ebs." Instead, I say, "You're looking pretty fly, too," which is true compared to his usual appearance.

Brad tries to flirt again, but he has absolutely no game. There's no way I'm gonna crush the boy's spirits, because I'm on a mission. After two or three minutes of indulging him, I get to the point.

"So, I heard we won't be able to get in unless we're on the VIP list. Is that true? Because that would suck."

"Yeah, it's pretty packed in there, but I'll take care of you," he says.

"And my girls?"

"No probs. All of you just have to save me a dance though."

"Sure," we say together.

I try to sound enthusiastic, but don't even convince myself.

It's enough for Brad. He takes us out of the line and gives us gold VIP wristbands.

"These will get you into the party and give you access to the VIP lounge," he explains.

The big dude at the door, who's probably some guy from the wrestling team, let us right in.

The girls thank Brad and so do I. As we pass him, he says, "Don't forget our dance, pretty ladies."

Without saying anything, I smile and brace myself for a long, uncomfortable night dodging Brad.

When we enter the building, I'm amazed at how they transformed the old school gym into something that looks like a nightclub. There are two DJs on a stage that is surrounded by a circular dance floor. They've got some special lighting effects. A large roped-off seating area immediately on the right when we walk in has a sign that says, "VIP LOUNGE." We show our wristbands and another wrestler-looking guy waves us through. We walk past Essence and her friends who, I'm sure are wondering how we went from nobodies to VIPs without their approval. I'm tempted to flaunt my gold wristband in her face, but *I Like It* comes on and Mercedes pulls me out to the dance floor.

Kendra joins us moments later. The new girls look on. After a fairly good music set, the DJ starts spinning some dub step stuff that we hate. We head back to the VIP Lounge and enjoy complimentary cocktails and snacks. Essence and her friends look annoyed that we've encroached on their territory. But so what? We're having fun. We snap the first few dozen of many party pics and the posting mania begins.

When the DJ plays *Sicko Mode*, everybody in the place loses it and rushes the dance floor. Even Sofia and Danielle. He follows that up with some more Drake, Queen Bey (of course), Khalid, Cardi, and Lizzo. Everyone in here is turnt up. The DJ plays an old song by Sza, who Mercedes loves, and she is in her own world . . . until a cute guy rolls up next to her and they start dancing. Then, here comes Brad.

"C'mon, Ebs, let's get it." I guess by the way he's gyrating in front me he wants to dance. We dance for about fifteen minutes. For a white boy with no rap game, Brad has a few respectable dance moves. He gets a five for originality and confidence, but loses points for getting too close to me. I give him a look that says, "Don't even try it," and he backs off. He behaves himself after that until some maniacal song comes on that makes him and a bunch of the boys around us gets amped. That's my cue to exit.

"Brad, I'm out."

He doesn't hear me until I yell it in his ear. He waves goodbye and I narrowly escape what once was a dance floor, but what now looks like a bunch of hyenas celebrating the crowning of their new leader.

I find Kendra sitting with Sofia and Danielle in the VIP area, far enough from Essence and the DWBs so that we shouldn't have to breathe the same air. No sign of Eye Candy. Mercedes is still dancing with the same guy. I squeeze in next to Sofia who hands me a bottle of water.

Kendra says to me, "You must be thirsty after all that. I thought you were gonna sweat your hair out."

"Nah. You know I'm too cool for that," I say, laughing.

Sofia shows me some of the videos she took of me dancing with Brad. Most of them are hilarious. Others are actually kinda sweet, but still embarrassing. "No posting those," I order.

From where we sit, we have a great view of a group of guys who seem to be enjoying their view of us. They're looking in our direction and talking to each other, probably planning out how they're gonna make their moves.

Kendra says, "Hey, Eb, you see that guy over there? The one in the white t-shirt. You think he's cute?"

"You mean the one who's been rappin' to every chick in here? Yeah, I see him. He's just a'ight."

I'm trying to make her not want to be interested in him anymore than she already is. He's quite attractive, but I'm not gonna tell her that.

"A'ight? That boy is fine. I think I'm gonna talk to him."

"Why?" I say in objection. "He's all over the place. Didn't you learn anything from that Randell mess?"

"Yes, I did. But this one is perfect."

I don't understand her logic, but she must know what she's doing. Kendra somehow gives the guy a signal. Maybe she smiled, maybe she winked. She could have blown him a kiss for all I know. Whatever she did works. He dismisses the future ex-side-chick that he's talking to and makes his way over to Kendra. He asks her to dance and before long, she captures him in her web. He spends the rest of his time at the party with her. She got him. Game must recognize game.

Mercedes finally returns from her dance-floor date.

"His name is Enrico, but he goes by Rico. He's a Senior and I gave him my number," she says looking and sounding like a kid on Christmas.

"That's nice, but isn't he kinda short for you?" I say. "You usually go for the really tall ones, with your short self."

"I don't care how short or tall he is Debbie Downer. He's really nice. And I'm not short. I'm just two inches shorter than you. Let me have my moment."

"Wow, didn't know that was such a sensitive subject. My bad."

About this time Brad returns to us. "Mind if I join you lovely ladies?"

We feel like we have to say yes since he did let us in free and give us VIP access. And, it is his party.

"Not at all," Sofia says, sliding over to make room for him to sit next to me. That wasn't necessary.

Brad tries to talk to me, but I pretend I can't hear him over the music. Kendra comes back and sits down when the guy she connected with leaves. Once we're back together Mercedes announces that we all need go to the bathroom to freshen up for round two. Brad laughs but promises to be waiting for us when we return.

Chapter Twenty-One

F irst topic of conversation when we get into the bathroom is
Brad, of course.

"Girl, that boy is into you," Mercedes says.

"Yeah, you got the vanilla swirl appeal," Kendra adds, teasing.

"Y'all know I don't date white guys so miss me on that."

Danielle says, "I do. I'll take him. He seems cool."

I tell her, "I'm not sure it works like that, but go for it."

Mercedes asks me if I've seen Eye Candy here tonight.

"No, but you know I'm looking," I say.

AFTER SPENDING WAY TOO MUCH TIME IN THE BATHROOM
talking and fooling around with our hair and makeup, we go back
to the party and turn all the way up for of the rest of the night.
Brad and I dance again. It becomes a group experience when
Danielle and Sofia join us.

Mercedes and Rico have reunited and Kendra is . . . being
Kendra. I'm recording a video of us acting up when I get a text
message from . . . Donovan? I haven't heard from him since he
dropped me off after that situation we had in the park.

D: Tell that boy 2 let u go & come talk me

I almost drop my phone. Donovan is here? Why? Where?

My mind and body start spinning looking from side to side, searching for his face in the crowd. Unfortunately, the room is too dark. He's gotta be close if he sees me dancing with Brad.

"Everything okay, Ebs? You're not grooving anymore," Brad says.

"Yeah. But I gotta go handle something. You keep grooving with Danielle and Sofia."

Immediately, I move away from the crowd and reply to Donovan's message.

Me: Where r u?

D: Behind u

My heart drops. When I turn around, Donovan is standing in front of me. I forgot how good he looks. He comes close to me and kisses me on the cheek. My eyes close and I'm taken back to our night in the park. A chill goes down my spine.

"I see you're still beautiful," he whispers in my ear.

Stay calm, Ebony, I tell myself before speaking to him. "Why are you here?"

"For the party, of course. My boys are part of the crew giving it, so I had to support them. Dance with me."

Donovan doesn't wait for a response. He takes my hand and walks me deep into the center of the crowd and the music takes us away. Everything about him right now – his touch, his smile, the way his body moves to the music feels sensual and inviting, despite me wanting it not to be. Without any warning, Donovan spins me around and pulls me in close to him so that my back is up against his body. He places his hands on my hips and guides them as we move in sync to the music. I can feel his warm breath on my bare back. I'm cursing this backless dress right now. He plants a few soft kisses on my neck. He pulls me closer and holds me tighter. Because so many people are dancing around us, I doubt that anyone can see how sensual our dance has become. And I'm really glad no one can see how good this feels.

The DJ changes the song. The people around us disperse and

I move away from Donovan. He takes my hand and leads me away from the crowd and says, "Let's go talk."

We pass Mercedes and Kendra and they give me the thumbs up sign. *If they only knew*, I say to myself. Brad and Danielle have gotten cozy in the lounge area. At least he's no longer a worry for me.

Donovan and I walk outside and stand near his illegally parked his bike.

"Still breaking rules, I see."

"Guilty as charged."

He leans close to me and says, "You still feel as good as I remember. Maybe even better."

In my mind, I've decided nothing more can happen between us than what has already happened. And that was more than I should have allowed.

"Whatever you're thinking of doing, stop," I say, pushing him away. "I'm gonna get back to my friends."

"Okay. Goodbye kiss?"

The word "No," is coming out of my mouth as his tongue is going in it. The kiss excites me and feels so good. I let it last too long, but I end it, even though I want more.

"Bye, Donovan."

"Later, Princess."

I walk away from Donovan and don't look back. I'm not sure if he even returned to the party. Mercedes and Kendra bombard me with questions about the mystery man.

"That was Donovan," I tell them.

"No way," Mercedes says in disbelief.

"That dude is absolutely fine," Kendra observes. "No wonder y'all ended up getting freaky in the park."

I'm not amused by Kendra's comment, but she's right. Definitely not mentioning the kiss we just shared.

"What did he want from you, Eb, besides what's in your panties?" Mercedes asks, bluntly.

"I don't know," I say. "He's friends with the Mafia guys so he came up for the party."

"He was feeling you up pretty good while you were dancing, so don't be surprised if you get a late night call to ride his bike or something else," Mercedes warns.

Kendra then says, "And we already know he gets them nasty girl hormones flowing. You best not let Cam find out."

"You two are terrible people and I can't stand either one of you."

They both laugh. Of course, I'm joking with them but still glad Kendra mentioned Eye Candy. He's who I need to focus on. If anybody is gonna get anything in me flowing, it should be him.

"Enough about Donovan," I insist. "Can we please get back to the party?"

The crowd has thinned out considerably so we easily find Brad and Danielle and join them on the dance floor. Losing myself in the music and my friends allows me to shake the thoughts of Donovan from my mind. At least for now.

Essence and her friends are dancing with a group of guys not far from us. They're constantly looking our way. In my mind, I imagine they're hatin' on us because of how dope we are. I hear Li'l Yachty in my head singing, "They wanna be us."

The DJ lights up the dance floor with another music set that is straight fire, definitely one of the best of the night. When the last song ends about an hour later, Essence and her friends walk out, talking loudly about the exclusive off-campus afterparty they're going to. Like anybody cares.

Brad announces that he wants to treat his dancing queens to breakfast at The Silver Spoon.

"A lot of the people from the party will be there," he tells us.

Hopefully, not Donovan.

We debate whether or not to go. We are hungry and he's offering free food. Sofia is the only one who acts like she doesn't wanna hang. She claims she's tired and wants to go to bed. We do what we do best and peer pressure her into coming with us. Mercedes and I also explain our rule to her, saying, "We come together. We stay together. We leave together. It's not optional."

Sofia finally agrees to hang and we meet up with Brad and his crew at the diner.

As expected, the Mafia afterparty takes over The Silver Spoon. At our table, about eight of us are talking loud. Laughing. Passing plates back and forth. Everybody wants to taste everybody else's food.

Other than stealing a few fries as they pass by me, I don't bother anybody's food, and keep my plate to myself. Food sharing with strangers ain't my thing. Depending on the food, sharing with people I know might not be my thing either. I keep my blueberry pancakes, eggs, and turkey sausage all to myself.

The Mafia guys are all pretty nice. Brad and Danielle have definitely made a connection. And how about Sofia? The one person who didn't want to come is hugged up with Connor in a back booth. My friends were clowning me about Brad making moves in my direction when they should've had their eyes on Miss Dallas.

By four in the morning, I'm ready to crash. Convincing the rest of my crew to leave takes another half hour. When they're ready to bounce, Brad and Connor offer Danielle and Sofia a ride back to campus with them, but Sofia wisely hesitates. She learned. We come together, we stay together, we leave together. Mercedes agrees to go with them.

"Since I invited you, I'll ride with you to be your chaperone to make sure you get back to school. After that, you're on your own."

"Ebs, do you and Ken need a ride? Kendra hates being called "Ken" as much as I despise "Ebs." But we both let Brad slide because his party was epic.

Kendra says, "Nah me and Ebs are good. I got a friend here who can take us back. But thanks."

I hit her arm for calling me Ebs. She just laughs.

Brad says, "Cool, hope you two lovelies had a good time. Make sure to send me your contact info so I can put you on my Special VIP list."

"We will. Thanks Brad," I say.

"Absolutely," Kendra adds.

ON THE RIDE BACK TO CAMPUS KENDRA MAKES AN interesting observation.

"This might be the first time our whole squad hooked up with guys at a party."

My interaction with Donovan, assuming that's what she means, hardly counts as hooking up in the same way that the rest of them did. But what happened with Donovan was something. Especially that kiss. Just thinking about it . . . .

Don't think about it, I tell myself. *Don't think about him.*

Kendra's friend drops me off and I head straight to the shower and wash all that partying off of me. Afterward, I check my phone before getting in bed.

Donovan sent a text message.

D: Hey Princess. Good seeing you tonight. Haven't stopped thinking about you. Forgot how good you taste. I need more of you. Will be in touch.

Boy, bye.

There's no more of me for you to have. I delete his message without responding. Erasing the memory of his touch and his kiss will be more of a challenge.

Chapter Twenty-Two

All the activity around the Mafia party yesterday wore me completely out to the point where all I've been able to do for most of today is sleep and binge watch my fave web tv series. I do make a journal entry.

Today I start fresh. I am better than I was. I am _____
I write **A VIP!**
Saturday, September 29, 2018

Hi. Thanks to my new friend Brad, we got VIP access to the MAFIA party. And OMG it was so lit. My crew plus 2 had a ball. Mercedes and Kendra both met guys, our plus 2 hooked up with Brad and another Mafia boy. D showed up and that blew my mind. We danced. He kissed me. I didn't want him to stop but real glad he did. He wants more of me. I really like that he's into me. It makes me feel special - like a VIP I guess. But I'm focused on Eye Candy and wanting our friendship to develop. I'll have to keep reminding myself that D is noise that I need to block out. As long as I don't see him, I should be able to do that. I pray that I can. ttyl

By seven o'clock in the evening, the walls of my room feel like they're closing in on me and I need to get out. Mercedes and Kendra are both with the guys they met at the party. If Eye

Candy wasn't at his tournament, I'd probably be with him. That thought prompts me to send him a text:

Me: Hey. Just saying Hi and good luck. LMK when u get back

After several minutes, he still hasn't responded, but I'm sure he's tied up with practice or a game.

Since I'm rollin' solo this evening, I make my way to The Row to get food. Reilly and her roommate, Hannah, see me and force me to eat with them. I end up being glad they do, because we actually have a great time.

"Why don't you come with us to the pub, after we eat?" Reilly suggests.

Hannah jumps all over the idea. "Whoa. That would be awesome," she says.

The pub is never the social destination of choice for me. The music and the people who party there are not my flavor. But I am having a nice time with Reilly and Hannah, and I have absolutely nothing else to do, so I agree to go. Then they tell me tonight is Techno Night. I'm so screwed. Techno, in my opinion, is the worst music genre on the planet. It's painful noise to me. I'd rather listen to any form of Trap instead. On second thought, I hate them both.

None of the excuses I come up with work, mainly because they're not true and Reilly can expose a lie within seconds. I would hate to be her man, or worse, her kids. As an alternative, I offer the truth.

"You guys, I hate Techno with a passion and I'll be miserable while you two are having fun."

They're still not willing to let me not go.

"Ebony, I thought that, too, the first time I went. But it was fun. You have to come. Please? We never hang out except in Forensics," Reilley says, increasing the pressure.

Forensics. That's right. I'm supposed to be focused on getting a good grade in that class and Reilly is the key to me doing that. For the sake of my GPA, I agree to take the "L" and get my Techno on, which makes Reilly so very happy.

The geeks and freaks at the pub tonight are pretty hardcore

and the DJ plays to their taste. As expected, I'm miserable, but amused watching Reilly turn up. Good to know there's more to that girl than crime and punishment.

The DJ announces "a sweat break," which clears the dance floor. Reilly comes to the table where I've been sitting since we got here. She's surprised to find that I haven't moved.

"I was keeping an eye on our stuff and saving our seats," I tell her. She accepts that.

"Where's Hannah?" I ask.

"We ordered wings and Sangria so she's picking it up."

If I was with Essence, I'd have to ask if the Sangria was spiked, but since alcohol isn't served on campus, I'm safe. Hannah comes to the table with a platter of buffalo wings and fries. The pubman, he prefers that to bartender, follows her with the Sangria, cups, plates, and utensils. He lays a pile of napkins on the table and says, "You're gonna need these. Enjoy."

"Dig in Ebony," Hannah insists, as she and Reilly do just that, without washing or sanitizing their hands or even saying grace.

Before they contaminate all the food and doom me to hell, I say, "Mind if I say my grace first?"

Thankfully, that freezes all the action at the table. Pretending it's a ritual, I pull out my hand sanitizer first, use it myself, then pass it to them. Then I bow my head and pray silently because I think they're both Jewish based on comments Reilly has made.

"Amen. Thanks, guys."

"No problem," Hannah says as she returns to the wings.

Before her or Reilly's hands touch too much of the food on the platter, I get what I want and push the tray closer to them. This food sharing with strangers . . . Uggh.

"Y'all enjoy the rest. This is enough for me."

The pubman walks by and notices we haven't poured our Sangria, so he does it for us.

"Messy hands must mean you like the wings," he says.

Reilly and Hannah nod. The wings are pretty good, but the fries are what would have me coming back up in here. They've got a perfect crispness, which for me defines a good fry. The

Sangria is the bomb too, much better than the 'Kool-Aid with fruit cocktail' experience I expected.

My head is totally blown when I see Reilly take a flask out of her bag and pour something into her cup.

"It's just vodka, you want some?" she says, offering it to me and Hannah.

"Nope. I'm good."

Hannah says, "Fill me up."

Note to Self: Don't let Reilly or Hannah ever serve me a beverage at a party.

Shortly after midnight, I reach my limit and leave Reilly and Hannah. My head is pounding and I've got indigestion from those wings. When I get to my room, I eat some antacid tablets and throw back some headache medicine. Then I take a long hot shower and go to bed. The ringing noise in my ears doesn't ease for at least an hour. Eventually, I fall asleep with every intention of allowing my body's natural alarm to awaken me from my slumber.

THE NEXT DAY, I SLEEP UNTIL ALMOST ELEVEN O'CLOCK, grateful for the rest I obviously needed. It will serve me well as I face a marathon study day. Before dealing with that reality, I check on my friends who have been M.I.A., Eye Candy included. Still no response from any of them.

Right now, it would be around four o'clock in the afternoon in the UK, so I decide to check in with my bestie in London. Tay and I haven't had much luck talking by phone lately with the time difference and internet issues on her end. We've definitely kept each other fully updated on our lives through messaging. When I call her today, she actually answers. My heart starts leaping for joy when I hear, "Ebbieee."

"Tay. Oh, my God," I scream. "I miss you."

"I miss you like crazy, too," she responds.

We run through the basic stuff. We're both doing fine. The

families are fine. London is great. Bryce not so much. We're both happy-ish.

"Any update on this Eye Candy guy?" she asks.

"He's good. They have a tournament this weekend so he hasn't been around. We're moving slowly, but that's good. He's really sweet and he gets me. I'm still not sure about the girls that hang around him, but I like where we're headed."

"That's great. Your dream is coming true."

"Or my nightmare," I say in a more serious tone. "Donovan showed up at a party here on Friday."

"What the? What was that about?" The alarm in her voice is totally understandable.

"Who knows. He surprised me. But girl, we danced and then we kissed. I promise you I had no intention of getting physical with him, but once it happened, I didn't want it to stop. I'm glad we were in public because who knows what I might've done."

"Hole up," Taylor says. "I thought you didn't want anything to do with him after that night in the park. And didn't you just say Eye Candy has some good potential?"

"Crazy, right?"

"Ebbie, listen." Uh oh. Here comes the lecture. "Donovan knows how to turn you on physically, but that's all he wants. You said that yourself. Actually, he told you that. Why are you wasting your time?"

"I'm not doing it on purpose."

How do I explain to her what being around Donovan does to me when I don't understand it myself? And, it's not like I invited him to the party. He just showed up.

"You can't let him back in, no matter what he does," she says. "Leave him alone or you might mess up something good with Eye Candy."

"Yeah, yeah, yeah. I've told myself all the same things. And I'm not looking to have anything with him. It's just crazy that he can get me going just by being around me."

"That's called lust. Even more reason to leave him alone."

"Yeah, I guess. Enough about that. What's up with Mr. Ethan

Jeffrey?" I ask turning the spotlight onto Tay and her British beau.

"He's really good. We're officially dating." I can hear the smile in her voice.

"Wow, that's awesome. So, what made it official?"

Silence.

"Tay?"

I'm trying not to jump to any conclusions, but she still hasn't responded and I know she heard me.

"Tay, did you..."

"Ebbie. Don't finish that question," she says quickly. "There are people here. I'll tell you about it later. It's not what you think though. Let's talk about something else."

I'm not sure what to say because the answer to that question is really all I'm most interested in talking about. With no place else to go with the conversation, I ask about Tay's fashions. She always loves talking about her designs.

"Okay. So, um. When will you have some sketches you can share?"

"Soon, I hope. My creative process is a lot slower under all these rules."

"That sucks," I say. Knowing what a non-conformist Tay is, I can imagine how she's feeling.

"Yeah, but it will pay off. I'm learning a lot but it's a drag sometimes."

"Hang in there. Isn't that what you would tell me?" I say.

"LOL, absolutely. Hey, Ebbie, I'm sorry, but I gotta run. We're doing afternoon tea. Can we talk tomorrow?"

"Of course. Enjoy it. *Cheerio.*"

"Hahaha. You're crazy. Love you."

"Love you, too."

Tay has a lot going on and I've got lots of questions that need answers. No time to deal with that, because now Mercedes is calling. "Hola, Chica! KK is on the call, too." She sounds more cheerful than usual.

"Well, look who finally resurfaced. Y'all both got some serious explaining to do."

They giggle like kindergartners with secrets they can't wait to share. Mercedes suggests we meet at The Cove to get food and they promise to spill all the tea.

"See you there in thirty," I tell them.

THE THREE OF US MEET AND THEY SHARE ALL THE JUICY details of their blossoming romances. Mercedes is ready to marry Rico and Kendra thinks she might have to turn in her player card and give this guy Thompson a real shot.

"But what about your man at home?" I ask. It seems I'm the only one ever looking out for him these days. And I don't even know him.

"He might get cut. That's what I need to figure out," she says.

"Wow, KK, that's deep. Thompson must be like that." Mercedes says.

"Yeah, he actually is."

The way she perks up as she talks about him has to mean something good.

"How can you know that so fast? You just met yesterday," I ask because for me, a day wouldn't do it.

"When you know, you know. That's all I can say. You know Cam is the one for you, right? Or is it Donovan?"

"Dang, KK, that's dirty," Mercedes says, seeming to be on my side. "But it's real talk. So, Ebony Morgan," making her voice sound like a TV announcer and putting a pretend microphone in my face, "whose rose will you accept?"

"That's a joke right?" I ask. Because she says it with a straight face, I'm not sure.

Then they both start laughing.

"Y'all are ridiculous. I'm Team Eye Candy all day. But KK is talking about ending a relationship she's had for almost two years for a guy she just met."

"That's a valid point, Chica."

Glad to have Mercedes back on my side. "How do you respond KK?"

Kendra turns to me and says, "Let me ask you this. Would you throw away your chance to with Cam to get with Donovan?"

They both notice my hesitation.

"Do we have a problem here, Eb?" Mercedes asks with real concern in her voice.

"Absolutely not. But Donovan does something to me. If he just stayed away I'd be fine."

Kendra is bent over, laughing. "He probably just tapped into your inner freak. Don't worry, that'll wear off."

"Taylor said the same thing. She called it lust."

"If that's what it is, and that's probably right, he's not good for you, Eb," Mercedes advises, "That's what I said after the first time and I'm saying it again."

"Yeah, I think I have to agree with her," Kendra says.

"You're both right," I say, "but I'm not trying to create anything with him. There's just some kind of energy when I'm around him."

"Get that in check before you see Cam. Dudes can smell other dudes on you," Kendra warns.

For a moment, I actually believe her. When she cracks a smile and starts laughing I breathe a sigh of relief. She's still right about needing to defuse this pull Donovan has on me.

Wanting to do that and actually accomplishing it are two very different propositions.

Chapter Twenty-Three

E ye Candy has been ghost since Friday. The tournament might have taken up most of his time over the weekend, but the team got back Sunday night and he still hasn't responded to any of my calls or text messages. I'm hoping this is just part of his competition routine. Kendra did tell me some athletes isolate themselves when they're playing. That's the only reason I haven't gone knocking on his door.

I don't like this and I let my journal know how I feel before I leave for class.

Today I start fresh. I am better than I was. I am ____

I write **WORRIED**

Monday, October 1, 2018

Hi. Eye Candy is radio silent and I don't know why. I have a feeling something is up, not just the stress of the tournament like KK says. I hope he's 1) ok 2) not dating somebody else 3) still interested in me. I'll be so bummed if this is over before it really even gets started. ttyl

WHEN I GET TO CLASS ON MONDAY, EYE CANDY ISN'T IN HIS usual seat. He's not in any seat. Before class starts, I send him a text.

Me: Hey. U coming to class?

EC: Yeah

Yeah? That's all he has to say. At least he finally responded.

Me: U ok?

EC: Yeah

Another one word answer is not good. Class is starting so I can't deal with this situation right now. As soon as class ends, I'm gonna have to find out what his problem is.

The lecture today is long and boring, and I'm distracted for most of it thinking about how to approach Eye Candy. All that planning ends up being pointless because he leaves the room without giving me a chance to talk to him. He's definitely mad, probably at me, but I'm clueless as to why. I spend my entire Forensics class replaying in my head the past few times that we've been together or talked and still can't figure out what I could've done to make him cut me off like this.

As soon as I leave class, I text Mercedes and Kendra for help.

Me: 911 Eye Candy hates me I think

K: WTF?

M: Why?

Me: Don't know.

M: Calling u now

Mercedes does a group call, but she has no help to offer me.

Kendra tells me to track him down and force a conversation. That may be my only option at this point.

AFTER TUESDAY PASSES WITH NO COMMUNICATION FROM HIM, out of desperation, I take Kendra's advice. Knowing Eye Candy goes to Central Dining before Public Speaking class, I get up super early on Wednesday morning and wait for him in front of his dorm.

When he walks out the front door, he's startled to see me.

"Oh. Hey. What brings you here so early?" he asks.

"You do. Can we talk?"

"Going to eat. We can do it on the way."

Eye Candy and I walk together, but it feels like we're strangers. The familiarity we had just a few days ago is gone.

"How was the tournament?" I ask, trying to create some line of communication between us.

"Great. We won. I got Tournament MVP," he says proudly.

"I'm not surprised," I tell him.

We walk in silence the rest of the way to Central Dining and separately get our food. Once we're seated, I ask Eye Candy what's going on with him.

"What do you mean?" he asks.

"You haven't talked to me since last Friday. You don't answer my calls or texts. And right now, it's like we don't even know each other. What happened?"

After some initial hesitation, he says, "I saw you at the party on Friday."

How Eye Candy could have been at the party and not me nor my friends see him blows my mind.

"Okay. Why didn't you say anything to me?" I ask him.

The expression on Eye Candy's face becomes uncomfortably serious before he speaks.

"If you must know, the way that white boy had you all pinned up, I really thought that coulda been somebody you were messin' with. But then I saw you with that other dude. Figured if you and White Boy had a thing, that dude was gonna be a problem for him. I wasn't tryna get involved in none of it. Either way, I don't mess around in other people's playgrounds."

Whatever Eye Candy saw me doing with Brad is of no concern, because Brad's attention truly meant nothing. Knowing the interactions I had with Donovan, I'm immediately panicked hearing he saw us together. There's no way to imagine how we appeared to the outside world, but I know how it felt. I understand now why he stopped talking to me.

"Me and White Boy, as you call him, that's nothing. His name is Brad by the way. He was one of the guys who gave the party and he let me and my girls in for free. He asked me to dance with him, so I did."

"Yes, you did. For a while," he notes.

"A while, okay. But he's just a friend and he actually hooked up with one of the girls I came with so he's a non-issue."

I wait for Eye Candy's reaction.

"Okay," he says. "And that other dude? Another friend?"

From the way he says "another friend," I have the sense that he's already come to his conclusion about Donovan. What I tell him probably won't change it.

"He's a guy I met on campus the day we moved in. We went out once and hadn't seen each other or talked since. Until the party."

Eye Candy says, "Really? The way y'all were dancing, I thought y'all knew each other better than that? Didn't think you got down like that with strangers."

I could give Eye Candy the whole Donovan story or just admit to being a slutty dancer. My chances with him would be squashed either way. Some form of both of those explanations will have to work.

"Technically, he's not a stranger in that sense. But I probably got caught up in the music and the moment while we were dancing. That's not my usual behavior. He's in the past and that won't happen again. Not a whole lot more to say."

I'm satisfied with my explanation and actually breathe a sigh of relief until Eye Candy says, "What about the kiss?"

The color feels like it drains from my face and I stop breathing. Eye Candy saw us kiss? I'm cursing Donovan and myself in my head.

"That kiss looked like it was very much in the present," he says.

I'm feeling so defensive about a kiss that I tell myself meant nothing, knowing it meant everything in that moment. But Eye Candy can't know that. He doesn't need to know that because in this moment Donovan is nothing to me.

"The kiss shouldn't have happened. I'm sorry it did. Even more sorry you saw it."

Eye Candy looks at me like he has more questions. Or

perhaps he just doesn't believe me. What I need to do right now is convince him that I'm not interested in Brad or Donovan. I'm only interested in him.

Before I can get those words out, he leans across the table and says, "I'mma be straight with you Ebony. I came to Bryce planning just to focus on my game and school and not mess with no girls 'cause it's always some drama with y'all."

I can't disagree with that.

"Seeing you that day had me rethinking that. I was really feeling you and wanted to take a shot at having something special. Thought you did, too. Then I saw you at that party with your so-called friends. You kinda shocked me. Didn't think you were out there like that."

"I'm not," I say in my defense.

"Coulda fooled me."

The finality in his tone makes me feel like he's not going to hear anything else I say.

"Here's the deal," he continues, "you can mess around with different guys if you want, but I won't be one of them. I don't share my girl and hell if I'm gonna compete with anybody for her attention."

"You're not competing or sharing me with anybody," I assure him.

"I wanna believe you. Guess I'm not completely there yet."

"How can I get you there?"

"You can't. I gotta do that." he says. "Look, we need to get to class right now. Gimme some time with this."

Chapter Twenty-Four

For the rest of the week, Eye Candy doesn't say much to me when we see each other. He definitely doesn't sit with me in class. It's hard to resist stealing glances at him when he's not looking. A few times, I've seen him staring at me. Mercedes suggests I give him something his eyes can't resist and lure him back in that way. I'm willing to try anything at this point; even letting Mercedes put an outfit together for me. Why did I do that?

"He seemed to like you in that yellow dress, you wanna try that again?" she suggested, last night.

"You, of all people, know I can't be an outfit repeater. Besides, that's a sundress, I have some yellow capri pants if you think that's the color I should wear."

"No. Gimme a sec."

The combination she eventually came up with looks much better on me today than it did laying across her bed last night – black leggings, colorful patterned top with zebra-striped trim. Simple, but eye-catching.

We videochat while I dress so she can style me.

"Wasn't expecting this shirt to look so sexy on me," I tell her.

"It's the fabric. Hugs in all the right places," she says. "Now, lemme see your face."

To me, this ensemble requires only a light face beat so that's what I did. More is less. Besides, I'm still just going to class, not the club.

"Don't you feel like doing a little bit more with the eye make-up?" Mercedes asks.

"Nope. Besides, I gotta go so I'm not too late."

"Go get your man, Chica!"

Before I leave, I make a quick journal entry and set my intention.

Today I start fresh. I am better than I was. I am ____

I write **DETERMINED**

Friday, October 5, 2018

Hi. I haven't told you this yet but I screwed up big time. Eye Candy saw me kiss Donovan at the Mafia party and he decided he didn't want to continue whatever we were doing. It was stupid of me to kiss Donovan. But I'm determined to get Eye Candy back on track. And I know, Donovan is off-limits. DANGER. I see that now. ttyl

My plan was to arrive to class later than normal so Eye Candy would see me walking into the room. That plan was busted because he and I end up walking up to Lawrence Hall at the same time.

"Hey," is all I'm able to say to him. The butterflies in my stomach keep me from getting any other words out.

"Hey, Miss Ebony, let me get that for you."

Walking through the door, I can feel his eyes on me and I'm sure he likes what he sees. We're almost late for class. My regular seat is occupied, forcing me to find a different place to sit. I spot a row with two vacant seats and head there. If Eye Candy follows me, I'll take that as a good sign. If he doesn't, he might just need more time, but at least he was pleasant today.

Professor Powell calls the class to order just as I reach the seat.

"Please sit down, close your mouths, and open your minds."

He's got to be the most annoying person on earth.

Eye Candy does sit next to me but maybe because he didn't have time to get to another seat. Either way, I'm jumping for joy on the inside, but playing it cool for him or anyone else watching me. We have a few assignment-related interactions during class and exchange more than a few glances at each other. When class ends, he doesn't get up. I'm trying to find the courage to ask him to walk me to class, but one of his boys calls him to the back. He flashes a smile at me and goes off in the opposite direction. His smile does give me hope.

When I update Mercedes and Kendra, they're hopeful, too.

M: Told you, Chica. He needed to see what he was losing

K: Def a good sign. He still feeling u

Me: We'll see. Walking into class. ttyl

If I wasn't sure about my weekend plans before Forensics class, I'm sure about them now. My every waking moment will be spent studying. Professor Kendall scheduled a timed take home test that's due by midnight Sunday. Reilly wants to have a marathon review session tomorrow and she assigned chapters for me and Jenna to outline, which means I'll be in the library for the rest of today and all through the night studying to be ready for her.

But first, I go to my room, chill for a minute, and change clothes. After that, I hit Central Dining to load up on food, snacks, and caffeine. By the time I get to the library, all my preferred reading areas either have too many people or too much activity for me to work effectively. I'm forced to go down to that dreaded room in the library basement, known as the stacks or, the "unhappiest place on earth."

The stacks room is a weird place because it's literally filled with rows and rows of bookshelves of old books and periodicals. But it's super quiet and there's no cell reception, which makes it a great, distraction-free place to study.

Everyone down here is doing serious work and the energy is

intense. This vibe works for me and for hours and hours, I read articles on evidence collection, scientific analysis, and criminal investigation. Then I review dozens of crime scene photos that Professor Kendall showed us in class to practice my observation skills. Reilly told me this exercise would be a huge help in getting more points on the test. Unfortunately, it requires me to stare at these gruesome pictures, looking for all the clues hidden in plain sight.

The sudden activity of the students sitting nearby causes me to ask one of them what was going on.

"Stacks closes at midnight. You gotta move upstairs," he says.

"Thanks. Didn't realize it was so late."

"You musta been having too much fun," he jokes. Fun is exactly the opposite of what I've been having.

When I reach the main level of the library, my phone buzzes with text messages - and missed call notifications. A lot went on in the world while I was in the dungeon. Before dealing with any of it, I find a comfy place to spread out in the first floor atrium lounge.

The first message I scroll to is from Mercedes. It's a video of her, Kendra, Rico and Thompson dancing at a party with a message:

M: U should B here!

This video of them is ridiculous.

OMG. Eye Candy sent me a couple of messages too.

6:14pm

EC: Hey Miss Ebony. U got plans later ? Hit me back.

8:39pm

EC: Not sure if u got my txt earlier. U free to meet up?

11:15pm

EC: Guess u had plans. Catch u later.

I'm jumping up and down, in my head, at the fact that he texted me so many times. Maybe there is hope for us. But now, he might think I'm ignoring him, which any rational person would know I'd never do.

. . .

Me: Hey. Sorry to be so late in responding. Been in the stacks studying all day. Still @library. #struggleisreal

He doesn't respond, so I go back to my crime files. Some of the more gory images are burned in my brain and I'll probably never be able to unsee them. After half an hour or so, my eyes are so tired that the pages look like blurry ink splatters. It doesn't take a genius to know that I'm done. My study time was productive, but I'm hardly ready to face Reilly. I'll figure that out another time. Right now, my bed is calling me, so I pack up and head out.

As I'm leaving the library, I see Eye Candy walking up the steps.

"Fancy seeing you here," he says when he reaches me. He takes my bag from my shoulder and puts it on his.

"Yeah, it is? What brings you to the library at this hour?" I ask.

"You," he says matter-of-factly. "Got your message. Didn't like you being here alone this late at night."

"Aww, you care," I tease.

"Actually, I do," he replies with more seriousness in his voice than I expected.

"Well, thank you." I smile sincerely to show my appreciation.

As we walk, Eye Candy asks if I've eaten anything.

"Not since earlier," I tell him. "Those books made me completely forget about food."

"Wow. That's some serious studying," he says. "We need to get you fed."

"I'll be okay. I'm more tired than I am hungry."

"Well, you owe me since you ignored all my messages today."

"You know there's zero signal where I was," I tell him. "I'd never ignore you."

"I'm playing," he says. "If you're tired, I can walk you to your dorm. If you're hungry, I can take care of that, too."

Hearing him say he "can take care of" anything that involves me makes my stomach flutter, especially after the challenges we've had this week. I am tired and not all that hungry. But I'm extremely interested in letting Eye Candy take care of me.

"Okay. Let's see how good you can take care of me. Where shall we go?"

Eye Candy pauses before saying, "Come back to my room."

Wow. I guess he's showing his true colors now.

"Really?" I ask in disbelief.

"No. Not like that," he assures me. "I'm just gonna get my roommate's car and take you to The Silver Spoon. You been there right?"

"Yeah, once or twice," I say, recalling hanging out there with the Mafia Crew. "I love their blueberry pancakes," I add.

"Then you're about to get blessed with a nice hot stack of them joints right now," he announces.

Feeling more comfortable with our plans, I say, "Lead the way. "

BY THE TIME WE GET TO THE SILVER SPOON, SIT DOWN, AND order, I'm starving. We both order blueberry pancakes. I add eggs and turkey sausage to my half stack. He adds bacon, eggs, and hash browns to his full stack. This boy can put away some food and I'm amazed he stays in such good shape eating the way he does.

"Where does all that food go?" I ask after he clears his entire plate.

"Playing ball burns a lot of calories. Plus, I work out a few times a day. Gotta keep it tight," he says, flexing his biceps.

"Yeah, it's tight," I say, adding, "but I'm sure you hear that from your fan club all the time."

Eye Candy dismisses my comment about his fan club and starts talking about me.

"I'm just an average guy," he says. "But you? You're next level fine."

I'm blushing hearing him talk about me like that.

"First time I saw you," he continues, "was the day my folks

moved me in. I told you I saw you in that dope ass *Crooklyn* shirt. I'm a huge Spike fan and was like who is that beautiful brown sister reppin' my boy, Spike, at Bryce College? My uninformed self expected all the women here to be stuck up."

"A lot of them are. My sister probably leads the pack," I say.

"That's not a nice way to talk about your identical twin sister." He emphasizes the "identical twin" part of his statement, which makes me laugh.

"So you were listening to my Public Speaking presentation."

"Every word of it. What did Jerry McGuire's girl say? 'You had me at hello'."

"Wow. I'm flattered, but that movie came out before you were born, didn't it?"

"Yeah, but I became a Cruise fan in my teens so I've seen all his movies going back to *Risky Business* and *Top Gun*."

"So is my older brother, that's the only reason I even knew what you were talking about."

"Bruh sounds dope."

"He is," I say, smiling.

After a few minutes of us just eating, Eye Candy says "I might've messed up, Miss Ebony. Seeing you with those guys that night sent me to a place that had nothing to do with you. You know my folks split up about three years ago. Basically, I walked in on my mom with another man while she was still married to my dad. All I saw was them kissing, but it was obvious other stuff had gone on. My dad moved away as soon as he found out and left me with her. My mom and I didn't speak for months because I was so mad at her for doing that.

"One day, I left. Ended up living in my boy's basement for my entire eleventh grade year. His parents never knew. My mom thought they did. Eventually, my coach found out and he convinced my mom to let me stay with him so he could train me for my Senior season. Winning State and getting a scholarship to get the hell away from her was my mission."

I'm speechless listening to Eye Candy's story. I can't imagine how devastating that was for him at that young age.

156

"Wow, that's awful. I'm so sorry."

He continues. "Yeah. It was. It is. But I'm telling you this so you understand; not for pity. When I saw you with those guys at the party, I thought I had you all wrong. Maybe you were cold-hearted like my mom or one of the thirsty chicks that's trying to get with as many dudes as she can."

I have to interrupt him to declare in no uncertain terms, "That's absolutely not who I am."

"Yeah, I know that now. But that's how it seemed and that made me want to be as far away from you as possible. It brought back a lot of pain. But I'd bet money it was the attention or the validation that got you . . . caught up. Isn't that what you called it?"

Having done the self-analysis already, Eye Candy is right. But I can't use that to justify kissing Donovan, or rationalize the way I felt kissing him. At least not to Eye Candy. My issue with Donovan has some other layers that even I don't understand.

"That's what happened, but - "

He stops me mid-sentence. "Let me finish."

"We both been through some shit and it's gotta make us better, not weaker. You gon' have to look to yourself for valida-tion and love, not some dude. And I know I gotta stop thinking every woman is as heartless as my mom."

That's harsh, but he has a right to feel that way about his mother.

Eye Candy leans back in his chair and pauses before saying, "There's a lot that I do well, but other stuff I suck at. Guess, I'm not perfect."

"And who said I was?" I ask. "We don't have to be perfect. Who said two imperfect people can't be perfect for each other?" That felt like a mic drop moment.

"Wow, that's facts," he says. "Look, I'm willing to try to make this work if you're willing to give me a chance."

A chance? Does this boy not realize he has infinite chances and if those run out, he could have even more?

I smile, nod my head, and say, "I'm definitely down for that."

Eye Candy reaches for my hands across the table and we just sit, not saying anything with words, but definitely connecting on deeper level.

Somewhere in the neighborhood of four o'clock, we leave The Silver Spoon and Eye Candy drops me off at my dorm.

We hug goodbye and I melt a little. I think he does, too.

Chapter Twenty-Five

"Bunnie, wake up. Bunnie, come on. I need you." Essence is standing over me. My eyes try to make sense of her uninvited and unwanted presence.

This has to be a dream. Actually, more like a nightmare.

"Do you hear me talking to you? Get up," she says even louder.

"Stop yelling," I shout back so she can feel how disrespectful being screamed at this early in the morning feels. "What do you want, Essence?" My grogginess masks the contempt I feel about her intrusion.

"Bunnie, get up," she commands. "Come on, pleeeeeeze. I need you. It's an emergency."

I don't move. None of this feels right.

After several seconds, I sit up in my bed, hoping that will give me a better perspective to understand why the person who couldn't be bothered being my sister all this time suddenly needs me, of all people, to help her with this emergency.

"Why can't this wait until the sun comes up?" I ask.

She hesitates, then says very matter-of-factly, "If it could wait, it wouldn't be an emergency. Bunnie, come on. I have to go to New York."

"Then go," I tell her. "You don't need my permission." I lay back down and bury myself under my covers.

"Bunnie," she says in a calm, quieter tone, while pulling off my covers. "You have to go with me."

For a fleeting moment I get excited at the thought that Essence wants me to go with her to New York, one of our favorite places going back to when our mom first took us there as young teens. I doubt she's proposing this trip as a way for us to relive those memories, but wouldn't that be amazing?

I'm really too tired to try to understand my sister's motives, or to continue this pre-dawn battle.

"Fine. I'll go"

"Great. If you hurry and get dressed, we can catch the eight-fifteen train. I already scheduled a car to take us to the station. It'll be here in forty-five, probably now forty, minutes. Do something cute." Then she disappears out the door, slamming it behind her. She rushed out before I could fully process the fact that she wants me to go to New York, like right now. She was so sure I would I say yes. Am I that predictable or is she just that manipulative?

The clock is ticking. I get up and move through my morning routine with one eye closed, barely able to stand upright. Essence commanded me to "Do something cute." Luckily, I can do cute in my sleep and that's pretty much my situation right now. While I do multiple outfit changes, I check myself out in the mirror several times, for my own stamp of approval.

If I had time for a journal entry today, my word today would be **HOODWINKED AND BAMBOOZLED.**

Once I'm Big Apple worthy, I drag my exhausted cute self out the door to the waiting car and immediately start pressing Essence for answers.

"Why in the world do you have me up at the crack of Saturday morning rushing off to New York? Are you in trouble with the police or something?"

"Of course not," she replies. "I'll explain later."

. . .

THE CAR PULLS UP TO THE STATION AND WE HAVE LESS THAN five minutes to board our train. We put our high school track skills to use. We sprint fast, hurdle high, and jump long, landing not-so-gracefully on the departure platform. The conductor makes the last "All Aboard" call as we reach the last door of the last car. We take the first two seats together that we see.

"Do I need to buy my own ticket?" I ask after we settle in.

"No, I got it," Essence says, indignantly.

"Okay. Do I need to prepare myself for any of your lovely friends to join us for this emergency trip?"

"No, Bunnie, but your sarcasm is noted. It's just us."

"So tell me why is 'just us' rushing off to New York?" I ask again, hoping now she'll finally give me the full scoop.

"Didn't I just say I'll explain later. No more questions," she says dismissing me. "Now let me go to sleep."

Sleep? The nerve of her. All I can do is shake my head at the irony of her wanting me to let her sleep when she ripped me out of mine an hour ago. Something tells me whatever Essence has planned is not good. I close my eyes and try to get any amount of rest I can before this adventure jumps off.

THE NEXT VOICE I HEAR COMES FROM THE CONDUCTOR announcing our pending arrival at New York's Penn Station. When I open my eyes, I'm holding my sister's hand. Our arms are intertwined, which always happened when we slept close to one another as kids. When I start untangling us, she wakes up. We both look at each other and reach for hair brushes and makeup bags and get to work. I guess the look on her face seeing me, and the look on my face seeing her, said all either of us needed to know.

Faces beat, hair did . . . Now, we cute.

Putting aside everything about how I ended up here, I got that Empire state of mind now and I'm energized and ready to hit "the concrete jungle where dreams are made of . . ."

We pull into the station and the train slows with that classic screeeeeech. Music to my ears. As we come to a stop, I figure it's late enough to quickly text my squad and let them know where I am.

Me: In NYC on some secret mission with Es

M: WTH?????

K: GTFOH. LOL

M: SMDH

Me: Will talk lata.

When the train doors open, the real fun begins. Hundreds of people pile onto the station platform. We push and squeeze our way along with throngs of other people to the single functioning escalator. So typical of Penn Station. We all make our ascent to civilization; or what most people call Midtown Manhattan, which can be anything but civilized at times.

"So what are we gonna do?" I ask.

"I don't know." Her reply is short and dismissive.

"Can we find some food? I'm starving."

Essence doesn't verbalize a response. She just starts walking down the street. I join her. She enters a diner not far from the train station and finds a table. After we order and get our food, we just eat. We don't talk, we don't make eye contact, we don't share food. I might as well be here alone because that's how I feel. I'd rather not spend an entire day in this great city feeling this way.

While she figures out how next to make my life miserable, I get a call from Eye Candy. On the low, I try to explain to him why I'm in New York, when just six hours ago I was with him. Essence makes a rude comment about me talking on the phone. She wants everything to be about her. If she had been nicer about it, I might have shortened my conversation, but her attitude sucks. So Eye Candy and I talk until he ends the call.

AFTER WE EAT, WE WALK THROUGH THE STREETS OF NEW York in no particular direction, with no actual purpose in mind for hours. We pop into and out of stores and end up in Times Square.

"Why don't we go to the TKTS booth and see if there's a show we can catch?" I suggest.

"Not interested."

"Then suggest something else."

"Let's just walk around."

So, this was the emergency? Wake up at sunrise to get on a train and come to New York to walk around with no plan. This is so ridiculous. Right then, I decide to make this trip fun for me, however I can. When I see a store I like, I go in and browse, whether or not she comes in, too. When I see an art stand with pictures I might want to purchase, I stop.

After walking aimlessly for hours, I'm ready for lunch. There's a great sushi place nearby and I lead Essence in that direction. On the way, we pass a funky little art gallery that's featuring polaroid photography, which I love. I tell Essence I'm going in to check it out. She comes in with me, but gets a call as soon as we get inside. She spends our whole time in the gallery on the phone and barely looks at any of the exhibition. When she ends her call, we leave.

"That exhibit was great, wasn't it, Bunnie?"

Her mood has changed. Whoever she just talked to needs to call her more often.

"It was, but you don't have to pretend you liked it."

"I'm not pretending," she says.

"You wanna tell me about the phone call, since it obviously put you in a good mood?"

"So listen . . . there's this guy I met when I was here before. He invited me to meet him this afternoon in Harlem, so we're gonna go there now." Even though Essence ends her statement with a period, I hear a question mark, and respond accordingly.

"No thanks. I don't wanna do that. What else you got?"

"No, Ebony. That wasn't a question. That's what we're doing."

It turns out Essence met this guy on a trip to New York with the DWBs Labor Day Weekend. From what I gather, she lied and told him last night that she planned to be here today, trying to see if he would ask her out. He didn't commit to wanting to see her until early this morning, which meant she had to frantically take a pre-planned trip that she hadn't planned. She brought me along to make herself look less desperate. I bet she told him she came to New York to chaperone me, or something just as ludicrous. But once again, I'm a prop in her life story.

A visit to Harlem sounds great, except for the part that has me sitting around with Essence and some guy. Briefly, I consider the idea of letting her go alone, but "We come together, we stay together, we leave together." Essence gives me a few minutes to process our new plans before she calls for our ride.

Moments later, "Bunnie," she says, "the car's here. We should go." I get in the car with her and we take a silent car ride through the streets of New York.

Chapter Twenty-Six

W hen we pull up in front of The Red Rooster on 125th Street, Essence jumps out of the car and into the arms of a guy waiting by the entrance. He's tall and gorgeous— Essence's two favorite flavors. But he looks old . . . I mean really old; like paying taxes and annual physical, old. I'd say he's at least thirty. Whatever his age, he looks like way more than Essence might have bargained for and that worries me.

He pulls her body close to his and starts grinding like he's trying to make a baby. Essence leans away and tries to give him a "we just friends" type of hug. But he holds her tight and then shoves his tongue so far down her throat, he can probably taste her toenail polish. He definitely catches Essence by surprise with that one. She tries pushing him away again. From the look on her face, she's not at all comfortable with that display of affection. Yeah, this guy looks like trouble to me.

Even though I'm now standing next to her, Essence doesn't bother to introduce me to her friend, so I do it myself.

"Umm, Hello. I'm Ebony, her twin sister."

He gives me a very dry, flat response, not the usual "Wow. Twins" reaction people have when they meet us.

"Oh, hi. I'm Rex," followed by, "Is she staying?"

He directs his question to Essence, but an answer falls out of my mouth before she can say anything.

"Yes, Dex, she absolutely will be staying." I refer to myself in the third person to make him realize how out of order he sounds. Hopefully, he hears every bit of my resentment, too. Essence definitely hears it and glares at me, which means she wants me to behave.

"It's Rex, not Dex," he says, sounding like he's scolding a child.

As we walk into the restaurant, Rex complains about Essence bringing me along without telling him.

"The reservation I made is for two. I even requested our favorite table. Waiting for a table for three will take another hour, and I don't have time to be waiting around like that with you."

As soon as those words hit the atmosphere, I see the change in Essence's body language. Her face hardens ever-so-subtly, like she might be holding back a more violent reaction. She looks at Rex as if to say, 'What did you just say?' She doesn't actually say that, so I take advantage of her silence to get him in more trouble with Essence.

"No time to wait? Really, Dex? That's rude."

"Ebony," Essence yells.

"What? He's the one you should be yelling at, not me," I shout back.

Rex grins like a Cheshire cat and starts hugging on Essence again. He looks like he has something sneaky on his mind. He's rubbing on her butt, either trying to turn her on, or arouse himself. It's comical to me because whatever he was planning, ain't happening. He majorly insulted the object of his passionate desires and probably lost any chance he thought he had with my sister.

Rule Number 1. You never tell Essence you don't have time for her. She has a thing that she no doubt learned from *The Code* that any guy who can't make time for her without complaining or wanting something in return, doesn't deserve her.

Even though Essence may plan to write this guy off, she seems intent on enjoying his company right now. Rex tries to convince her to send me off, because he "Can't get with my attitude."

I remind them both, "I'm not leaving until Essence leaves. We came together, so we're leaving together."

Rex mumbles something that I can't hear. Whatever it is, his words harden Essence toward him even more, which I notice immediately, but to which Rex still remains oblivious. I'm not seeing any more lip locks or body grinds in the future for Sexy Rexy.

"Essence, I didn't know Rex had his heart set on having you all to himself today. I shouldn't have invited myself."

Essence knows I didn't invite myself, but I say that to see who's team she's on right now, his or mine, so I can direct my misbehavior accordingly. To test her loyalty further, I say, "Why don't I go sit at the bar and have dinner alone so you two can have your romantic dinner at your favorite table?"

I emphasize that last part in case she thinks I missed Rex mentioning that. These two apparently have a lot more history than she let on.

Essence shakes her head, letting me know she understands that I have no intention of leaving them or of eating by myself. But Rex quickly latches on to my offer.

"That's a great idea. Why don't you do that?" he says.

Essence kills that idea fast. "Ebony, you're not going anywhere." Turning to Rex, she says "Have you lost your damn mind? How you gonna treat my sister like some stranger off the street? That's so foul. I don't know if I can stand to be around you. If you can't manage to be gracious to her and show some respect, then why don't *you* go sit at the bar. She and I will enjoy that romantic table you reserved."

We both look at Rex like, 'Whachugondonow?'

"Fine, Es. You win. She can stay."

I know I can. Glad he finally recognized that. Rex is now standing next to Essence in all his six feet of chocolateness with his arms folded, lips poked out, pouting like a two-year-old. He looks like a straight punk.

Essence takes pity on him and gives him a "thank you" kiss on his cheek. He perks right up. She whispers something to him that puts a slimy smile on his face. Now he's standing up tall looking like a grown man should. I can only imagine what she said. But actually, I'd rather not.

Rex offers to get us all drinks from the bar "since now we have a bit of a wait." He had to throw that out there.

I decline. Essence asks for a specialty cocktail with a shot of tequila on the side. What? Last I checked Essence and I are the same age and I'm too young to drink . . . legally. It seems that she might have missed that memo. But I leave that alone. As my mom would say, "Not my circus, not my monkeys."

Rex and Essence get their drinks and become lost in their own private world, so I move to the bar area and sit down. To pass the time, I call Eye Candy but get no answer. Then I check my socials and send a couple messages to my friends. My face is buried in my phone and the bartender now standing in front of me startles me when he says, "Excuse me, Miss. Would you like some water?"

"I'm sorry, what?"

"Water. Would you like some?" He offers me a glass and says, "I noticed you didn't order anything with the rest of your party."

"Oh, sure," I take the water and say, "Thanks."

"Would you like the same cocktail your sister ordered?" I almost ask how he knew we were sisters. I laugh at myself to myself.

"Nope. I'm not drinking," I say politely.

"Okay. If you change your mind, you can open a tab or add it to the tab Rex has open."

Did he say Rex opened a tab?

"On second thought," I say, "do you have that really expensive sparkling water?"

He laughs. "We sure do."

"I'll take one of those please, and definitely put it on Rex's tab."

A FEW MINUTES LATER, THE BARTENDER COMES BACK, BOTTLE in hand.

"One expensive bottle of sparkling water for the lovely lady," he says as he places a glass in front of me and fills it with water. Hmm. He's actually really cute, but let me not even go down that road.

"Thank you" and a smile is all he gets.

About that same time, the hostess waves at me to let me know our table is ready. As we walk to be seated, Essence whispers to me that Rex gave her fifty dollars to seat us at the first available table, which turns out to be circular table in the center of the dining room that could easily seat five or six people. Essence and Rex sit close together on one side of the table and I sit on the other side.

Could they make it any more obvious that I'm the third wheel in this party?

"Let's order quickly," Rex insists. Either he's hungry or anxious to get to the afterparty part of this date. We all study the menu, then I order the Yardbird with mac and cheese and collards on the side. Essence orders a salmon combo, and adds cornbread and fried green tomatoes as appetizers for the three us to share. Rex gets the shrimp and grits with stewed cabbage.

While we wait for our food, Rex talks about his high post job as a cybersecurity analyst, his international travels, fancy cars . . . as in more than one, and his custom-made designer suits. Clearly, he's trying to impress my sister. She's pretty materialistic so he's definitely scoring points with this conversation. Thank God the apps arrive.

The cornbread isn't as large as we expected, so Rex says, "Give that one to her," pointing to me, "and bring one for me and my lady. And another round of drinks for us, too."

His lady? More drinks? This thing is heating up right

before my eyes. And, Essence having another drink . . . having *any* drinks? That's a problem. She better know what she's doing.

The server asks what she can get me to drink. I'd like to ask her to have the cutie bartender bring me another water, but I order a peach tea instead.

After blessing my food and taking that first melt-in-my-mouth bite of my personal serving of cornbread, I'm grateful to Rex for being so petty and giving it to me. If I'm being rude eating and enjoying it as much as I am while Essence and Rex wait for theirs, good. They have other food and each other to munch on. Before Rex gets too disgusting doing just that, the second cornbread order arrives. That was quick. They must've gotten someone else's order.

Essence asks Rex to bless their food, which she's used to having the oldest male at the table do in our family. Rex is an old man so she probably expects him to fill that role. Or, knowing Essence, this might be her way of punishing him for his earlier misconduct.

Rex looks at Essence like she asked for the passcode to his checking account, and says, "I don't do that."

She and I both look at him with the same question on our face. *How do you say no to thanking God for your food?*

"I'm not eating until you bless the food, Rex. It's a simple request," Essence says in a brash tone.

He says, "I'm not into religion like that."

"You don't have to be into religion to be grateful," she says pointedly.

They have about a ten second standoff, which Rex ends by eating.

If I had a yellow flag like the football referees use, I'd throw it on the table and give him an unsportsmanslike conduct penalty for eating without saying grace, and put him in a fifteen-minute time out. Then I'd throw another flag and call a personal foul for eating before your date and give him another fifteen-minute time out. Actually, I'd toss him out of the game.

Essence calls him out in a different way. "You're going straight to hell Rex, you know that, right?"

Then she prays aloud for their food and his salvation and starts eating. For several minutes, no one speaks. Essence acts like she's mad at Rex for being a heathen, but then he starts feeding her. Suddenly they're annoying lovebirds again.

The arrival of our entrées about ten minutes later changes the dynamics at our table again. My entire focus turns to my plate, which I pretend I'm enjoying with people I actually like. At some point, Essence and Rex start having food sex. Feeling super uncomfortable, I excuse myself from the table as soon as I finish eating.

"I'll be back to order dessert when you guys are ready."

Essence waves me off.

Without many places to go for refuge, I walk over to the bar and find a place to sit to pass some time. The bartender from earlier sees me and comes over and greets me.

"Hello again. What can I get you, another expensive bottled water?"

"No actually I've upgraded to the peach tea."

"Oh you fancy, huh? Peach tea coming right up."

When he brings my tea, he starts a conversation. "I'm Khalil, but everyone calls me Black."

"Because of your complexion?" I ask. He is dark as midnight.

"Actually, my last name is Black," he says, laughing, "but that, too. And what's your name?"

"Ebony."

His eyes light up, and he smiles a huge grin. "Ahh, for that beautiful brown skin."

He bops his head and starts rapping a song by Remy Ma. "Got that melanin magic, brown skin poppin."

"Yeah. Like that," I say. He got me laughing and bopping, too, as I imagine hearing the song.

"Hold that thought." He leaves to take an order from another patron, then another and another. I watch as he glides back and forth between each end of the bar, taking orders, mixing drinks, talking to people. It's like a well-orchestrated dance, the way he moves. Pretty smooth for a guy who looks like he could be a linebacker on a football team.

By the time he returns to me, I figure Essence and Rex have finished eating and should be ready for the final course.

"I gotta get back so we can order dessert," I tell him.

"Understood. Desserts here are great. Holla at me before you go."

With a smile I say, "Okay."

Back at the table, I'm floored to learn that Essence and Rex ordered dessert without me. Essence claims she didn't expect me back so soon.

"They way that bartender was checking you out, I thought you would want to hang out with him for a while. Get to know each other maybe."

"Essence, the plan was for me to have dessert with you. Isn't that what we said?"

I give her the evil eye, completely ignoring Rex, trying to bring her into agreement with me.

"Sorry, girl. You must've misheard me."

She makes me wanna scream sometimes. Many times actually. This is definitely one of those times. Just when it seemed like we were gonna make it through the rest of this meal with no more drama, Essence switches teams. Now she's the one treating me like an unwelcomed visitor.

I'm fuming and storm away from the table and end up pacing near the hostess area because, once again, I have nowhere else to go. Khalil sees me and motions for me to come back to the bar. He directs me to a seat and greets me like a long lost friend. That's part of the job, I guess.

"Welcome back, Ebony."

I barely respond. It doesn't take a genius to see that my mood has changed in the short time I was gone. He doesn't press me with questions; he just brings me a glass of peach tea.

"Let me know if you need anything else. In addition to being charming, I'm a great listener."

As I sip my tea, I regret not saying no when Essence forced me to join her for this escapade. She's been manipulative and selfish from the beginning, why am I so bothered that she's acting like that now? Maybe because I keep hoping she'll change. Khalil's voice pulls me out of my thoughts. "Can I get you another tea?"

"No thanks, but how about something sweet instead?"

He gives me a flirtatious look. "Okay, I can show you the dessert menu or give you my number."

Oh, he's smooth. Didn't see that one coming. I'm flattered but nicely request, "The menu please."

He hands me a dessert menu and says, "It was worth a shot, right?"

As he glides away to help a nearby customer, he winks at me. He is really cute. *But Eye Candy is, too,* my inside voice says. Right. Duly noted.

"You need help deciding?" he asks when he returns.

"Actually, I do," I say.

He proceeds to give me his review of every dessert offered. "The coffwe and donuts are a favorite and a safe bet. The cobblers are just so-so right now. We got this red velvet cake today, and that thing is the truth."

Red velvet cake is my absolute favorite dessert and I don't require much convincing when it's an option.

"Sold. I'll take the cake."

After he puts in my order, Khalil alternates between talking to me and taking care of the other people at the bar. For the bar to be as busy as it is, I'm impressed with how attentive he is to everyone, including me. He's the only one today to treat me like I actually matter. He even brought me a pre-dessert cappuccino because he saw that I was fading after eating all that food.

About fifteen minutes pass and finally my dessert arrives. I try to stay classy because I know Khalil is watching me, but when it comes to good food, especially sweets, I sometimes have no chill.

"How you like that dessert, Miss Lady?"

"Oh my gosh, it's so good."

"Awesome. Glad you like. Can I get you anything else?"

"No, but can you charge my dessert to Rex's tab?"

"Nah. This one is on me. If you gimme your number, I'll do it right next time and buy you dinner first."

I'm not trying to start anything with this guy, especially after the conversation Eye Candy and I had last night.

"Actually, I'm seeing someone so I probably shouldn't."

He apologizes and says, "No disrespect."

"None taken."

I'm sitting here in front of another plate that I've practically licked clean, feeling stuffed as a Thanksgiving turkey. I'm too full to move, but Essence is probably ready to leave. Slowly, so as not to pop, I lift myself to a standing position and get Khalil's attention to say good-bye.

He rushes over and says, "It was pleasure spending the afternoon with you, Ebony. Take my number in case your status changes."

"Thanks for your company and I'll keep that in mind."

As I walk back to the table, I wonder what my status even is.

"Dang, Ebony, we thought you left," Essence says, sounding surprised to see me.

She knows I didn't leave. I couldn't leave; not without her. I'm basically her hostage. Rex has the nerve to say something under his breath that sounded like, "I wish she would leave and stop blocking."

My eyes turn into daggers and I fix them on him.

"Excuse me? Did you have something to say to me?" I ask him.

I shock myself when I hear those words out loud because they were supposed to stay in my head. Oh well, too late now.

Essence asks me with her eyes to chill and play nice a little while longer. I would have done that, for her, even after the way she's treated me.

But Rex says, "I have a lot I want to say to your whiny ass, but your sister won't let me."

Oh, for real? I'm steaming now and ready to unleash on him. But before the first syllable of the first word that I want to say even forms in my mouth, Essence goes into warrior twin-sister defense mode. She stands up, leans down, and gets in Rex's face. This stance looks familiar (having been on the receiving end of it before) and I know what comes next.

"Rex. Stop it," she says firmly. "We've already been through this."

"Es, you need to lower your voice and sit down."

To my surprise, she does. That never worked for me.

"That's better. Look, you know I just wanted to enjoy some time with you. You coming at me for having a problem that your sister invaded our time. That's some bull. I got a right not to like it and I ain't gonna let no chick, not even you, tell me otherwise. I don't care if either one of you has a problem with me feeling that way. That's some tough shit for you."

Essence gets quiet. She closes her eyes, then she starts nodding her head and clenching her hands together almost like she's praying. I watch and wait her transform as she listens to Rex. It's coming and it won't be pretty. Then she speaks, not just with her mouth, but with her entire body – chest puffed up, neck rolling, and fingers pointing. She delivers the message that this whole experience is about to come to an unpleasant end.

"Okay, Rex. That's it." She's loud and doesn't care.

Everything around us stops. All eyes are on her.

"I've had enough of your crybaby shit for a lifetime and I'm over it now. I came all the way down here to see you when I could have gotten as much enjoyment staying home doing laundry. And this is how you thank me? By throwing temper tantrums and fits like a spoiled baby. I thought you were Mr. Bigshot with the nice car, high post job, flexin' here, flexin, there. News flash. You're a big joke. Having all that stuff that you brag about doesn't make you a man. Being a man makes you a man. You fail in that department."

Essence stands up and takes a few steps away from the table

and heads toward the door. I follow her because I think she's done, but she turns around and starts in on him again.

"And by the way, Rex. I don't appreciate the way you disrespected my sister or me. Probably the best thing you can do at this point is to, go screw yourself, because you certainly won't be doing me. Ever."

The manager, our server, and Khalil are at our table by this point trying to restore order. I'm speechless, watching this unfold and I'm not the only onlooker in that state. In my head, I'm giving Essence a standing ovation because in a tasteful, not-making-a-scene-while-making-a-scene kind of way, she just read Rex up one side of his big, chocolatey old self and down the other.

Rex stands up and moves toward Essence.

Khalil steps in and says, "Hey, man, why don't you leave it alone."

The expression on my sister's face says, "Try me. I dare you."

Rex raises his hands in surrender and again tries to appeal to Essence.

"Can you please calm down Es, so we can talk, privately?" He knows all eyes are on him and he speaks gently. "I don't want to fight with you. I think we all need to calm down, have a seat, and talk like adults."

"Adults?" Essence says in disbelief. "Now you want to act like an adult? Rex, go straight to hell."

Essence grabs me and we storm out. She angry-walks for about two blocks, causing me to have to jog to keep pace with her. Tears begin to replace her rage. I hate seeing my sister cry, even tears of anger. There's nothing I can say or do to fix this, so I offer silence. After about four blocks, I get her to sit down in a nearby tea shop. We need time to figure out what to do next.

When Essence begins to sob loudly, I slide my chair close to hers. Recalling the many times as kids that she sat by my side when I had sorrows and hurts, I cradle her in my arms and offer words of encouragement.

"It'll be okay, Sisi. You'll get through this. Cry as much as you need to."

The tea barista, or whatever she's called, brings over what she refers to as a calming tea.

"It's on me," she says.

"Thanks," I whisper.

Essence cries for several more minutes. I'm able to convince her to drink the tea. It does seem to settle her agitation and restore some semblance of peace. We sit quietly for another half hour, then she gets up.

"I wanna go now," Essence announces then marches out, not concerned about whether I'm with her. As I hurry to catch up with her, I thank the tea barista and place a tip for her on the counter. Essence has already hailed a cab when I reach her outside.

"Where are we going?" I ask as gently as I can.

"As far away from here as possible," she replies.

TURNS OUT, PENN STATION WAS AS FAR AS WE NEEDED TO GO. The next train to Connecticut leaves at six o'clock, and we'll be on it. We find seats in a quiet section of the passenger lounge to wait for the next two hours. Other than one brief phone call that ended with Essence saying, "Go to hell, Rex," and throwing her phone into her bag, she's been sitting in tearful silence this whole time. I'm trying to be present for her and don't even answer my phone when Eye Candy calls.

After we get on the train and Essence falls asleep, I have a chance to text him and my girls to update them on today's happenings.

By the time the train gets us back to Bryce, it's only eight, but my body and mind have nearly shut down from exhaustion.

"You need me to walk you to your room, Sisi?"

"No," she says. "You've done enough damage for one day."

Me? What did I do?

I absolutely can't with her.

177

. . .

As I lay in bed, wondering why God punished me by making me her twin, I pull out my journal and make an entry for today.

Today I start fresh. I am better than I was. I am ____
I write **USED AND ABUSED**
Saturday, October 6, 2018

Hi. That might sound extreme to you but do you know what I've been through today? I was snatched from my sleep to go on a mission with Essence to NY. Really, she just wanted to see a guy who turned out to be a total asshole. He was rude and disrespectful and wouldn't pray. He even made her cry. It was an awful experience and she's really hurt. Somehow, she's making this my fault. I only went because she forced me to and didn't tell me why. I'm so over her using me and then throwing me away. Karma is real. She'll get hers one day. ttyl

Chapter Twenty-Seven

※

The day after my New York adventure starts off as well as can be expected. Although I got about six hours of sleep, that trip drained me physically and emotionally. I'm rested, but my mind is weary.

After showering and getting dressed, I check on Essence. Bianca is with her, so she dismisses me. Then Reilly calls to tell me she's putting me out of her study group for missing our session yesterday. Due to what she called my "neglect, laziness, or whatever the hell," she had to prepare the chapter reviews she had assigned to me. Knowing Reilly the way I do, she had already prepared an outline of my chapters, her chapters, and everyone else's, so I don't feel bad for her at all. But I'ma still let her know to watch how she comes at me and never again to call me lazy.

She gets a pass today because I just don't have the energy for any more conflict.

What I need to do before I get up under these books, is to eat and talk to Eye Candy. He sends me a text just as I'm about to send one to him.

EC: Hey wassup over there?

Instead of responding by text, I do a video-call.

"Hey, Miss Ebony," he says with the sweetest smile.

"Hey, Mister Cameron."

"Glad you're safe," he says.

"Thanks, I'm just glad to be off that rollercoaster my sister had me on."

Eye Candy throws what feels like a million questions at me about New York. I'm sure it was probably only five or six, but my head spins at the thought of rehashing all the drama to provide him the information he wants. I'm hoping he'll be satisfied with my condensed version of the highlights.

"Essence basically kidnapped me and made me go to New York because she wanted to see this guy who turned out to be the biggest jerk. He was so rude and disrespectful to me. Anyway, Essence got mad at him because of how he acted about me being there. They had a huge argument. She cursed him out and we came home." I get that all out in one breath.

Eye Candy's looking at me with his mouth open. "What the hell?" he finally says.

"It was bananas. But can we talk about it another time? I'm trying to get my head ready to study for my Forensics exam."

"Oh, right. How's that going? Were you able to study on your trip."

"Not a bit. My plan for today is to read and review all day and take the test at around ten o'clock tonight. It's supposed to be a one-hour test, but we have two hours to complete it. There's some stuff I don't really understand so that's gonna take some time."

"Can you get with your girl from class?" he asks, trying to be helpful.

"You mean the one who put me out of the study group because I ghosted her yesterday? Doubt it."

"Damn, you taking hits left and right."

"I know, right? Sucks to be me today."

"Let's fix that. Meet me for a quick breakfast. Promise I'll have you back by noon."

"That's tempting, but I have so much to do," I whine.

"You gotta eat."

He flashes that winning smile and there's no need for any more discussion.

Excitedly I say, "I'll be ready in twenty minutes."

Eye Candy greets me in front of my dorm with open arms.

"Hey, beautiful. You shining this morning."

I collapse into his embrace. If his stomach hadn't started growling, I probably would've stayed in that position until his arms fell off.

"Thanks for that," I say to him, speaking of our hug. "I might need another one of those before this day is over."

"Plenty more where that came from," he says, grabbing my hand. "You good with Mocha Café? My boy, Hayes, is working there today. He can get us a table so we don't have to wait."

"Works for me." I'm a little giddy from Eye Candy's hug and would be agreeable to pretty much any place he suggests.

We walk to Mocha Café, my hand in his. His grip is gentle yet firm, which dissolves the angst that built up over the past day. Suddenly nothing else in the world matters to me. I memorize this moment in time and store it in my heart.

The Sunday Brunch line at Mocha Café is easily thirty people deep. Thankfully, Hayes brings us in through a side entrance and seats us in the Private Dining Room, or PDR. I've never eaten in here before. Apparently, this area is for those people who make advance reservations, which my friends and I never do. It must cost more, too, because the table settings are nicer and the buffet food is fresher than in the main room where we usually dine.

"Enjoy. Let me know if you need anything," Hayes says after he reviews the PDR protocol.

Eye Candy thanks him and they give each other dap.

After saying grace, Eye Candy says, "A'ight, let's eat."

The food, the service, the ambience are all so much better in the PDR. We shamelessly stuff ourselves on everything from wings to salmon to prime rib, and gourmet side dishes galore. The desserts blow my mind. And to my surprise, we get an entrée to go, "to extend the culinary experience," as Hayes reminds us. He recommends the braised short ribs for Eye Candy, because it's a good amount of food and suggests the shrimp and grits for me. Uggh. That's what stupid Rex ordered yesterday.

"May I have the short ribs instead?" I ask.

Eye Candy asks Hayes to hook him up with some more wings, and a crab cake sandwich as well.

Before I can tease him about how much food that is on top of the ginormous amount of food he already ate, he says, "Don't even go there. I work out twice a day and put in my time practicing with the team."

Instead of responding verbally, I just shake my head and laugh.

Eye Candy and I leave Mocha Café with four take-out bags. Three belong to him; only one is mine.

"Most of that food is yours, so you get to carry the bags," I tell him. "But that shouldn't be a problem since you work out so much."

"These bags ain't nothin'," Eye Candy boasts. "I could carry them and you without breaking a sweat."

"You might have to carry me at this point as sleepy as I am."

"You got the 'itis," he jokes. "You need a nap."

"Actually, I need to study," I remind him. "You promised to have me back by noon and it's almost one o'clock. No time for a nap now."

"It ain't my fault you got greedy."

"Whatever," I say, brushing off his comment.

When we reach my dorm, Eye Candy pulls me in for a hug and says, "Don't worry about the test or the studying. You got this. Go knock that test out like you knocked out those wings."

In a half-hearted way, I push away from him as if his comment insulted me. It didn't because I did kinda bumrush the chicken wings and mumbo sauce we ordered. The taste took me back to my favorite carry-out in D.C. and I definitely got my eat on. But so did he.

"Excuse me, but I know you're not talking. Didn't you eat half the order while I was still on my first wing?"

Eye Candy belts out a loud laugh, probably recalling how he had his face in that platter.

He pulls me back in close to him and holds me.

I don't want him to let me go either, but duty calls.

"Good luck," he says when he releases me.

"Thanks. I'm gonna need it. And thanks again for today. It was nice and right on time. Just what I needed."

"No worries. It's what I'm here for."

WHEN I GET BACK TO MY ROOM, I'M BARELY ABLE TO KEEP MY eyes open. I grab an energy drink from the vending machine and within ten minutes, I feel like all of my brain cylinders are on rapid fire. I'm hyper-focused and make good progress on my chapter reviews. I even complete a practice test and score a passing grade.

Jenna sends me a text at around five o'clock to let me know she and Reilly just finished the test and she emailed me the study group outline.

J: But don't tell Reilly I gave it to U UR still on punishment w her. LOLOL!

Me: I know <<eyeroll>> but OMG! #lifesaver tysm

I log into my Bryce email account and Jenna's email is right on top. As I read through the attached document, I hear harps and an angelic chorus rejoicing and giving thanks for this master-piece. It's obvious Reilly prepared the entire outline, which she would have done even if I had worked all day on my chapters. I'm not gonna waste any time bad-mouthing her now because her micromanaging is paving my way to a higher grade on this test. I'm definitely in my bag now.

By eight o'clock, the energy drink has worn off and my brain is fried. I'm tempted to take a quick nap but with my luck, I'd oversleep and miss the test. The other option, another energy drink, would have me awake until the sun comes up. My body can't survive another night like that. The take-out bag from Mocha Café sits on my dresser, staring at me. Since technically, I missed dinner, nourishment might be the solution to my fatigue. When I look in the bag, I see that Hayes hooked me up with way more than I expected. Not only do I have short ribs, but he gave me shrimp and grits anyway, wings, sautéed spinach, and dessert. My stomach is ready to devour it all, but I know the 'itis is lurking in the shadows, so I just sample a bit of everything. During this mini-feast, I videochat with Eye Candy.

"You eating again?" he laughs, asking as soon as he sees my face.

"This is my dinner," I reply. "Your boy loaded me up with food."

"Yeah. Me, too. How's your studying?"

"Great. Jenna sent me the study outline and that made everything so much easier. I'm probably gonna go take the test earlier so I can be done with it."

"That's wassup."

Eye Candy is stretched out on his bed, chillin'. What I wouldn't give to be laying there next to him right now.

"You look like you're about to crash." I say.

"Yup. Just ate and you know what that means."

"That means sleep tight."

He laughs and says, "You right, sweetheart. Good luck."

At exactly 9:45pm, I enter the testing center and login to the exam. Over the next hour and fifteen minutes, I dump a day's worth of cramming into what I'm sure are all correct multiple choice responses, thorough essays, and a cleverly-solved whodunnit. After hitting submit, I shout "Yes," and a great feeling of relief comes over me.

With my mind free of the stress of this test, Reilly, Professor Elaine Kendall, and Essence, I rush back to my room and I'm pretty sure I fall asleep before my head hits the pillow.

Chapter Twenty-Eight

To celebrate surviving my weekend from the depths of hell, Eye Candy suggests we do something fun after class today. We decide to head downtown and go bowling, which I'm surprised to find out he enjoys as much as me. We also pick out a cool place to eat not too far from the bowling alley on the Riverfront.

As I change into my going-out-on-a-date outfit, all I can think about is how exhausted I am. My tank hit empty halfway through Forensics and I've been running on fumes since then. The thought of cancelling this outing crosses my mind but immediately gets extinguished.

"This is Eye Candy," I tell those detracting voices. "This date is happening." Hopefully, just being with him will invigorate me.

When I walk outside, Eye Candy is waiting for me at the back path near where he parked his roommate's car. This is the same spot where I met Donovan for our bike ride. I quickly shake the thought of him out of my head and focus on Eye Candy and the beaming expression on his face. Oddly, as I get closer to him, he looks at me with concern.

"You okay?" he asks me.

"Yeah, I'm good."

"You don't look so good."

I'm slightly insulted by that comment and say in response, "Gee. Thanks."

Eye Candy takes quick action to get me out of my feelings. "Whoa," he says. "That came out wrong. Dial that attitude back. You know you look amazing as usual. But you don't seem real energetic compared to when I saw you a few hours ago. That's all I'm saying."

"Glad you cleared that up because I was about to say . . . "

"So what's up?"

"I'm just tired. It was a rough weekend, but I'm ready to beat you in bowling, so let's go."

"That fatigue got you delirious if you think you can beat me at anything, but that confidence is kinda cute."

The smirk on my face says, "Thank you and I know."

Eye Candy looks intently at me. "Joking aside, everybody has a limit. You might be at yours. Maybe we should do this another time."

"Or," I propose, "how about we just do something different that's low energy." This seems like a reasonable compromise to me.

"How about I just get you to bed instead?"

We both know what Eye Candy means by that question, but he lets the ambiguity linger.

My cute confidence stirs the pot by asking, "How is that low energy?"

Eye Candy stares right at me and says, "I'll do all the work."

Suddenly, I'm not sure what we're talking about, but whatever it is, in my head, I'm with it.

"What are you suggesting?" I ask with interest.

"Let's go up to your room and I'll show you."

I'm saying "no" in all kinds of ways . . . in my head. But those words don't come out of my mouth. Actually, no words do. Without any thought, I turn around and lead Eye Candy up to my room.

"This dorm is even nicer than I heard," he comments as the elevator doors close. "You must be well-connected to get a spot up in here."

"Not me. It's my sister who has the connections. I just get her crumbs."

"Crumbs? This looks like a full course meal to me."

When we walk into my room, I'm thankful I cleaned up the mess I made getting dressed.

Eye Candy's first comment is, "Yo, this room is tight. And you got a view."

He surveys my books, the wall art, and the few photographs I have around my desk. He asks so many questions.

"What's up with the posters of all these art museums? Have you been to any of them?"

"Is that kid on the monkey bars you?"

"Who's with you in those polaroids, because they're comical?"

I'm flattered he's so interested in me and my stuff. We sit on my bed and I tell him as much as he wants to know.

The polaroids he asked about are mostly of me and Taylor so he gets to hear all about my best friend and her current adventures in London.

"I'd love to travel to Europe one day," he says, pensively. "But my first trip outta the U.S. has to be to Africa."

He closes his eyes, probably imagining what he'll feel like planting his feet in the Mother Land. I've fantasized about that as well.

"Africa is on my list, too," I share. "Actually, everywhere is on my list."

Eye Candy's playful side comes out as we continue to talk, especially when I tell him about me jumping off those monkey bars in the picture and becoming the playground superhero.

When we get to the end of that conversation, Eye Candy caresses my face and says, "Thought you were tired."

His touch takes my breath away.

"I am. Or I was. You might've energized me," I whisper as I lean into the warmth of his hand.

He shifts his body closer to mine, and says, "Oh yeah? What you plan to do with all that energy?"

"Good question," I say, gazing into his eyes. Unconsciously, I part my lips slightly. Eye Candy looks at me provocatively, then bends down and kisses my lips two, maybe three times. Then he leans away.

"Your lips are even softer than I expected," he tells me before kissing me again. He gives me what starts as a nondescript, 'he could be kissing anybody' kiss. But then he makes it more personal. In fact, he kisses me like I'm the first and only person he would ever want to kiss. As far as I'm concerned, there's nobody I'd ever want to kiss again. In my head, there's music, and dancing, and fireworks, and people rejoicing in the streets because of our kiss. Just like I always imagined it would be.

When the magical kiss ends, I feel like I'm floating. I'm glad Eye Candy is still holding me, otherwise I might drift away.

"I could kiss you all day," he tells me.

"Okay."

He laughs. "Okay what?"

"Kiss me all day," I reply, perhaps more seductively than he, or even I, expected.

He smiles a naughty grin.

"You sure?" he asks.

This time, I answer his question with a naughty grin of my own. He wisely perceives this as an invitation, better yet a challenge, to kiss me all day. The mischief in his eyes speaks for him. Challenge accepted.

WHEN EYE CANDY FINALLY LEAVES SEVERAL HOURS LATER, I lay down and close my eyes. His scent covers every part of my bed and I roll back and forth in it like a puppy playfully rolling in the grass. When I open my eyes, I reach for my journal to document this momentous occasion.

Today I start fresh. I am better than I was. I am ____

I write **BREATHLESS**

Monday, October 8, 2018

Hi. OMG Eye Candy and I had our first kiss, followed by the second, third and fourth one too. He's such a great kisser. I'm literally dying. I'll be dreaming about him and his lips all night. ttyl

Chapter Twenty-Nine

I n the almost two weeks since our first kiss, Eye Candy and I have become a lot closer and more intimate. Not intimate in the sense of having sex, because that's still not an option for me; but more in terms of our becoming better connected as friends. We share an adoration for each other that's sometimes electric. And no matter what madness might be happening around us, we're able to stay in our vibe. Mercedes and Kendra tease me by saying that I've become so consumed with him that I'm ignoring them. They're right to an extent.

But even though Eye Candy and I spend most of our free time together, we give each other space to do our own thing. So I don't get annoyed when he wants to spend his entire Sunday watching sports. And he never complains when I want to hang with my girls, who now have hot love interests of their own. They're as tied up with their boyfriends as I am with Eye Candy so having lunch and dinner on a regular basis, going to parties together, or just kicking back doesn't happen as often as it used to. We do try to meet every Friday for breakfast, which we'll do today, and catch each other up on anything our daily texts and videochats don't adequately convey.

. . .

BEFORE MEETING KENDRA AND MERCEDES, I TAKE A MOMENT
to celebrate my romance in my journal.

Today I start fresh. I am better than I was. I am ____

I write **HAPPY**

Friday, October 19, 2018

*Hi. TGIF. Sorry It's been a minute since I've written here. I'm
deep into this thing with Eye Candy and I'm overjoyed. I never
expected to find anybody like him. He's perfect. And he thinks I'm
perfect so that makes us perfect for each other. There's a strong
physical attraction too but right now, it's under control. I'm not sure
if that will last. ttyl*

MERCEDES SHOWS UP TO BREAKFAST TODAY FULL OF
excitement because Rico said "those three little words."

"I'm telling you it was so cute," she gushes. "We were just
walking and he was telling me how he's never met anybody like
me and he feels like our friendship has changed him. Then he
said it."

"Aww. That's sweet," I comment. "What did you say?"

"What do you mean, what did I say? I said, I love you, too."
She glares at me like that should have been obvious.

"Don't give me that look. How was I supposed to know? Do
you really love him?"

She says, "Yeah, I guess. But for his purposes, I do."

"Wow. That makes no sense. If you don't really love him, you
shouldn't say you do," I respond. "That's the worst thing you
can do."

"Don't worry about it, Chica. I got this," she assures me.

"You know that changes the game?" Kendra says. "He's probably gonna wanna hit it now."

"Shut up, KK. You can be so common sometimes," Mercedes
shoots back. "Everybody isn't freaky like that. Besides, we
already had that conversation so he knows what to expect and
what not to expect."

Ever doubtful, Kendra says, "If you say so. We'll see how long he lasts."

To give Mercedes some moral support in this conversation, I mention, "Eye Candy and I haven't done it yet either. We've gotten close, but I'm not ready. He's okay with waiting too, especially since he knows it would be my first time."

"Y'all both gon' find out soon enough. At some point, it comes down to a decision to go all the way or walk away. You might not be there yet, but just wait."

"Maybe that's how it is in your world KK, but it may not turn out that way for us," Mercedes declares.

Kendra just shakes her head and stuffs some eggs into her mouth.

Mercedes turns to Kendra and inquires with deep interest. "So does that mean you and Thompson did the thing?"

"Did the thing? If you mean did we have sex . . . Nah. Not yet. But we're not talking love either."

"But, you're seriously thinking about doing it?" she asks.

Kendra shuts down any further discussion about her actual or potential love life.

"Why don't we talk about Eb and Cam and how she got him to go to Sunrise Yoga?"

Mercedes gets the message and doesn't pursue the topic. Her interest comes from a place of concern, I'm sure, because she doesn't believe in sex before marriage. Kendra is, or would be, okay with it I guess. Who knows? But she might be all talk. As for me, I still don't know.

"How'd you do it, Eb?" Kendra asks.

"Basically, he lost a bet so that was what it cost him. But he liked it, so he came again. Now he's a regular. Hey, why don't we all go and make it a triple date?" I suggest.

Kendra shuts that idea down fast. "No thanks. I'm not feeling that yoga thing and definitely not at the butt crack of dawn."

"Forget her, Eb. I'll see if Rico would be interested. It might be a fun couples thing to do."

. . .

Considering how intensely Kendra opposed the idea of Sunrise Yoga a week ago, I'm stunned that she and Thompson show up at all today. As expected, Rico and Mercedes arrive fashionably late. Luckily, I saved them spaces near us. This yoga class has gotten more crowded since I first started coming, which changes the whole mood of it. The setting is still beautiful and calms most of my internal busyness, but only if I can block out the people who aren't serious about yoga. If Eye Candy hadn't embraced class the way he has, I would stop coming.

"Yo, this class ain't for suckers, fellas. It might look easy, but take my word for it," Eye Candy warns Thompson and Rico.

They laugh, but they'll find out . . . the hard way.

Bey Bey begins as she always does. "Namaste, Yogis."

We say together, "Namaste."

No surprise that Kendra checks out of the class ten minutes in. She made it through the warm-up and intentions phase, but her downward dog never got up. She and Thompson leave before the class ends. At least they tried it.

After the class Mercedes tells me that all the girls were gawking at Eye Candy, like he was Magic Mike.

"Really?" I ask in disbelief. Once I get into my zone, I'm oblivious to the people around me. "I had no idea. That explains why this class suddenly got so popular. Please don't tell him or he won't want to come back."

"My lips are sealed, Chica."

After gathering up our mats, Eye Candy says, "We usually go to the Juice Bar after yoga. Y'all down?"

Rico nods and Mercedes responds, "Sure, why not."

When we get there, Rico says, "This is my first time hittin' up this spot."

"You're a senior. How is that possible?" Mercedes asks. "Especially since you're working out here all the time."

"They just opened a few months ago," Eye Candy offers.

"That and these prices are whack," Rico remarks. We all laugh, but it's true.

The overly excited juicerista belts out his usual greeting. "Morning, Morning, Morning. Good Sunday morning. You guys want your usual?"

Eye Candy glances at me for a response and I nod. He turns back to the juicerista and says, "Yessir, and then whatever our friends want. It's all on me."

"Thanks, man, but I got it," Rico tells him.

"No worries. You can get it next time. I got a sports allowance I need to use up."

"Oh. A'ight cool."

AFTER WE GET OUT DRINKS, MERCEDES AND RICO SUGGEST WE meet for yoga again.

"Sounds like a plan," I say. "And we'll try to get Kendra to stick around a little longer."

"Good luck with that one," Mercedes exclaims, as she and Rico walk off.

On the way to my room, Eye Candy and I see Essence and some of her DWBs heading toward us. I dread the encounter we are about to have. Because we don't talk, I haven't told her about my relationship with Eye Candy. She's seen me with him on campus, so I'm sure she knows something more than friendship is going on between us.

Please let them walk past without saying anything.

"Isn't that your sister headed this way?" Eye Candy asks.

"Yeah, but let's just keep walking and not give her a chance to ruin my day."

He thinks I'm kidding, but I'm not.

We end up not having a choice about interacting with her because her friend Suraya eyes us. Suraya is probably the meanest of the mean girls, not just to me but to everybody outside of their clique. She might be the reason Essence turned on me, now that I think about it.

"Dayum. This must be my lucky day," she shouts from a distance. "Hey Cam-G, I've been wanting to meet you up close and personal. I'm a huge fan." Ignoring me, Suraya stands uncomfortably close to Eye Candy. So close, in fact, that her breasts are brushing against his arm. He tries to create distance, but when he moves, she moves.

She starts talking about how attractive he is and how she can't wait to see him play this season. She offers to help him work out. Essence and her other friends find the scene amusing, until I say, "That won't be happening." They stop laughing.

Suraya's head spins in my direction. She stares me down but addresses Essence.

"Es, you betta check your twin."

Essence moves toward me. I stand in front of Suraya, not backing down from her or Essence. Eye Candy takes me by the hand and walks me away from them. As we leave, I hear them laughing.

Suraya yells, "Call me when you're ready for a real woman, Cam."

Eye Candy waits several seconds before saying anything.

"What the hell?" he finally asks.

I'm so mad and want to scream.

"Why would your sister let her friend - "

"Humiliate me? Good question. That was a new low, even for her." So much for her always having my back.

"That's foul," he says. "Y'all need to work that out. If something ever went down you wanna be able to count on family."

With a long sigh, I just say "It would take a miracle to fix my relationship with Essence."

We walk the rest of the way to my dorm in silence. I'm fuming on the inside, wishing I had said something to Essence, and not just Suraya.

"I'll send her a text," I blurt out.

"Send who a text?" Eye Candy asks.

I laugh, realizing he wasn't a part of the conversation that just happened in my head. After catching him up, I repeat my plan to send Essence a message letting her know how disrespectful she and her friends were.

"That's right. Handle your biz," he says, encouraging me.

The message I send is short and to the point.

Me: You & yr friends went 2 far. How u gon explain 2 mom&dad?

"Done," I announce.

"Good. How do you feel?"

"Actually, I'm okay. She'll get hers."

"Uh oh. They better watch out. My li'l Mayweather is ready to kick some butt!"

"Hey, don't come for me," I say.

Eye Candy laughs and playfully shadow boxes with me. Then with a single kiss makes me forget about everything wrong in my world.

Chapter Thirty

I t never fails. No matter how good I may feel one day, or for several days, like I have for the past week, lurking around every day, is a tomorrow like the one I had today.

I thought Essence had finally accepted that we could co-exist without her actively trying to ruin my happiness. Apparently, I was wrong. We ended up fighting today. It started over me not letting her borrow a pair of my jeans. That was my payback for how she just watched while her friend, Suraya, tried to seduce Eye Candy in front of me. She was already mad because I told our parents and she got lectured by both of them, which she hates.

My saying no to her about my jeans escalated to name-calling and turned physical. I pushed her into the wall and she swung and hit me so hard across my head, the room started spinning and I fell to the floor. As she stormed out, with my jeans, I threw a book at her and got her good in the back.

That happened like three or four hours ago. All I've been able to do since then is lay in bed. My head is pounding, my emotions are raw, and my thoughts are chaotic. Eye Candy and I had planned to have dinner tonight, but there was no way he could see me in this condition. When I cancelled "because I wasn't feeling well," he said he understood.

I've been drifting in and out of sleep and now, the sound from someone knocking on my door gets incorporated into my dream. I'm in deep enough sleep to be dreaming but awake enough to know I'm having this conversation in my head. The knocking stops and so does my dream.

When the door opens, I figure it's Essence and even in my sleep, I get mad.

"Hey, Ebony? It's me. Can I come in?"

Eye Candy's voice takes a while to register.

By the time I open my eyes fully, he's sitting next to me on my bed.

"I came to check on you. How you feel?"

"Not great," I admit.

"You wanna talk about what's going on?" he asks.

I should talk to him and let him be my friend; better yet, let him be my man. But I don't want talking. I just want quiet.

"I'm not really up for that yet. It's been an horrendous day. There's a lot of noise in my head and I need that to settle down. The only way I know to do that is just to be still."

The room is dark so I can't see his expression, but I can hear in his voice that he understands.

"Do whatever you need," he says. I let out a sigh of relief.

Then he says, "Can I stay and be still with you?"

Is he not perfect?

"Sure. If you don't think that would be too weird."

"Nah, it'll be fine," he says as he lies in my bed next to me. In stillness. In quiet.

At some point, we both fall asleep. I awaken when he gets up to answer the call of nature. I do the same since now I'm up, too. He makes it back to the room before me and sprawls out in the middle of my floor on top of a makeshift palette he created using my comforter, some pillows, and a blanket. He's already undressed down to his t-shirt and boxers and has gotten real cozy. I tease him about taking up so much space being so tall. I change into a pajama shirt and lay down next to him.

We've had more than a few late nights together, but tonight

feels different. Maybe because mentally I'm in an unsettled, fragile space. With Eye Candy here, though, I feel very supported.

As he moves around trying to get more comfortable, I whisper, "Thanks for being here."

"No need for that," he says. "You know I gotchu. Always."

Yeah, I do know that. And that gives me all kinds of feels on the inside. I lean over and kiss Eye Candy softly. He takes hold of my kiss and turns it into something far more sensual than he and I have ever shared. I can tell the passion is rising for both of us. He starts touching me in places that I had locked down very securely since Donovan. I feel those locks falling off fast.

Eye Candy pulls my pajama top off, leaving me in only my panties. He spends a lot of time acquainting his lips and tongue with my bare shoulders and back. I had no idea I could get so . . . aroused by anybody doing that. With one hand he caresses my breasts, while the other hand starts an exploration of its own around my inner thighs. My body is literally on fire. My brain starts sending out those warning signals like it did that time with Donovan, but this is different. *I* choose to be here and *I* am choosing to do this. *This* is fine. I am comfortable with *this*. But what if doing *this* leads to him wanting to do *it?* Eye Candy is talking to me while I'm talking to myself.

He's telling me how beautiful I am and how nice my body feels.

The voices in my head are reminding me that I've traveled this road before and it ends at a place I'm still not sure I want to be.

Meanwhile, my body is proclaiming YOLO and giving me permission to surrender my whole self to Eye Candy's affection. As I feel myself doing just that, the noise becomes even louder. It's too much for me to endure and I shout, "Stop."

I startle Eye Candy and he . . . stops. All the chatter . . . stops. Everything . . . stops. That's not what I intended, but here we are.

Eye Candy stares at me, maybe waiting for me to say something.

"Sorry," I say. "I didn't mean to yell like that."

"No apologies needed. We don't have to do anything you're not ready for. I just thought..."

He doesn't finish his sentence. Instead, he gives me my pajama shirt to put back on.

After laying quietly for several seconds, Eye Candy tells me how hard it is to keep his hands off me.

"But, there's no rush," he adds.

"I didn't think we were rushing." That's the truth. And I wasn't telling him to stop. But I probably should have been, so thank you to my angels, and maybe even his, for running interference. "I'm just not mentally ready for what my body wants to let happen," I tell him.

"Totally understandable. I'm cool waiting until you're ready body, mind, and spirit."

After a few moments of silence, Eye Candy announces that he's gonna head back to his room.

"Why do you want to leave?" I ask.

This better not be one of those situations where he's feeling some kinda way because I said no.

"I don't, but I wanna respect your decision."

"Can't you do that and stay with me?" I inquire.

Apparently he's forgotten that we've spent nights together before and had no problems.

He says, "Something feels different tonight. Your body is giving me these signals. Can't quite explain it. But it's hard to resist you."

"Please stay. I promise not to send out any more signals."

Eye Candy wraps me in his arms. "I'm not sure it works like that, but okay."

As we lay together, our bodies quiet themselves. The energy between us becomes less charged. Soon we both doze off to sleep.

Chapter Thirty-One

A few days ago, Mercedes proclaimed "You and Cam are so cute. You're like two little lovebirds."

She's become such a fan of love now that she and Rico have professed their love to each other. She wants everybody to experience what she feels.

"Slow down there," I tell her, when she brings the topic up again today. "I don't think we're at that level yet."

"All that freakin' you two doin', it better be some love up in there," she insists.

"Wow. You're absolutely too much. I can't say if it's love. But if it's not, it's definitely close."

That should satisfy her enough to drop the subject.

What I could have said to Mercedes was that my feelings for Eye Candy are growing stronger by the day and maybe what I feel is love. I'm just not sure what love would feel like. And I have no idea where he is on the spectrum of emotions.

He did give me one of his practice jerseys the other night, which apparently is a big deal, even in college. He said it means we're officially a couple and I'm supposed to wear it so everyone knows I'm his and he's mine. Of course, I commemorated the occasion with a journal entry.

Today I start fresh. I am better than I was. I am ____

I write **IN A RELATIONSHIP**
Tuesday, October 30, 2018

It's official. Eye Candy and I are in a relationship. He gave me his #23 jersey on the 23rd and asked me to be his girlfriend. I changed my status to "In a Relationship with @CamG23." This Princess finally got her Prince Charming. ttyl.

EVEN THOUGH EYE CANDY AND I HAD ALWAYS BEEN PUBLIC about our relationship, announcing it on social media took it to another level. Like, it was for real before, but once we came out on the socials, it was for real for real.

I'm learning that dating the school's marquis basketball player comes with many challenges, some of which I expected; others take me by surprise. Practice, workouts, team meetings, and games take up a lot of his time. And they will always come before me. This much I knew.

But groupies constantly trying to get his attention and maybe his time, I didn't expect. I knew there would be haters but these chicks go hard with the shade and can sometimes be cruel. "Don't bother reading that stuff," everybody advises me. It's hard not to when it's thrown in my face. To make matters worse, a few of the more thirsty ones will flirt with Eye Candy right in front of me, like Suraya did, except these girls are serious. Suraya was just being jerk.

Usually, I'm able to convince myself that the wannabe baes and side-chicks are meaningless. Occasionally though, when my self-confidence has been bruised or beaten by the ups and downs of life, the attention Eye Candy gets from these other girls annoys me. It doesn't help me that he's genuinely nice to everybody so he lets these girls say and do almost anything they want.

"That attention don't do jack for me," he insisted when the topic came up at dinner a few nights ago. "Girls have been acting like that around me since junior high. I've learned to block it all out."

"Maybe you can do that, but I can't. This is new for me," I reminded him. "And it's embarrassing and disrespectful to me when they get all in

your face and touch you, especially when we're together. It's like I'm invisible."

"You're too fine to ever be invisible."

He was playing, but I was seriously bothered, which he realized when I didn't smile at his comment.

"Listen, it doesn't matter what anybody says or does, I don't want to be with anybody but you. None of those comments even registers with me. I'm so tuned out of all that hype. You're in your feelings for no reason."

As much as Eye Candy tries to assure me that I have the one and only spot on his roster, my own self-doubts and insecurities often work against me. These are probably just more fallout from my sister's efforts to live her best life by wrecking mine. But just as I have to decide every day not to let Essence control my happiness, I have to remind myself that Eye Candy picked me and that must mean I've got something special, even if only he sees it.

With my head held high and rocking his jersey, I walk into the library today and make my way to our usual study area. He's at the table surrounded by yet another group of fangirls. Really? It's Saturday morning and they're at it already? I laugh to myself and shake my head. So, this is really my life now? When Eye Candy sees me, his face lights up. He could easily have any one or all of these girls, but they don't make him smile like that. I walk past all of them and directly over to him.

"Hey, babe," I say, as I plant a kiss on his lips. Someone watching this might say I'm marking my territory, or flexing, as he calls it. Yes, I am.

"Hey, you," he says after our lips part. "You make my jersey look good, girl."

I do a little twirl to model it for him; but really for them. Then I give Eye Candy and everyone who's minding our business my 'I know I look cute' smile as I take my seat next to him. With my eyes, I ask what he plans to do with his fan club.

He reads me well. He dismisses his groupies by announcing that, "We," pointing to me and him, "gotta hit these books."

"If you need any tutoring . . . or anything let me know," this one chick says.

Or anything? She's definitely a problem.

"Nah, I'm good," he tells her.

"Bet you are," she says under her breath but loudly enough for him to hear. And of course I hear it, too. That's really what she wanted I'm sure. It feels like she's sending out a message to let Eye Candy know she's available to take care of him because she thinks I can't. Suraya did the same thing. And they both remind me of Essence and how she disregards my relevance and diminishes my importance to serve her needs. None of them think I'm enough.

After they leave, Eye Candy says, "Sorry about that. You good?"

"Yep. Occupational hazard, right?"

I'm trying to show him that I can handle his popularity without getting upset, so I open my book and start reading.

"You mad?" he asks.

Without looking up from my book, I say, "Nope."

"What's up then? You usually have more of a reaction when that happens."

"It means nothing, right? I'm trying not to let girls like her bother me."

"It's not really working," he says, teasing. "I can see the steam coming outta your head."

He makes me laugh.

"At least I tried. But honestly, she wasn't even cute. Why would she think you would need her for anything. I got this. That's what I shoulda told her."

"Nah, let me take care of this."

"How exactly do you plan to do that?"

"I'll figure it out," he says with finality.

Our study session is quiet and more serious than others we've had. But there's no tension or hard feelings between us. I'm just in my head, thinking about how he plans to handle this. Every so often, when I go deep into thought, I end up staring off into the distance for several minutes.

Eye Candy touches my hand to get my attention and says, "Hey. Where you at?"

"Just thinking," I answer.

"You wanna talk about it?" he asks.

I smile and say, "Nope."

He returns to doing his school work and I do too. After about three more hours, he's ready to shut it down so we pack up our books and head out. Our original plan for today was to study together for a few hours, then he was going to work out with some teammates, and I'd probably just go back to my room or try to hook up with Mercedes or Kendra.

When we get outside of the library, I'm expecting him to walk me to my dorm, so I head in that direction. But Eye Candy takes my hand and says, "Come with me."

"Where?" I ask.

"My suitemates have an away LAX match so they're gone till tomorrow morning. Come chill with me."

"You have that workout, I thought."

"It can wait."

THE ONE THING I HATE ABOUT COMING TO EYE CANDY'S room is that his suitemates are slobs. He, on the other hand, is a neat freak. He's always cleaning the common spaces in the suite, in addition to keeping his own room nearly spotless. Whenever the other guys have an away game, Eye Candy sanitizes their entire suite. Knowing that, I'm prepared for the smell of bleach and disinfectant that slaps me in the face as soon as he opens the door.

"Sorry, it's so strong. I'll open a window."

"Who you tryna kill?" I ask.

"Not who. You mean what. There was a science project or

something growing in that kitchen sink," he jokes. "My room should be okay."

He's right. As usual, Eye Candy's room is an oasis. He spreads out a blanket on the floor. The Thai food he ordered on our walk here arrives about fifteen minutes later.

"What's your favorite picture of us," he asks while we eat.

"That's random," I say. "I don't know. They're all my faves."

"Please pick one," he urges as he scrolls through the pictures of us on his phone.

I narrow my selections down to two. "A'ight. I'll go with this one."

What he's doing with the picture, I can't tell. But shortly afterwards, I start getting tag alerts on my phone. When I open the notifications, he has posted a picture of me on all his social media pages with the caption that says:

@EbonyGabs has my whole heart #MyOne #MyWomanCrush #Wifey

Then he adds a picture of the two of us all snuggled up with the caption:

Boo'd Up

He makes this one his profile pic and then so did I.

"This might not stop those girls from doing all the silly stuff they do," he says. "But if you ever doubt where I stand, this can be your reminder. Hopefully, you don't feel the need to question my commitment or to judge yourself against any damn body."

I have no words but hope my face expresses how much I appreciate him for doing this. He takes my hands in his and brings them to his lips and kisses them both softly. He might as well have kissed me directly at the center of my heart because that's where I start to feel myself melting.

Chapter Thirty-Two

I end up staying with Eye Candy all night. To avoid possibly encountering his roommates when they get back from their match, I leave him sound asleep at daybreak.

The campus is beautifully quiet right now. Only the joggers and people like me – the ones creeping to our rooms from where we were last night – are out at this time of morning on a Sunday. This girl I don't know and have never seen before runs toward my direction and stops in front of me, blocking my way. Apparently, she missed the lesson on personal space because she's all up in mine and it's not cool.

"Hey, where you been?" she asks.

Thinking she might try to rob me or something, because that does happen here, I maneuver around her and jog away. She follows me.

"Wait up. We was just partying together on Friday. How you gon' play me?"

Then it dons on me. She thinks I'm Essence.

"You sure it wasn't my twin sister you were with?" I ask.

My face remains completely serious, but she laughs.

"Stop playin'. We were just partying together in Brooklyn. You forgot about it already? Oh, right, you and your man, Rex was pretty lit up, so maybe you don't remember anything."

I know shock and confusion are plastered all over my face as I try to process what I just heard. Brooklyn? Wasted? Rex? After the big fight we had with him, I knew for sure Essence had cut him out of her life. Why would she ever want to see him again? And what's this about her getting wasted? And in Brooklyn?

While I try to figure out the answers to these questions, this girl rambles on about the party, probably trying to refresh my memory, or rather Essence's memory. There were people drinking, getting high, and apparently engaging in all types of ratchedness. Somehow Essence and Rex fit into this decadence. The longer she talks, the more uncomfortable I feel. It's like I'm eavesdropping on somebody's private X-rated conversation.

I can't listen anymore and stop her mid-rant. "You really must have me mistaken for my twin sister."

She stops walking and talking to stare me up and down. She leans her head back and squints as she examines every feature of my face. Her raised eyebrows tell me she still has doubts.

"Stop playing, Es," she says, swiping at the air like she's swatting a fly.

"I'm not playing," I assure her. "Essence is my twin sister. We're identical. I promise you I wasn't in New York with you and if I was, I surely would not have been anywhere near that Rex guy. He's a super asshole."

My disdain for Rex convinces her I'm not Essence.

"Dayum," she screams before she starts cracking up laughing. "Y'all just look alike."

Did she not hear the part where I said we were identical twins?

"It's fine, it happens all the time." Then I let her know, like Jenna said, "We're identical twins, but we're nothing alike."

Now that she knows I'm not Essence, our conversation should be over. I start walking toward my dorm again and she calls out to me.

"Wait up, Twin."

I'm pretty sure I roll my eyes with my entire body when I

turn around to see what she wants. She's unfazed and pleasantly introduces herself.

"I'm Zola."

"Hi. I'm Ebony."

"Ohhh, I get it. Ebony and Essence." I watch as she unravels the concept behind our names.

"That's wassup," she says as she nods. It takes her a few more moments to move past the name thing and get back to the reason she accosted me.

"What's with your sis? She alright?"

"What do you mean? Why wouldn't she be alright?" I ask.

"Well, she got pretty wasted at the party so I wanted to see how she was feeling. They were into some strong shit, so I can only imagine how bad she felt yesterday. If she felt anything," she adds with a laugh. "After my first night of drugs, booze, and mayhem, I was Sly and the Family stoned. Took me two days to recover."

My shock deepens listening to her talk about doing drugs and alcohol so casually, like it's an everyday thing. It's not a laughing matter in my opinion. And I'm feeling some kind of way about her putting my sister in the middle of that type of situation. Essence will break some rules, but she wouldn't do the kinds of things Zola is describing, except the drinking part because I witnessed that myself. Zola was probably the one too high to know what really happened.

"I'm not sure I believe all this stuff you're saying about my sister, but if you're so concerned call or text her?"

Zola sets me straight. "Look, Twin, I ain't got no reason to lie. If it wasn't you, it was her. Unless there's a triplet out there."

"Besides," she continues, "I did all that calling and texting. Even sent a DM. No response."

I'm worried hearing that but pretend I'm not for Zola since I don't know her and am not liking her at this moment.

"Well, I'm sure she's fine. She can be moody sometimes and anti-people." *Ask me how I know.* "I'll stop by her room when I get to our dorm."

I walk away from Zola again hoping to end this chance encounter. She lets some distance grow between us and then runs up to me handing me her phone.

"Before you talk to Es, there's something else you should know."

I can't imagine that this story could get any worse, but I still ask, "What else is there?"

"A video."

Those words cause my breath to stop and my heart to skip a beat. I close my eyes and shake my head in disbelief. I don't want to take the logical next step, but I know I need to.

"Let me see it," I say.

"Twin, this is not a good look for your sister, so be prepared."

I watch the eight-minute video in horror. The entire time I wish I could say the person in this video is not Essence but it one hundred percent is. My own anger rises watching Essence go from sitting and talking normally while she and that asshole, Rex, are drinking and getting high, to slurring her speech, stumbling, and letting Rex and some other guys grope her without fighting them off.

Zola says, "He musta given her some kind of pills because she went from being chill to acting like this in seconds. They mixed a lot of intoxicating substances at one time, which I never woulda done, but I figured that's how they got down."

The video ends with Essence and Rex going into a room and closing the door. My eyes fill with tears. I'm so hurt and disgusted and embarrassed for Essence but pissed off with her at the same time. I told her Rex was trouble. She wouldn't listen. She just ridiculed me.

"Bunnie, what do you know about men? Have you even dated anybody out of diapers?"

A crushing feeling of dread comes down on me imagining what might have happened to Essence in that room. And what if the drugs she took damaged her permanently?

Panicked, I take off, sprinting to my dorm, praying the entire way there, that she's safe. Zola follows close behind.

When we reach Essence's room, I knock and get no answer, then call out and get no response. I'll have to use her key code to open the door. As much as I hope Essence is in here, because at least I'll know she's alive, the wrath I'll incur if she is, almost turns me away.

I enter the code and open the door. Essence is sitting on her bed, talking on her phone showing no signs of impairment or injury. I'm thankful and relieved, but now bracing myself for her anger. Fortunately for me, Zola walks into the room first and I follow, closing the door behind me.

The expression on Essence's face goes from "I know you didn't just barge into my room without my permission," when she sees me, to 'Oh shit,' after she sees Zola.

Essence ends her call.

"Do y'all see the time? What's this about?" she demands.

I look at Zola to respond. After all, she was at the party and has the video.

"Yo, Es. I been trying to catch up with you to see how you were doing. I ran into your sis and thought she was you."

Essence is unaffected by Zola's concern, probably because she's trying to figure out what I know.

"I'm doing fine as you can see and I don't appreciate y'all breaking into my room. It's six-thirty in the freakin' morning."

She directs that remark to me and threatens me with, "I got something for you, Ebony."

"Es, don't rail on her like that. She did it because I kinda told her how wasted you were at the party. And we were worried."

Essence brushes her statement aside and says, "I wasn't that bad, Zola. I just had a few drinks. No big deal."

My first thought was Essence is downplaying her unruly behavior in front of me to keep up her perfect image. But through my twin-sense, I can tell she genuinely believes what she's saying. Zola looks at me, I guess wanting my permission to give her the truth. I nod my head.

"Come on, Es," Zola says easing into a conversation that

hopefully will trigger some memory. "Do you really not remember? It was more than a few drinks. You were white-girl wasted."

I'm surprised that Essence doesn't kick Zola out, or worse, for insulting her with that characterization. Essence has always prided herself on maintaining her bougie, and "white girl wasted" is the complete opposite of that. My guess is she knows some of what Zola is telling her is true, but she won't admit it in front of me.

"Like I said, that's not how I remember it. But it doesn't matter because as you can see, I'm fine. Now can you both uninvite yourselves from my room?"

"It's on video," I blurt out.

Instantly, her whole demeanor changes. Like with me, those words first halt her motion and then, make her lose her breath. I imagine her heart probably also misses a few beats.

Her venomous, angry face transforms into a palette of shock, worry, and fear. She turns to Zola.

"What video?" Her speech is slow and deliberate.

Zola sits with Essence on her bed, while I stay across the room. Essence looks horrified as she watches herself doing and saying things she never would have done sober. Her next words destroy me.

"How can that be me? I don't remember any of this."

Zola gently says, "Your man musta slipped you something because you went from talkin' and chillin' to being pissy drunk in a few seconds. Then y'all disappeared into that room."

"Why didn't you help me?"

She's rightfully angry with Zola. Friends don't let friends get drugged and possibly . . . I can't even think about it.

"Hold up," Zola says becoming defensive. "How was I supposed to know you needed help. You came with him and I figured he would take care of you. Not to mention, I was very intoxicated myself. I would not have been any good to you."

Essence sits frozen. Her eyes don't move from Zola's phone even though the video has stopped playing. I move closer to give her a hug or hold her hand because that's what I would want her to do for me.

"How could he do that to me?"

Zola says she has no answers, but suggests Essence ask Rex herself. After sitting motionless for a minute or two, Essence does a video call to Rex. She's not concerned about Zola or me hearing their conversation.

"Why'd you hang up on me?" he asks when the call connects.

"My sister came in."

So she was talking to that creep when we walked in.

"Oh. What did the annoying crybaby want?"

As soon as I open my mouth to call him some ungodly name, Essence silently warns me not to say anything.

"She actually came in with Zola, remember her? The one who invited us to the party on Friday."

"Oh yeah, she was cool. Wassup with her?"

"She wanted me to see a video she had of me from that night."

I'm surprised at how calm Essence is while she talks to Rex, especially when she mentions the video.

Rex says nothing.

"Hello. Did you hear me?" she bellows, less calmly now.

"Yeah, I heard you. Stop yelling. What kind of video?"

"Why don't you tell me?" she asks angrily.

"I don't know about no damn video," he claims. I can't see his face, but he sounds too defensive to be telling the truth.

Essence still speaks evenly, but her breathing pattern is changing and she's clenching her fists. She's definitely getting mad.

"Do you know anything about drugging me up?"

He pauses, then says, "Look baby, we were both getting high, drinking and doing all kinds of shit. I might've put something extra in one of your drinks. I was just trying to have a good time with you, but you kept fighting with me. Telling me not to touch you."

"Why didn't you just leave me alone then?" she screams.

"Hell nah," he responds smugly. "You talked too much shit about what you wanted me to do to you and I wanted to make sure you got all that and more. But then you tried passing out on me. We still got it in." He has the nerve to laugh when he talks about how Essence acted after he drugged her.

Essence is speechless. She reaches for Zola's hand, tears streaming down her face as she listens to Rex recounting some of the things he watched her do. When I can't take any more of his account of the events, I snatch the phone from her and yell into the camera,

"You're a jackass, Rex and our parents will be pressing criminal charges."

Then I hang up and throw the phone on the bed. My heart breaks as I watch Essence whimper helplessly and hopelessly in the arms of a girl she hardly knows. I would give anything to be able to hug her and nuzzle our noses right now.

When I try to talk to Essence, she completely loses it. She puts Zola and me out, saying she never wants to speak to either one of us again in life, so we leave her.

"She doesn't mean that," I tell Zola as we walk down the hall. "If you decide you wanna be bothered with her, give her a few days. Otherwise, it is what is. Just promise me you won't show anybody that video . . . ever."

"I'm cool, Twin. No hard feelings. And you got my word, this won't be seen by anybody."

ALONE IN MY ROOM, I DESPERATELY WANT TO BE WITH Essence. At the same time, I so mad at how she carried on, not just that night, but it seems like this is her usual behavior. I just wanna punch her. How did she stray so far away? How could I not have known? If I had been less annoying, maybe she wouldn't have pushed me away. Then I would have been able to stop her. Guilt overwhelms me on top of everything else. If this were any other situation, I'd call my mom and she would tell me how to handle it. Mom isn't an option. No one is. I collapse into tears.

Several hours later, I wake up to multiple messages from Eye Candy, Mercedes, and a few other people. The thought of talking to anybody right now puts me on the verge of a panic attack, which means I definitely need to bring my emotions down. First, I meditate. Then, pray. I'm led to my journal to release my feelings.

Today I start fresh. I am better than I was. I am ____

I write **HORRIFIED**

Sunday, November 11, 2018

Hi. Something awful happened to Sisi but I don't know how bad it was. She doesn't remember because she was doing drugs and drinking. I can't believe it. I'm so pissed at her. How could this happen and how could I not know she was into this crazy stuff. This could all be my fault as much as hers. She needs help – maybe medical and legal help. But she is so mad at me now and I'm probably the last person she would want involved in her mess. Our parents need to know what happened, but she would kill me if I told anybody. I'm stuck here helpless and afraid. ttyl.

SORROW FOR MY SISTER FILLS MY HEART THROUGH NIGHTFALL and I cry myself to sleep, fearful of what the coming days will bring.

Chapter Thirty-Three

E ssence was really torn up about Rex for exactly forty-eight
hours. Bianca stayed with her most of that time. I heard
she cried, pitied herself, and asked why. Then she got really mad.
That lasted another forty-eight hours.

That's when Bianca finally tapped out emotionally and
suggested that Essence let me help her through this because I'm
the only other person, besides Zola, who knows about it.
Essence agreed, no doubt because she was tired of Bianca. So,
for the past day and a half, I've been her sounding board, her
confidante, and her cheerleader. It's been weird because she's
treating me like a new friend, not someone she's known all her
life. Maybe I should just be grateful for whatever I can get.
Hmmm. Grateful? That can be my journal word today.

Today I start fresh. I am better than I was. I am _____

I write **GRATEFUL**

Sunday, November 4, 2018

*Hi. It's been a long time since Sisi, and I have been able to be
together and not fight or want to fight. We worked that out and now
she actually sees me as somebody. Not a problem but as a solution.
Better than before when she just used me. That's not how it is now.
Never stopped loving her. Even when I hated her. But I like her*

again. We're still rebuilding our friendship but I'm thankful we are moving in the right direction. ttyl

THIS DAY BRINGS A SURPRISING MORNING MESSAGE FROM Essence.

Es: About 2 change everything. Hair 2. Will tell u more after I get back from church.

Change? Church? These words make no sense in relation to Essence, but I want to stay encouraging.

Me: K. Happy for u

ESSENCE RETURNS AROUND FIVE O'CLOCK AND IMMEDIATELY summons me to join her for dinner. She's brought pizza from Antonelli's, I think because she knew I couldn't refuse it. When I walk in her room, I ignore the waiting food because she's given her room a complete makeover. She purchased a new bedding set, accent pillows, and an area rug. She also took down her black and white prints of the Empire State Building, Brooklyn Bridge, and Apollo Theater and hung a reprint of the U.S. Capitol portrait of Shirley Chisholm by Kadir Nelson and a picture of Beyoncé. I'm not sure what her thinking is, but maybe it's some kind of girl power theme: "Unbossed" meets "Who Runs The World." Makes sense.

While we eat, Essence expresses how she needs more happiness in her life.

"Major change is how I plan to get that," she says. "Obviously, you see I redecorated my room. What do you think?"

It's not clear to me how these new purchases will have any lasting effect on Essence's contentment, but for now, I'll continue to encourage her.

"Looks good," I reply and add, "It's brighter now and looks and feels more like your room at home."

"You think so? I hadn't realized that. Cool. Maybe I'll still change out the lamps and get a different desk chair."

Essence also mentioned that she wanted me to change her hair. That's why really I'm here. She needed my help taking out her crochet braids. This would ordinarily be Bianca's job, but they're "taking a break" while Essence "resets," as she says, but I know the real deal.

I'm just here to be a supportive friend, not to judge, so we tackle her hair after we eat our fill of pizza.

"What's the plan for this hair after these braids are out?" I ask Essence as we both dissect out rows of crochet braids that have been latched into her own hair.

"Natural . . . kinda like yours?"

Hmm. She definitely put a question mark at the end of that sentence.

"Are you asking for my permission? Because I have no control over you so don't fake like I do," I comment.

"I'm not asking permission because you're right I don't need it. But we're gonna end up looking more alike once I go natural. How you gonna feel about that?"

"It's whatever. But so much for the individuality you fought so hard for all these months," I say, rolling my eyes.

"That was less about how we looked and more about who we are. We'll still have our different personalities. I'm probably gonna change my hair color eventually anyway. Or cut it really short. I feel like doing something crazy."

Umm. . . something *else* crazy. But I don't say that.

The one change Essence is making that I applaud and receive without questioning is in her attitude toward me. She doesn't treat me like an enemy. Now I'm more of a friend, working my way back up to sister. I'm sure it's because she knows I can dime her out to our parents at any moment. And not a day goes by when she doesn't beg me not to tell them her secret.

"Bunnie, I swear, I'll do anything for you, but please don't ever tell Mom and Daddy what happened."

Each time, I assure her I'm not going to say anything, but she better not still be seeing that creep. And I remind her constantly that she should press charges against him.

The issue of going to the police is still a sensitive one. Zola and I both told Essence she had enough evidence to show he committed a crime. But the evidence is mainly the videotape and she won't let anyone see it for any reason. Bianca hasn't even seen it, but she knows it exists. Rex still needs to be punished. I'm tempted to call Khalil to find out if he knows anybody who can beat him up or at least break out the windows of his fancy cars. He'd probably think I was the one who needed to go to jail. It's still a thought.

Listening to Essence talk about her new attitude and changes to her life makes me wonder if she's just expressing how hurt she still is over Rex. That situation would have anybody to' up from the flo' up. But her denial is deeper than the river in Egypt. Until she conquers that, she can change the outside all she wants. She'll never fully heal.

"Thanks for helping me with my hair, Bunnie. It's such a chore," Essence says two hours into the process.

To that, I respond by saying "No problem. I do nice stuff like this for people all the time."

"So you're suggesting I've missed out on that because we haven't been on good terms? That's what you're getting at?"

"You said it, not me. But yeah. Why would I do nice things for somebody who hated me the way you did?"

Essence doesn't seem bothered or surprised by my comment. It's almost as if she expected it after all these months of her abuse and negativity. Yet, she says nothing. She just leaves my words hanging like leaves dangling on a tree limb after brisk autumn winds.

When Essence finally responds to the question I asked more than a minute ago, she turns to me. Her eyes are downcast, but her tone is light.

"I never hated you."

"Then what was with the cruel and unusual punishment you inflicted on me this past year?"

"That's a bit much, Miss Drama Queen."

Now she wants to be offended by my characterization of the

abuse I've endured at her hands. My words reflect how I felt so, whatever.

"The simple answer is I was angry." She continues by admitting, "And you were the person I took it out on."

"Because I made you angry?" I wonder aloud.

"No, not directly. My anger grew from never being seen apart from you. For years, I just wanted to be me, not anybody's twin. Apparently, that was blasphemy according to your parents."

"Oh, now they're mine?" I say with a slight smile. "But seriously, why couldn't you be you and be my twin?" I ask.

Essence snaps. "Because when I tried to do that you went all crybaby on me and I knew I was gonna have to keep you by my side, or at least close behind."

Wow. That hurt.

"Whoever told you to do that didn't ask me," I snap back.

She breathes deeply and calms down. "Nobody told me to do it. It was just a natural response, I guess," she explains.

"But you got all Daddy's attention. I got none. That should've been enough to make you feel like you existed apart from me."

The smirk on Essence's face tells me there's a story behind our father's hyper-interest in 'all things Essence.'

"You know why Daddy started paying more attention to me? Because one day, when we were fourteen or fifteen, Mom told me I couldn't do something unless you came along. You didn't wanna come so she made me stay with you. I cried to Daddy about how Mom never gave me any attention because she was always babying you. After that, he started picking up her slack."

"He's gone to the extreme with it now, don't you think?"

"Maybe, he has. But that's more because he doesn't know what to do with you, Bunnie."

"Wow, that makes me feel good."

I shake my head knowing my own father doesn't care enough to try, just a little bit, to be my father. He'd rather just let me struggle out here while he watches, waiting to criticize me.

"Don't take it the wrong way. Look, you know Kingston lived

in Daddy's shadow and followed in his footsteps, so he was easy for Daddy to raise."

"And it's the same with you," I interject. "Point you in the direction and off you go being fabulous, exceeding everyone's expectations, mastering the universe. But not me, right? Isn't that what you're gonna say?"

"Yeah, kinda. But that's not bad. Well, maybe it's bad for Mom and Daddy, but if that's your reality, own it. Besides trying to live up to somebody else's hopes for you will guarantee that you'll never be happy. What does Grandma Patsy always say, 'You can't fit a square peg into a round hole?' You're a square peg and maybe Daddy's idea of you is a round hole that you'll never fit into."

Essence just blew my entire mind with that nugget. I still think about the fact that my own dad has such a misguided idea of who I am that he can't help but have misinformed expectations of who I can be. Funny, my mom seems to get me. I guess they're just as different as me and Essence.

"Okay. I'm with you on the square peg thing," I tell Essence, "But I'm stuck on why you had to be so mean to me. If you wanted space, you could've just told me."

"That didn't work. Trust me, I tried," she says.

She's probably right about that. If she had told me to give her space, I'm not sure I would have known how to do that since I was so socially dependent on her at that time.

"And don't forget, how you hijacked my whole college experience. That had me in my feelings, too."

"That's not fair," I say. "You know I never wanted to be here. They made me come. I'd be done if it wasn't for Mercedes and Kendra."

"And Cam," she throws in.

"Yeah, and Cam." Just saying his name makes me smile.

"Whatever, so when Mom and Daddy told me you would be coming to Bryce, too, I was so pissed. They didn't tell me it was their idea, so I just figured it was yours. There were so many things I wanted to say to you and to them, but I held it inside.

That probably made me feel worse. Daddy told me it would be okay if we lived in different dorms, had different friends, and stayed in different social lanes. So that's what I tried to do. What I didn't expect was that everybody here would be obsessed with 'the twins.' The very thing I tried to escape had followed me here."

The more Essence explains her motivations, the more I wish she just hated me. All these other feelings she had about me and about our relationship were completely opposite of what I felt. It's hard to grasp everything she's telling me now, but looking back on the past year, it definitely explains why she acted like such a . . . not nice person.

"And I'll tell you one last thing, Bunnie, only because it's really what put me over the edge and convinced me I had to do something drastic. There was a super cute boy who I had been crushing on from the first day of my freshman English class. He started being real nice to me and had me thinking he wanted to go out with me. One day, he told me he really just wanted me to introduce him to you. Girl, I was so bent. No guy had ever chosen you over me, mainly because we didn't go after the same guys. No shade. Different tastes. My self-esteem plummeted and it felt like everything I had imagined my college experience would be was about to be tanked . . . by you."

"You know I had no idea about any of this," I remind her.

"Yeah, but that's a rational thought and I wasn't having those then. Anyway, to save myself and my dream college life, I created an alter ego as different and as separate from you as possible so people would never expect to see you when they saw me."

"So, once again, you sacrificed me to benefit yourself."

Saying that out loud makes it all make sense. It doesn't make it right, or any less painful. And it still feels like she did all of this because she hated me, no matter how she disguises it.

"Yeah," she admits. "Putting it like that sounds harsh, and I know it was. Obviously, I messed up and I was an awful person. But I apologize. I honestly didn't set out to hurt you. Please tell me you forgive me."

As much as I want to be mad and punish her for the pain she caused me, I feel nothing but love. Actually my entire body is flooded with emotions of love and forgiveness, which something in me, perhaps my angels, force me to pour out into her.

"Of course I forgive you, Sisi. But understand, I don't want to be you. Besides, I couldn't be you as well as you can. And I don't want your life because I couldn't live it like you. Even though I'm still figuring myself out, I know I'll be much happier being me and not following anybody else's blueprint. Obviously, I'll never be part of your Bryce world, and I may not live up to Daddy's plan for me ever, but that's not what I want anyway. My Bryce life and my own dreams work for me."

Essence looks relieved and says, "I love you, Bun, and I'm really happy to be your twin."

"Yeah. Me, too."

AFTER THAT TALK WITH ESSENCE, I NEEDED A DAY OR SO TO process our conversation and the new emotions Essence's words caused to flow, especially relating to my dad. I took that time away from her to . . . heal. I'm feeling better now and I'm ready to embrace this better relationship with her.

ESSENCE HAS COMPLETELY CHANGED HER ATTITUDE TOWARD me. Now, we speak to each other in public and she lets me borrow her clothes without asking for personal references or requiring a security deposit. We still don't hang out together socially, mainly because I'm not a fan of any of her friends. We also don't fight anymore. If we disagree about something, and often we do, we try to work it out or politely agree to disagree.

The best improvement has been that we have what I call our "twin-time," where we just hang out in her room or mine and enjoy being sisters. It's just enough time to keep us both grounded and connected, but not so much that I become dependent on her or she feels she needs to return to her antagonistic ways. And it's in private, so her reputation is preserved.

Sometimes we're together for just fifteen minutes; other times we spend hours together. No matter how long it is, for that entire time we are once again interchangeable, indistinguishable, inseparable twins. I celebrate this development in my journal.

Today I start fresh. I am better than I was. I am ____

I write **RECLAIMED**

Tuesday, November 13, 2018

Hi. I've neglected you over the past few days. There's been so much happening. The result of it all is that Sisi and I have been working to fix what was broken between us and we're becoming friends and sisters, and hopefully one day, twins again. It's different this time because even though we're identical, the parts of us that are different are what we love the most and we'll let the world see more of that side of us. I really do believe that I am enough now. She recognizes it too. Now to work on Daddy. SMH. ttyl

Chapter Thirty-Four

At breakfast this morning, Kendra brings news about a protest the BSU is organizing. The plan developed after a Black Bryce soccer player got thrown off the team because he knelt during the national anthem at a game. The player was inspired by Colin Kaepernick to take a stand against racial injustice and police brutality because, the week before, his own brother was arrested under false pretenses and badly beaten by the cops. They claimed he was resisting, but dashcam video showed he wasn't.

On top of that, there have been more instances of racial profiling by Campus Security. Bryce Security Officers still don't seem to understand that Black students have the right to enjoy any and every part of this campus.

The BSU wants all people of color to protest these injustices by kneeling during the national anthem at the next Bryce home game, which happens to be tomorrow's basketball season opener. The school administration already warned the team that any player who "disrespects this nation and The Star Bangled Banner could face discipline, including loss of school-sponsored scholarships." For the Black kids, that could mean having to leave school.

Everybody wants to know whether or not Eye Candy plans to

participate in the protest. He's been stopped and detained by Campus Security more times than a few, so it would make sense for him to do it. And he's friends with the soccer player who got in trouble last week. He hasn't told me or anyone what he plans to do. BSU leaders and others associated with the protest not only hound him daily, but now they're pressing me to convince him to join the cause.

"We really need them all to take a stand," Jax said when he cornered me at The Cove earlier today. "He's the leader on the team. If he does it, I'm sure his teammates will follow him."

"But he's really worried about getting kicked out of school," I explain.

"That won't happen. The lawsuits would bankrupt this place, especially if they all did it."

"I'm not sure it's that simple," I replied.

He pleaded, "Just talk to him. The game is tomorrow and it would be great to know in advance if he'll do it."

I agreed to try but don't plan to bring anything up with Eye Candy unless he does. I'm trying to be his safe place away from the madness in these streets, not another person stirring up controversy.

Lucky for me, the subject of the protest hasn't come up when Eye Candy and I have talked or texted today. But that might be about to change based on the text message he just sent me.

EC: Can u come by after your class 2nite? Need 2 talk

Ordinarily, Eye Candy would come to my room to hang out because he has suitemates and that limits our privacy. And he hates me being out alone at night, so this is an odd request.

Me: U don't wanna come to me?

EC: Can't leave.Too much noise out there but wanna c u

Me: K C u soon

WHEN I GET TO HIS ROOM, EYE CANDY IS IN BED, STREAMING a web series on his laptop. I kick my shoes off and slide next to him. We watch a few episodes of the show, which is about strange things happening in a small Indiana town after some kid disappears. Our conversation is light. We talk about the 80's throwback vibe of the show, his love and my hatred for thrillers and horror movies in general, and the plot twists that have my brain spinning.

After three episodes, Eye Candy closes his lap top and says, "That was a nice escape."

This feels like an opening for a conversation about the protest.

"You wanna talk?" I ask.

"This thing is weighing heavy on me. The game is less than 24 hours away and I haven't figured out what to do. I'm definitely down for speaking out against the effed up system we got, but I can't lose my money."

"Jax doesn't think that would happen," I say, hoping to offer some assurance. "The school could get sued."

He laughs cynically. "What the hell does that rich pretty boy know about that?" he asserts in a condescending way. "Maybe that would work in his world, but my pops would kill me before any lawsuit papers got filed in court."

"But wrong is wrong," I reply.

"Easy for you to say, too. What do you have to lose? It's not your scholarship that's at risk. Your spot on the team isn't in jeopardy. It's my entire future on the line, so wrong might end up getting a pass this time," he snaps back.

I don't take his tone personally because this is not about me. Rather, I let him continue to speak freely and without interruption.

"Some of my teammates have already publicly said they'd never do it. They support the cause but can't jeopardize their scholarship eligibility. It's messed up we have to make that choice."

"What do you plan to do?" I ask.

"Wish I knew. But that's all everybody wants to talk about. Everywhere I go, people saying do it. Then some saying don't. Nobody wants to talk about basketball. Y'all forget we have a game to play tomorrow, a game we wanted to win. Now, with all this B.S., who knows."

"Don't say y'all. I'm on your side."

"I know. My bad on that. Let's stop talking about it. How about we watch one more episode then I'll get you back to your room because it's almost lights out for me."

One more episode turns into three. At eleven o'clock, Eye Candy turns the lights out, but with me asleep in his arms.

Chapter Thirty-Five

The next morning, I wake up super early and sneak out of Eye Candy's room and return to my own, while he's sound asleep. After I shower, I send him a message since by now he should be up and getting ready for Public Speaking like me.

Me: GM babe. what's good?

EC: U

Me: :-) u must b feeln ok 2day

EC: Not really

Me: Coming to class?

EC: Nah. gotta lay low & clear my head

Me: Need anything?

EC: your hugs

Me: LOL c u after class

AFTER SITTING THROUGH THE LONGEST TWO CLASSES IN THE history of my college education, I pick up some food from The Cove and take it to Eye Candy. When I walk in his room, he's sitting on the floor listening to classical music looking very relaxed.

He motions for me to join him.

"Nice music," I say as I sit down. "Is it helping?"

"Yeah. I needed a reset after talking to my dad."

I'm unable to read his face to tell whether or not the conversation with his dad went well so I ask, "What did he say?"

"He told me to make the responsible decision."

"Did he say what that was?"

"He didn't have to."

We don't linger on the subject. He asks about the food he smells, since I hadn't mentioned that I was bringing anything to eat.

"Brought you a little snack," I say, passing him the bag. "Wasn't sure if you had eaten today."

Turns out he hadn't. I'm glad I prepared for his appetite because he inhaled the first sandwich and had started on the second before I knew it. He worried me when he started reaching into the empty bag looking for something more.

"You can't still be hungry," I say. "What are you looking for?"

Jokingly, he says, "Thought you were bringing me a hug. Where's that?"

I laugh and extend my arms. He falls into them and I hold him hoping to take away his troubles and encourage his spirit. We move from the floor to his bed and lay together quietly until we both fall asleep. When we wake up, it's almost four-thirty.

"Guess I need to get to the gym," he announces, sounding resigned, no longer enthusiastic about his long-awaited Bryce debut.

"Whatever you decide to do, I gotchu," I say, while hugging him as tightly as I can.

He thanks me with a sweet, tender, emotion-filled kiss.

Mercedes and Kendra are coming to my room to hang out before the game. In the few quiet moments before they show up, I write an entry in my journal.

Today I start fresh. I am better than I was. I am ＿＿＿

I write **AFRAID**

November 16, 2018

Hi. Today is the big game and all the Black and Brown kids are ready to riot. What's happening is wrong and we all should have a right to speak against it – even the student athletes. I know Eye Candy wants to support the cause, but he can't lose his scholarship. I'm praying whatever angels he has watching over him lead him to the right decision. I'm scared for what might happen today. No matter what choice he makes, he'll be miserable. And I will too. ttyl

MY GIRLS ARRIVE WITH GOURMET BOX MEALS THE ATHLETIC department distributed as part of the tailgate event we're not attending. Mercedes and Kendra seem to be enjoying the food. I can hardly eat any of it. My stomach is in knots thinking about Eye Candy.

"Any word on what Cam's gonna do tonight?" Kendra asks.

"No. But he's getting a lot of pressure from everybody and he's real stressed."

"The school knows they wrong for threatening to take away the players' scholarships. That right there is racist, because it's us on scholarship."

"So true," I say.

"Well, Chicas, let's get going so we can get good seats," Mercedes says. "You know that place is gonna be packed."

AS EXPECTED, THE GYMNASIUM IS ALMOST FULL WHEN WE arrive and tip-off isn't for another thirty minutes. We're able to find seats close enough to the team bench so I can see Eye Candy. He's sitting by himself with his sound cancellation head phones on. Kendra says he's probably getting in his zone, but I know he's still trying to block out the protest noise.

A loud buzzer goes off and both teams leave the floor. The Bryce Cheer squad and mascot perform for fifteen minutes or so. Then the announcer introduces the opposing team and their coaches. All the gym lights go off after that and the DJ plays a sick music mix that begins with the chorus from "All the Way Up," as the Bryce team and coaches come back onto the court. The crowd erupts with cheers and applause, which build when the announcer introduces the Bryce starting line-up. As soon he says, "At guard, number twenty-three, Cameron Gregory," the place explodes again. Number twenty-three shows no reaction on his face, but he does pump his fist in the air.

Players and coaches from both sides stand in front of their benches.

The announcer says, "Please rise for the national anthem, performed by Nicole Lindsey, Senior Vocal Major from Los Angeles, California.

Most of the people in the building stand.

"O say can you see by the dawn's early light . . ."

Black and Brown people throughout the stands kneel.

Mercedes, Kendra, and I kneel.

"What so proudly we hailed . . ."

To my surprise, Eye Candy kneels. Harrison, the white team captain, also kneels.

When the song ends, the crowd chants "Black Lives Matter" easily for ten minutes delaying the game.

Eye Candy and Harrison walk to the bench together, but they're intercepted by the Coach and Campus Security, who send them to the locker room. They never return. The game proceeds and Bryce loses miserably.

During the entire game, I try calling and texting Eye Candy, but he doesn't respond. About twenty of us linger in the gym after everyone else leaves, waiting to find out what happened. Campus Security eventually comes and clears us all out.

Before going to my room, I go to Eye Candy's dorm to see if he's there, but I don't find him. He finally sends me a text at one in the morning.

EC: I'm off the team.

I jump outta bed and call him immediately. His voicemail answers. He doesn't respond to the text I send. I'm so undone.

By sunrise, everyone has heard that Eye Candy was cut from the team, but Harrison was suspended for just one game. The administration felt the reason behind Eye Candy's actions was "more divisive and justified a harsher penalty." We all know that's bull. On the real, Harrison's dad is a big donor and if Harrison got punished too harshly, his daddy would close the checkbook.

The BSU is already circulating a petition to demand Eye Candy be put back on the team. Only problem – nobody knows where he is. Not even me. He hasn't communicated with me since that last text. I'm so worried about him and write about that in my journal.

Today I start fresh. I am better than I was. I am ____

I write **WORRIED**

Saturday November 17, 2018

Hi. Last night was a disaster. Eye Candy did what he thought was right and got kicked off the team. He must be devastated. No one can find him now. I don't know what to do. I'm so worried about him. I'm praying the angels that led him into this situation are taking care of him. But I need to know he's ok. ttyl

At around nine o'clock this morning, Eye Candy finally sends me a message.

EC: ok 2 come by?

Me: definitely

EC: b there n a hour

One hour. That's means I have to move quickly. I'm able to shower, do my hair, and lightly beat my face. As I prepare to put on my clothes I hear a knock on my door. It's too early to be Eye Candy and anybody else who I might want to see knows not to come to my room unannounced this early on a Saturday.

I ignore the knock so I can finish getting dressed, but it continues. "I'm busy. Who is it?" I yell through the closed door.

No response just more knocking. I throw on my robe and

fling the door open, ready to call the person on the other side all kinds of names.

Before I can speak a word, my unwanted morning visitor says, "Hey, Princess."

"Donovan," I reply in disbelief. "Why are you here?"

"Is that any way to greet me? Can I come in?"

"No," I say, "now is not a good time. I'm not even dressed."

"I've seen your goodies already." He pushes the door open, walks into my room, and closes the door.

I tighten the belt of my robe and get back to trying to figure out what he wants, and more importantly, how to get rid of him before Eye Candy arrives.

"Why are you here?" I ask again.

"To see you. What's going on? You looking as delicious as ever," he says, licking his lips and moving closer toward me. "Take that robe off and show me what you're hiding."

I push him away and put as much distance as I can between us.

"You shouldn't be here. You need to leave," I tell him.

"Aww, come on. Can't we just hang out for a little while? Then I promise I'll go."

"No, we can't. I'm expecting someone any minute and you can't be here."

"Must be a dude." He's fishing for information.

"None of your business. Now go. Please?"

I try pushing him toward the door but any physical contact between us emboldens him. And he's not taking me seriously.

Finally, I just say, "Look, my boyfriend is on his way. So I need you to leave."

"Boyfriend? Wow. I didn't expect to hear that."

"Meaning what?" I ask, taking mild offense to his statement. "Never mind. It doesn't matter. I just need you to leave."

"Okay, Princess. I'll go. But a boyfriend? Wow. Lucky guy. Hope to meet him one day."

"Ummm....No. That ain't happening."

"Guess that would be awkward," he says, laughing.

Donovan leans in to hug me. I push him away and fold my arms across my chest to send what I hope is a clear signal that I'm off-limits to him. He gets the message. As he walks to the door, he turns back around, I'm thinking, to say good-bye. Instead, he looks at me, deeply and with the same desire he had that night in that park. For a split hair of a second, I feel myself being drawn in to his energy. Thankfully, by the grace of my angels, I snap out of it. I reach past him and open the door and say, "Please just leave."

He smiles and replies, "Okay. Be good, Princess."

I close the door behind him, relieved that Eye Candy didn't show up in the middle of that. Literally, within seconds, I hear a knock on my door again. Donovan better not be coming back. I take a deep breath and open the door.

"Didn't I tell you that you can't be here . . . Oh. Wassup?"

I try to turn my exasperated tone into a welcoming one. The look on Eye Candy's face tells me I didn't succeed.

"Why the hell was that dude leaving your room?"

"What dude?"

Why did I say that? I know perfectly well who he's talking about. And he knows I know.

"Don't play with me, Ebony. The guy I saw you kiss at the party. Why was he here? I thought you said nothing was going on between y'all."

"Nothing is going on. He just showed up a few minutes ago unannounced. When you saw him, he was leaving because I told him he had to go."

"Really? So he has it like that to where he can just show up on a Saturday morning uninvited? I don't even do that and we're supposed to be..."

Eye Candy doesn't finish his thought and it's not because he can't find the words. He's just mad.

"People I know have shown up at my room unannounced before. It happens to you, too. It's no big deal."

My attempt to minimize Donovan's intrusion goes nowhere as Eye Candy points out, "It is a big deal when a guy you had something romantic with does it twice and gets you so caught up that you lie to me."

"Hold on, I never lied about anything," I insist and actually am insulted that he would even say that.

"Oh, let me correct myself," Eye Candy says sarcastically. "You just pretended you didn't know who I was talking about just now when I asked about him leaving your room."

Before I can respond to that point, he fires another shot. "What makes this even worse, is that thing you got barely covering your body is very enticing to a man's eye. Especially to a man who knows what's under it, which I'm guessing he does."

He pauses, probably waiting for me to confirm or deny his supposition. At this point, the last thing I want to do is open that pandora's box.

When I don't comment, he continues. "He shouldn't get to see you like this. I know what it does to me and it makes me sick thinking he had any of those same urges."

There's no way to deny that Donovan was turned on seeing me, but I could've had on overalls and a lumber jack shirt. He would've had the same reaction. But Eye Candy makes a good point.

"Okay, when you say it like that, I totally get it. But I never thought this robe made me look any kinda way except covered up. That was my objective when I put it on. When I heard the knock on the door, I grabbed it thinking it was one of the girls on the hall."

Eye Candy is listening to me, but from the unemotional expression on his face, he's not hearing a word I'm saying, or he's just not interested in the truth. From his perspective, this looks bad. But he knows me and should know my heart. I'd never do anything like what he's thinking. Getting him to see that feels like an impossible feat.

"Something about this doesn't feel right," he says. "Maybe it's everything that's going on with me today or maybe I'm more scarred than I realized from catching my mom cheating on my dad."

"Or it could be all of that," I reply, trying to express the empathy I feel. "But please listen to what I'm telling you. He showed up here, not because of anything I said or did. We haven't had any communication since the party. He means nothing to me and he shouldn't be causing this tension between us, especially not today."

"Exactly. Not today. This was already one of the worst days of my life and now I gotta wonder about this guy coming between us."

"You definitely don't have to wonder about that because I would never do that to you or to us. I'm not interested in him at all."

Eye Candy then bluntly asks, "Did you kiss him today?"

"Of course not, don't be ridiculous. I would never do that."

"Did he try to kiss you?"

"No. He didn't try to kiss me," I say firmly. "There was nothing physical. It wasn't like that."

"That's the one good thing in this, I guess. But this is the second time he's come after you since we've been together. Either he's not getting the message, or you're not sending the right one."

"I've told him I don't want to have anything to do with him. It's not my fault if he doesn't listen. I'm not sure what else you want me to do."

"So he's always gonna be a problem for us?" Eye Candy asks, his tone becoming more abrasive.

"That's not what I'm saying. What I'm telling you is no matter what he wants or does, you're my only priority. Please believe that."

Eye Candy doesn't say anything, even as my pleading becomes more desperate. Every word I say seems to be falling on deaf ears and a hardened heart.

"You know what," he finally says, "I got way too much on me right now to deal with this. How 'bout I let you work this one out by yourself. I'm done," he says, brashly.

"No, please don't do that," I beg. "This is just a misunderstanding. I'm really sorry."

"You can keep that. I got enough sorry people in my life. I don't need another one."

Eye Candy walks out, leaving me in shock, standing in the middle of my room. As the reality of what just happened sinks in, the pain I feel intensifies. My head feels like it might burst from all the thoughts and words and feelings that can't find a way of escape or a place to dissolve into. I know the earth is spinning, but my world is at a standstill. I'm not sure if I'm even breathing. I suddenly feel very dizzy and light-headed and my body is pulled to the floor. Where I sit. Hurt. Dazed. Mind racing about so many things, none of which makes any sense right now. I'm lost. I'm at a loss. And now, I'm losing it.

A volcano of emotions begins to erupt from deep inside me - heartache, disappointment, regret, emptiness. All I have left are tears, which flow from my heart like a waterfall.

At some point, I must've cried myself to sleep because I wake up lying on the floor, surrounded by my own sorrow. Daylight has turned dark. I have no idea what time it is and don't really care. I find the strength to move from the floor to my bed.

In my half-sleep state, I think I hear Essence and her loud-talking friends outside my door. At first, I'm not sure if this is real or a dream. Essence dismisses her friends and my door opens slowly. She peeks inside my room before coming in and sits on the edge of the bed close to me. Ugly tears start flowing again. I know she wants to tell me to stop crying because it's a messy cry and Essence doesn't like messy. She says nothing, which says so much. I appreciate that she just sits with me and lets my tears have their way.

"You'll be okay, Bunnie." She whispers this every so often.

I try to hold on to her every word as if it's a pinky promise.

Essence tries to wipe away my tears with her hands, but they keep falling. She curls up by my side and wraps herself around me. Within minutes, our breathing, our heart beats, our beings fall in sync. We lay together, tightly wound until I have no more tears to cry.

"Are you ready to talk now?" she asks in a voice so gentle, I wouldn't have believed it came from Essence if I hadn't been laying next to her.

I take several deep breaths. "We had a huge fight over some stupid misunderstanding and he . . . " I try not to cry through this story, but the tears win again. "I think it's over, Sisi. He's so mad at me, but I didn't do anything. And I don't understand any of this." I ramble on, but my words get jumbled by my sobbing. I never intended to share any of this with Essence for a lot of reasons, mainly because she and I handle major disappointments way differently. She's more of the 'get up, brush yourself off, and get back in the game' person, like Kendra. I'm the total opposite; more like the 'falling out, torn to pieces, ugly crying' person. Essence usually has no patience for my ways, but today, she lets me be me.

As I lay with my sister, her presence eases the turmoil raging inside of me. Eventually, my pain diminishes and I fall asleep. Essence does, too.

SOME TIME LATER, COULD BE MINUTES, COULD BE HOURS, I wake up to find our arms and legs entangled again. Our hearts beating in sync. Our breaths sharing the same rhythm. We connect to the original source that gave both of us life in the same instant.

Her eyes open too, and she begins to unwrap herself from me. She kisses me then we nuzzle noses. Essence gets up and leaves. She doesn't say anything, she just walks out. I guess she's done enough sistering duty for one day and now she can return to her regularly scheduled programming.

Not too much later, as I start feeling totally abandoned, Essence comes back in her PJs with freshly brushed teeth and washed face. She plops back down on the bed next to me, shoos me over, steals my pillow, and kisses me goodnight.

I hate that I'm so bad off that Essence feels like she needs to spend the night with me, but I don't know how I would get through this if she didn't. I close my eyes and whisper a litany of prayers, thanking God for her and begging Him to get me through this ordeal quickly.

Before I start making deals with Him, saying what I will or won't do if only He does me this solid right now, I drift off to sleep, probably mid-sentence. That might have been a good thing because I'm never able to hold up my end of those deals anyway. And I already have enough trouble as it is.

Essence and I wake up the next morning around the same time. She looks pretty drained. I'm sure I look a heck of a lot worse.

"You didn't sleep too well, Bunnie."

"I know. Sorry if I kept you up."

"I'm cool." Essence pauses to wipe a tear from my cheek. It feels like she has something to say so I brace myself.

"You wanna tell me exactly what happened? I don't like that he hurt you like this."

Is Essence thinking about doing harm to my man . . . my ex-man? Uggh. I hate how that sounds. Whatever the case, I need to squash this.

"He didn't do anything, so please don't you do anything."

"Okay. Because you know I was getting ready. So what happened?"

I tell her the whole story. Now she gets why I say Eye Candy overreacted to the extreme.

"But honestly, Bun, guys are different. It's all ego with them. The worst thing a woman can do to a man's ego is cheat on him. Maybe cheating on him with one of his boys is the absolute worse."

"I didn't cheat. Nothing happened. But he won't believe me. He wouldn't even listen."

"In a sad way, it doesn't matter what you did. Think about it.

He just got kicked off the basketball team and then he catches you in a weird situation with a guy he saw you kissing a few months before? He's not thinking right."

"So I'm being punished for him getting kicked off the team, for his mom cheating on his dad, and for Donovan being an asshole. Why is that fair?"

"Hold up. His mom cheated?"

I'm hesitant to give out the details of Eye Candy's personal life, but I trust Essence not to blab her mouth.

"He caught his mom with another man, just kissing, but still. His parents split up after that."

Essence shakes her head and sighs deeply, then says, "This is bad."

"Duh, I know that," I yell.

Essence wants to check me for yelling at her, but doesn't. I appreciate that. She just says, "Give him a day or two, then call him. He might be less emotional and more rational. Whatever happens, I promise you, this won't hurt forever."

Essence's words always gave me hope when we were kids. I pray they still have that power.

"I gotta go," she says as she jumps up and heads to the door. "I'll check on you later."

I pray she does. When she leaves, I can still feel her presence and the comfort it brings me. I let that feeling cradle me all day and into the night, as the pain in my heart sharpens. I'm beginning to think that I must actually love him; otherwise it wouldn't hurt like this. I hate everything right now. My hope of hopes is that joy will come in the morning.

Chapter Thirty-Six

Today I start fresh. I am better than I was. I am ____
I write **BROKEN**
Monday, November 19, 2018

Hi. Whoever said "it's better to have loved and lost than never to have loved before," told a big fat ghetto lie. I would be so much better if I had never met him and never loved him. My heart wouldn't be shattered into a million pieces right now. I still can't make sense of what happened. Mercedes and Kendra have been really supportive. Sisi has too. But it still hurts so much. ttyl

IT'S BEEN TWO FULL DAYS SINCE WE BROKE UP. I HAVEN'T LEFT my room since. Eye Candy hasn't responded to my calls or texts. There's no chance I'm going to my Public Speaking class today. I'm not ready to see him and have him treat me like his ex-girlfriend. What if he doesn't speak when he sees me, or if he says something mean to me or about me to his friends? What if I see him with another girl? All these "what ifs" are why I'm skipping class today and maybe for the rest of the year.

A knock on my door takes me by surprise. It's too early for any visitors, not that I'm in the mood to see people anyway.

"Please go away," I yell.

"Bunnie, we're coming in."

That's my sister's voice but, she doesn't have a "we" that I want to deal with right now.

"No. Go away," I whimper.

Essence opens the door and Mercedes and Kendra walk in with her. I want to be mad at all three of them, but I'm actually glad they're here.

Mercedes says, "Hey, Chica," and comes to my bedside and hugs me. "Sorry to bust in on you. But we hadn't heard from you since yesterday. We wanna help you get through this," she explains.

"That's right," Kendra says.

Essence apologizes saying, "Bunnie, I'm sorry, but you need your friends."

Kendra signs on to that statement. "Yeah, Eb. We're here for you. Whatever you need."

"Come on, let us help you. Dealing with this alone will only make you feel worse," Mercedes says. "This is your first real heartbreak and it's hard. But we been through it before and we'll help you get to the other side. It will take time. But you'll have us."

She and Kendra sit around me on my bed. Essence sits across from us in a chair. The tears that start falling down my cheeks reveal how far away I am from the other side. Mercedes puts her arms around me again and lets me cry. She doesn't care that's its messy.

When this period of crying stops, we all sit quietly. Kendra suggests that we order breakfast and watch movies to cheer me up. It seems we're all blowing off class today.

"Sure," I say, even though I don't care about doing either.

She puts the plan in motion, logging on to her computer to find some place that will deliver us good food. "This is not a day for garbage," she declares.

While Kendra is busying herself doing that, Essence comes over to me and wipes my tears.

"You're gonna be okay, Bunnie. Pinky promise." Then she kisses me and nuzzles my nose.

"A'ight y'all. I'm out," she announces. "Let me know if you need anything."

After she leaves, Mercedes comments on how nice Essence was to me.

"Yeah, Eb. That was weird, but I'm glad," Kendra says.

I hadn't really thought about the fact that Mercedes and Kendra don't know what happened to Essence and how I ended up being the one person she turned to in her time of need. They also don't know how we've gotten closer through her mess. Essence would kill me if I put her business out there to them so I give them a short, simple, partial explanation.

"She and this guy she was seeing had a huge blow-up and some other ugly stuff went down, but I had her back then and now I guess she has mine."

"Dang, y'all both got man problems. That twin thing is real," Kendra says.

"Don't say it like that, KK," Mercedes scolds. "You'll just make it worse."

"It's fine," I tell her. "That is deep when put it like that."

"Okay then, Eb. Look at your sister. She's bouncing back from her man drama and putting that guy behind her. You'll get there, too."

I love Mercedes' optimistic nature, but if she only knew how much turmoil Essence has on the inside because of "that guy" she wouldn't be using her as the model of recovery after heartbreak. I go along even though nothing in me believes it.

"Sure. You're probably right," I tell her.

While Kendra orders our food, Mercedes suggests a shower would be good for me.

"How long has it been?"

"A couple days, maybe."

"Yuk. That's nasty," they respond playfully, almost at the same time.

"Whatever, y'all. I'll take a shower since you're here and I don't want to gross you out."

I'm moving in slow motion as I gather my bathroom essentials. Even though I usually keep them all in one place in my shower caddy, nothing is where I expect to find it. Suddenly, feeling overwhelmed, I stop in the middle of the room, drop everything, and start crying again. Mercedes consoles me, while Kendra picks up my toiletries. After I calm myself, Mercedes walks with me to the bathroom.

"There's nobody else in here so you have the place to yourself," she tells me. "You want me to wait here with you?"

"No, I'm fine," I say, even though I'm not. She promises to return in fifteen minutes if I haven't come out.

Once in the shower, I let the water run over my body while losing myself in my thoughts. When even the water begins to sting of sadness and pain, I release a long, quiet, emptying cry.

"EB, YOU OKAY?" MERCEDES ASKS TENTATIVELY, SOME TIME later.

"Yeah, I'm fine," I say, even though I'm nowhere near that.

"You been in here like twenty minutes. Just wanted to check on you."

That time went by fast. It feels like I just got in here.

"I'll be out soon," I say.

"Should I wait?"

"Nah, I'm okay."

"I'm giving you ten more minutes. Then I'm coming back."

Mercedes will do what she says and I wanna be out before she feels the need to come find me. With a few deep breaths, I finish my shower and make it back to my room before the search party returns.

"Oh my goodness, you guys cleaned up," I say when I walk in. "And you changed the sheets on my bed. You didn't have to do that."

"Yes, we did," Mercedes says. "It was kinda nasty in here. And we got food to eat."

I offer a teary, "Thanks."

"You feel any better?" Kendra asks.

"Kinda."

My friends being here, the shower, the cry, or a combination of all that, steadied some of the emotions I'm battling.

"I'm still sad and confused. It's still sinking in," I add.

Kendra spreads out our breakfast platters from the Waffle Shop on my desk.

"The crab grits are yours, Eb. Maybe they'll take your mind of your shit-uation."

"That's a clever word, KK. Thanks for the grits and they're still hot. Y'all got me feeling special," I say, pushing a piece of smile onto my face.

"You are, Chica, don't ever forget that."

Mercedes and Kendra spend the entire day with me eating, watching movies, and talking me through my sorrow. They're convinced Eye Candy will realize our relationship is worth saving and he'll be ready to put this misunderstanding behind us. How long that will take, who knows.

"Just be patient and give him space," Kendra advises. "Nothing's gonna happen til his shit-uation with the team is solid."

"You and that word. OMG. Have you guys heard anything about that?" I ask. I've avoided all social media and Bryce chatter since Saturday.

"Everybody's still demanding he get his spot back. My boy said he left campus on Saturday and has been home since then. The petition is getting a lot of signatures. BSU and SGA are planning a demonstration on Wednesday morning to protest the team's actions. Whenever it is, I'm there. My flight home isn't until Thursday." She also mentions, "A bunch of other folks are rearranging travel so they can attend."

"LATINX is joining, also, so you know I'm right there, too," Mercedes adds. "But I woulda been there anyway."

"Wow, that's crazy. I hope he knows how much the student body supports him."

Thinking about this fills me with emotion, and it's not all bad. I'm really proud that other people respect Eye Candy so much that they're protesting for him. At the same time, I miss him so much it hurts. Knowing the pain the team decision caused him and not being able to help him with it, makes everything even worse.

It's almost ten o'clock when Mercedes and Kendra leave. I'm exhausted, but I decide to call Eye Candy to check on him. His voicemail picks up and his mailbox is full so I hang up. I decide not to send another text because he hasn't responded to any of the others I've sent so what's the use? Besides, Mercedes and Kendra says he needs space.

I collapse into bed, praying sleep will come before sadness and hurt throw me back into this cruel game of keep away with my peace and joy.

Chapter Thirty-Seven

Tuesday comes and brings more darkness. Most of my day is spent pining for Eye Candy and cursing Donovan's existence. Now, as I prepare for bed, guilt is my new companion. If only I had . . . My mind ticks off a list of lefts when I should've gone right, yesses that should've been nopes, and hellos that should've been goodbyes. In my head, I am singularly responsible for my own pain, but worst of all, for Eye Candy's too. I can't even.

Guilt has me tossing and turning throughout the night trying to escape its weight. It won't let me go. I yell at it. Call it names. Beg it to leave. It likes tormenting me. I'm no match for it and I feel myself crumbling. By the grace of my angels, Essence shows up. Through her twin-sense, she must've felt my need for her energy.

We lay side by side, our hearts trying to find a common rhythm, but they never do. We're out of sync. Neither of us can fall asleep. We both wrestle against something from the time our eyes close until the sun opens them in the morning. Come to find out, her enemy was Rex; mine was myself. Somehow, we battle through together. She convinces me I'm not to blame for anything that happened.

"Shit happens, Bunnie" she says. "And unfortunately you stepped in it and right now it stinks. Pretty soon it won't."

"But Rex's shit will always stink," I say and we both laugh ourselves into tears.

Our conversation turns serious again when I ask her what she plans to do about him.

"It's complicated," she begins. "He's saying he loves me and he never meant to hurt me."

"Stop right there. You've been talking to him?" I ask, not hiding my shock and disapproval.

"Umm. Don't judge me," she says. "Yes. He needed to make sure I knew he was sorry and he would never let anything bad happen to me. Blah, blah, blah."

"Has he told you everything that actually happened?" I ask with some caution since I don't know if Essence wants to venture into this territory.

"I haven't asked. But I'm pretty sure he had sex with me while I was blacked out."

Hearing that makes me furious. "That's rape, you know that, right?"

"No it's not," she says, adamantly. "He said I told him I wanted to do it."

Now, I want to scream. Instead, as calmly and as firmly as I can, I tell her "If you're drugged or drunk, there's no way on earth, in heaven, or in hell that you can agree to have sex. Didn't you hear that at orientation?"

"Whatever. That's a different situation as far as I'm concerned."

She is seriously clueless and it angers me that she won't acknowledge that he violated her and possibly put her at risk of other dangers. Where were her angels? Or maybe she pissed them off, too?

"Do you know what else happened in the room after the camera cut off? There were other guys there. Did they . . . ?"

"Shut up, Ebony."

My comment struck something sensitive in her and now she's

back to being the angry, mean Essence I thought I'd never see again.

"Don't you even finish that thought," she says angrily. "Rex wouldn't let anything like that happen to me. He might take some liberties, but he'd never allow that."

"I'm sorry. Wasn't trying to upset you. I'm just concerned."

After sitting in silence a few moments, Essence calms down, then says, "He's really sorry about it and wants to make it up to me . . .and to you."

I shake my head. "Miss me on all of that. You're not considering it, are you?"

"Hell no. Honestly, you scared him when you said something about pressing charges. He's on damage control. Something about his security clearance."

Even more reason to file a criminal complaint, that would be perfect payback, but I'll save that conversation for another day. Essence still seems to be processing what actually did happen, and what else might have happened to her. She knows more than she's willing to admit, I think. Now is not the time to work through that issue, not to mention I'm so not equipped to deal with the emotional fallout when she does have her breakthrough. That level of adulting is way above my pay grade.

As we sit, I notice Essence becoming a little melancholy.

"Rex was a dream that turned into a nightmare because I was out of control," she acknowledges. "The whole time I pretended to be everything I'm not so he would like me. Turns out, I didn't like the me he wanted anyway. So he's got to go and so does she. That's hard."

"But I'm here to help," I remind her. "We'll get it done, together. Pinky promise."

As awful as I feel about the hurt we both experienced with our relationships ending, our break-ups strangely brought us back together. We've got a synergy now, where our combined power truly is greater than the sum of our individual strength.

We're together again and we're even better. I wish we could've gotten to this point without the broken hearts.

THE NEXT DAY, ESSENCE FORCES ME TO GET READY AND GO TO my Public Speaking class. If he shows up, this could be my first time seeing Eye Candy, since our breakup on Saturday, and my last chance to see him before Thanksgiving break. Part of me hopes that seeing me will make him want to work on fixing this mess of ours. Actually, all of me wants that.

I arrive early for the class to a partly empty room and take my usual seat. The chair next to me, where Eye Candy usually sits, is empty. Class begins. Class ends. The seat next to me is still empty. Eye Candy never shows up. I'm relieved and disappointed. Relieved that I didn't have to face him yet, but disappointed because I really did want to see him.

After my classes end, I stay far from any activity related to the campus protest, which has been going on for a few hours. Kendra and Mercedes call me, trying to get me to come, but there's no way I can handle the sadness, disappointment, and anger of the crowd. I have enough of that of my own. Instead, I take refuge in my room. To take my mind off of the activity outside and Eye Candy, I start my gospel playlist, which I usually listen to on Sundays. This list has old songs I heard at church when I was a kid as well as some more current tunes. As if divinely ordered, William Becton starts singing one of my Dad's favorite songs, *Be Encouraged.*

"... *I know right now it's impossible to see, But God is gonna work it out if you just believe...*"

This song and quite a few others have me on my knees calling on God and my angels to heal my heart and right the wrong that has fallen upon Eye Candy.

HOURS LATER, ESSENCE COMES INTO MY ROOM WITH FOOD.

"You haven't been out since your class, have you?" she asks.

My answer was obvious, so I don't bother to speak it.

"Didn't think so. I brought us jerk chicken sandwiches and ginger beers from Mo' Bay."

"You know I can't resist that combo."

"That's exactly why I got it."

She lays the food out on my desk, guides me to the chair, and literally sits me down.

"You can bless the food since you're already in prayer mode."

"How do you know?" I ask.

"Girl, I felt it as soon as I walked in the room."

If what Essence says is true, then my prayers just might make it to God's ears and maybe have a chance of getting answered.

As directed, I offer a blessing over our food and before I can say "Amen," Essence is already eating.

When I look at her and shake my head, she responds with "What? I was starving."

Essence and I don't say much while we devour our food, other than to comment on how these are the best jerk sandwiches we've ever had. We say that about every jerk sandwich we get from Mo' Bay. Then she casually announces that she talked to Eye Candy at the protest.

I almost spit out my food.

"Oh, God. He was there? What did you say?" I ask with fear in my voice.

"Nothing. Well, I did say 'Hi'."

"I hope that's all you said."

"Not exactly."

I'm ready to scream. Not exactly? This can't possibly have ended well.

She continues, "I also told him he was an idiot for walking away from the most beautiful love story I've ever seen and he needed to fix this."

"No. You. Did. Not." I'm frozen from shock.

"I'm sorry, but I did. Bun, I'm sick of watching you hurt. He's being a big baby and somebody needed to say that to him."

"Oh nooooo," I cry out. "What did he say?"

"He said I quote, 'You got a lot of balls, girl.' No lie. But then he said, I might not be wrong, except about the idiot part."

"Wow. What does that even mean?"

"I don't know, but maybe he's starting to see the situation differently."

"Doubt that. He was so mad at me."

"So what? That was almost a week ago. A lot has changed since then. Like he's back on the team."

"What? When? How?"

Now I'm jumping up and crying tears of joy. Essence is beaming like she orchestrated his return, but really all she did was deliver the best news I've heard in my life.

"The Athletic Director and Coach announced it during the protest. The school will find a way to let the athletes show solidarity, but they won't be allowed to kneel or anything."

Some of that sadness I was carrying for Eye Candy lifts from my heart.

"That's a step forward. I'm so glad he's back," I say.

While Essence continues to update me on the day's events, Mercedes and Kendra show up. They attended the protest and let me see some of the videos and pictures they took.

"That's a big crowd," I observe.

"Probably the biggest the school has seen on any issue of race," Essence says, "which is amazing considering it's the Wednesday before Thanksgiving. Most people are usually gone."

"Now we have to make sure we extend this kumbaya moment to address some of the other issues on campus. Let's see if they care about all of us or just the ones who bring them money on the court?" Kendra adds.

"You're becoming quite a radical, KK," Mercedes says. "I'm here for it, though."

"Haha. Cool. But, I'm about to take my radical behind to my room. Gotta pack. Early flight home tomorrow."

Mercedes says, "Guess, I'll head out with you. My Tia is coming to get me tonight so I can help her cook. I have some new recipes I want to try for Thanksgiving dinner."

We stand around saying goodbye for another fifteen minutes, wishing each other safe travels, promising to call each other every day, and warning each other about eating too much. Mercedes and Kendra encourage me not to give up on Eye Candy.

"Things are looking up, Chica." Mercedes says. "He'll get himself together over the break."

"Hope so," I whimper.

When they leave, Essence confirms our itinerary and offers to help me with whatever packing I plan to do, which isn't much.

"We're going home. Anything I need is already there," I say. "Plus, we're getting a ride so I can wear pajamas and no one would care."

Essence laughs. "The pjs are not the move. Your mother would kill us both. Just be ready to leave by five. And keep your head up. He'll come around."

"I'll try."

After Essence leaves, I decide to shut it down. I take a quick shower and grab a t-shirt from my clean-but-not-folded-laundry pile to sleep in.

The shirt I pick up happens to be one that Eye Candy left in my room. Even though I washed it, the shirt still has his scent. I debate whether or not to put it on, but the shirt ends up on me. I sit on my bed, wearing Eye Candy's shirt, checking the socials to see how everyone is reacting to the return of Cam-G. Eventually, I land on Eye Candy's story page. For whatever reason, there seem to be lots of pictures of him with various girls, I guess from today. They all seem pretty innocent, except one where he's hugged up on this cheerleader chick wearing his jersey, or a knock-off of one, with captions that say #crushin' - #futureMrs - #couplegoals.

As I look at the picture closely, the look on her face, his expression, his smile, the one that I thought he only had for me, make me wonder if this is really his new crush. That thought almost breaks me down emotionally, but the comments that people wrote are cracking me up. If this was a real thing, Eye

Candy definitely would've clapped back at some of these people, especially at the person who wrote: Dont do it @CamG23. That's a restraining order waiting 2 happen.

In response, he wrote, LOL Factz.

Someone else wrote, Dont let @EbonyGabs see this picture @CamG23. She'll kick yr as.

No response from him. I take a screenshot of the post and muster up the nerve to send it to Eye Candy with a question.

Me: futuremrs? ☹

Several minutes pass, but to my surprise, he eventually answers.

EC: Neva. Not my kinda flow

Me: Good

He doesn't say anything after that. I debate whether or not to send another message, maybe congratulating him on being back on the team. Before I'm able to put a coherent sentence together, a message alert chimes on my phone. A reply from Eye Candy.

EC: Didnt know u cared

Of course I care. Is that what his problem is? I respond to him immediately.

Me: always

I get butterflies in my stomach when I hit send. I hold my breath as I wait for him to react. Finally, he responds.

EC: wanna c u

I take a selfie and send it to him.

EC: Ahh nice pic. miss seeing u in my clothes

Me: I miss seeing u

After I send that message, Eye Candy calls me.

"Hey," I say when I answer.

"Hey back."

That familiar awkward silence follows. He needs to move us past it this time.

"Can we talk?" he finally says.

"Of course, when, where?"

"You still on campus?"

"I'm in my room," I tell him.

"On my way," he responds.

I'm surprised how nervous I am thinking about seeing him. Hearing him knock makes my heart beat a little faster. When I open the door, a rush of emotion comes over me.

I kinda fall into Eye Candy's arms as soon as he walks in the room. He holds me for what feels like forever, but not long enough.

When he relaxes his embrace, I'm breathless. I have so much I want to say, but can't find any words to express myself. Eye Candy chooses to speak to me with gentle caresses. With each tender stroke, our hearts reconnect. My eyes become tearful, which seems to be my new normal. These are not sad tears, though. They're more like tears of relief. Eye Candy wipes my face with his hands at first, then with his kisses.

"I'm sorry," he whispers. "I shouldn't have tripped like that. All these thoughts and feelings about my mom just rushed up on me. I got mad all over again. I tried hard to make my time with you special enough so you wouldn't ever have a reason to wanna hurt me like that. But seeing him and knowing y'all had history kinda made me crazy. And it kept me from really hearing what you were saying. You didn't deserve that."

"I'm so sorry, too. I didn't handle that situation well at all and I swear I never meant to hurt you."

"Yeah. I know. My ego might've got in the way of me showing that."

Tears flow freely down my cheeks.

"I thought I lost you," I confess.

"You can't lose me," he says. "I'm not the same without you."

"Me either," I reply, smiling.

After a long pause he gives me the most beautiful smile ever and says, "I love you, Miss Ebony."

With what I hope is one of my better faces, I look at him and say, "I love you, too." And I really mean it.

When our lips meet, there's dancing and singing and rejoicing again. Cinderella has found her Prince Charming .

. . .

THE MORNING AFTER EYE CANDY AND I GOT BACK TOGETHER, I'm up early preparing for the ride home. I watch the sunrise. As the sky becomes a mosaic of color, I grab my journal and make a new entry that says:

Today I start fresh. I am better than I was. I am ____
I write **ENOUGH**
Thursday, November 22, 2018
Hi. I get it now. I am something special and I AM enough. ttyl

THE END

Made in the USA
Las Vegas, NV
08 February 2022

43509178R00148